Possibilities

Possibilities

A CONTEMPORARY RETELLING OF
PERSUASION

DEBRA WHITE SMITH

BETHANYHOUSE
a division of Baker Publishing Group
Minneapolis, Minnesota

© 2006 by Debra White Smith

Published by Bethany House Publishers
11400 Hampshire Avenue South
Bloomington, Minnesota 55438
www.bethanyhouse.com

Bethany House Publishers is a division of
Baker Publishing Group, Grand Rapids, Michigan

Bethany House edition published 2018

Previously published by Harvest House Publishers.

Printed in the United States of America

ISBN 978-0-7642-3072-1

Library of Congress Cataloging in Publication Control Number: 2017961598

Cover design by Connie Gabbert

Author is represented by Alive Literary Agency

To my wonderful friend
Rose Blackburn.
You know the whole Smith clan
loves you!

Cast

Allie Elton: Based upon Anne Elliot from *Persuasion*. The daughter of Richard Elton, Allie is devoted to her family and to the legacy of Georgia Gold Plantation.

Brent Everson: Based upon William Elliot from *Persuasion*. Brent married Richard Elton's niece, who was killed in a tragic accident. Brent is in search of another rich wife.

Darren and Sophia Cosby: Based upon Admiral Croft and Sophie Croft from *Persuasion*. Darren is married to Frederick Wently's sister, Sophia. The Cosbys are personable, successful, and wealthy.

Evelyn Elton: Based upon Elizabeth Elliot from *Persuasion*. The eldest daughter of Richard Elton, Evelyn manages the Elton mansion and tries to manage everybody and everything else in her sphere.

Frederick Wently: Based upon Frederick Wentworth from *Persuasion*. Frederick joined the Air Force and was a fighter pilot in the war in Afghanistan. He came home a decorated hero. His love for flying is second only to his love for Allie Elton.

Helena Grove: Based upon Henrietta Musgrove from *Persuasion*. The younger daughter of Charlie Sr. and Martha Grove, Helena is considering marrying Craig Hayden.

Jim Bennington: Based upon James Benwick from *Persuasion*. A close friend of Frederick Wently, Jim mourns the death of his fiancée, Felicity Harvey.

Landon Russ: Based upon Lady Russell from *Persuasion*. Allie Elton's aunt, Landon is Allie's best friend and confidante. She believes she has Allie's best interest at heart.

Louise Grove: Based upon Louisa Musgrove from *Persuasion*. An incurable flirt, Louise is the eldest daughter of Charles Sr. and Martha Grove.

Macy Elton Grove: Based upon Mary Elliot Musgrove from *Persuasion*. A hypochondriac, Macy is married to Charlie Grove Jr. and is Allie Elton's sister.

Penny Clayton: Based upon Penelope Clay from *Persuasion*. Penny Clayton is the gold-digging friend of Evelyn Elton. She uses her friendship with Evelyn to further her chances of matrimony.

Richard Elton: Based upon Sir Walter Elliot from *Persuasion*. Richard is the third wealthiest man in Georgia. He is the father of Allie and Evelyn Elton and Macy Elton Grove.

Sarah Hamilton: Based upon Hamilton Smith from *Persuasion*. Sarah is Allie Elton's dear friend from high school. Although Allie's family disapproves of her relationship with someone from lower financial standing, Allie and Sarah share a "sister" bond.

One

"A yardman!" Landon Russ's thin eyebrows arched. "You're wanting to marry a yardman?" Her blue eyes couldn't have been wider . . . or more disdainful.

Allie Elton's face went cold. Even the afternoon heat suffocating the Georgia plantation couldn't stop the rash of chills. She never considered that her aunt would object to her enraptured news. Never. Allie's fingers tightened around her sweating lemonade glass, and she stared at the droplets trickling down the tumbler until her eyes stung and the lemon slices blurred. She ducked her head before continuing. "I thought you knew we were—"

"I saw you were friends, yes. We all saw that, your father included, but we thought that's all it was—that, plus the fact that you had to work together. But we thought you had the good sense not to—We never imagined you would—"

Aunt Landon sprang from the back porch's swing and hovered over her niece, only twelve years her junior. "Allie, this can't happen! It won't happen! Your father will never let it happen!"

Allie pressed her sneakers against the wooden porch. The swing stopped swaying. She blinked. Her eyes misted anew. A tiny blur of feathers and beak zipped into her peripheral vision. Afraid to lift her focus from the lemonade, Allie refrained from even glancing toward the hummingbird. The diminutive creatures gorged themselves on the sweet liquid Allie provided in the feeders hanging from the porch. She loved watching the birds and considered each of them her friend. But now she was beyond even their influence.

Aunt Landon's disapproval bore into Allie, ushering in a barrage of thoughts that tore at her heart. In the midst of the mental whirlwind, one thing became increasingly clear: She had misread the entire situation. She thought her family knew she and Frederick were falling in love. And she thought they would approve since they all seemed to like him.

"I don't understand how this happened!" Aunt Landon stewed. The boards creaked with her pacing.

"But I thought you all *liked* him." Allie's comment fluttered out like the whimpered wish of an undervalued child. She fumbled with the hem of her walking shorts and dared to lift her gaze. Her tall, lithe aunt observed Allie as if she were daft.

"We *do* like him, sugar," she crooned in her sweet, Georgian drawl. "He's a very nice *yardman*. But that doesn't mean you need to go off and marry him!"

"But I love—"

"Sshh! Don't even say that." Landon looked over her shoulder toward the mansion's closed door and hurried to Allie's side. Her long maxi skirt brushed her legs in cadence with the tap of sandals on antebellum wood. Accompanied by a waft of sophisticated perfume, she plopped back down on the swing and jostled Allie's beverage. A dollop of lemonade sloshed from the glass and dotted Allie's knuckles in cold droplets. She pressed her hand against her T-shirt and wiped away the liquid.

Aunt Landon tugged at Allie's hand and clutched her fingers. "Listen to me," she insisted as if Allie were on the verge of drinking poison. "You need to *think* about what you're doing! He's penniless. His parents are *nobodies*. He's twenty-five and hasn't even finished his education. He's got *dirt* under his fingernails."

"But he's joining the Air Force and wants to be a pilot." Allie's claims sounded leagues weaker than the passionate belief she held in her Frederick. "And he's smart, Aunt Landon. Really smart! He's got *some* college and wants to finish in the Air Force. He's already got his private pilot's license. I believe in him. I believe he'll make it."

"Ah, honey." Aunt Landon stroked the side of Allie's shoulder-length hair. "Of course you do. What woman your age wouldn't? He's got brown eyes you could drown in and a smile that would stop a tornado. And let's don't *even* start on all those muscles! They'd knock the socks off a saint. But good looks aren't what a solid marriage is all about. Can't you see? He's no match for you. You're the daughter of *the* Richard Elton, peach king of the South!"

"But Frederick's father wants to run for the state senate. That's *got* to be worth something."

"And how's he ever gonna do that?" Landon's mouth settled into a no-nonsense line. "That takes money."

"That's his whole point!" Allie gazed across the acres of rolling peach orchards called Georgia Gold Plantation. She glanced back at her mother's sister. When Allie's mom died nine years ago, Aunt Landon had become a second mother, big sister, and friend all rolled into one. She'd been nothing but Allie's chief cheerleader during those years . . . until now. Allie trembled at the very thought of arguing with her aunt. Nevertheless, she persisted.

"Frederick's dad s-says holding a public office shouldn't be about who's got the most money, but who's got the right *motives.*"

"I agree it should be about motives and dignity and integrity and all that," Landon said with a nod. "But you can have the best heart in the state, and you won't stand a chance at the senate or the House, either, for that matter—not unless you've got the money to back you."

"Sarah said—"

Landon held up her hand. "Don't start quoting that penniless twit," she stated. "I'm beginning to think we should have never tolerated your friendship with her. The whole thing with this yardman probably stems from her. Your best friend is from the wrong side of town, and now you think you should marry and move over there!"

Allie's shoulders sagged. She and Sarah had been friends ever since Sarah's mother, the Eltons' cook, was allowed to bring her daughter to work with her. Millie had promised the Eltons that the ten-year-old Sarah would be free help if the Eltons would just allow her daughter to come with her. Allie's mom, a dedicated mother herself, had agreed. And when Sarah hadn't been helping her mother, she and Allie had planted their own little garden and played with the cats and daydreamed. Neither was worried they were from different economic backgrounds and different races. They just knew they liked each other. The like had grown to love. Now the two were inseparable. And even though Sarah was a successful med student, she was still "from the wrong side of the tracks" in Landon's mind.

Allie set her lemonade on the porch railing, stared into her lap, and clicked her thumbnails against each other. She'd been digging around the roses without her gloves and reaped the benefit—traces of soil under her cuticles that hand-washing hadn't remedied.

Up until now, Sarah Hamilton had been the only person

who knew that Allie and Frederick were close to marriage. Sarah had been everything Aunt Landon wasn't: supportive, excited, and truly happy for Allie.

"Listen, Allie," Landon continued, "if Frederick's going into the Air Force, he'll drag you all over creation. You'll live on one base and then another, with almost no income. *You'll* be the one supporting the two of you with your trust fund. Who knows where you'll be next, and who knows if he'll ever do more than *clean* airplanes. The way I see it, a good marriage doesn't happen until *both* partners bring an equal share to the table. And in this case, you'll bring all the clout while he brings nothing but . . . but . . ." she wiggled her manicured fingers, " . . . but dirt under his fingernails."

Allie dug at the smudge of dirt under her unpolished thumbnail.

"Or if he *does* become a pilot, the next thing you know he'll bless you with half a dozen kids and fly off and leave you alone with them." Landon grabbed Allie's arm and gasped. "Oh my word!"

Allie met her aunt's startled gaze. "What?"

"You're not pregnant, are you?" Landon's horror-stricken question pierced Allie to the center of her soul.

"Aunt Landon!" she shrieked. "How *could* you! I thought you knew me better than that." Allie jumped to her feet, balled her fists, and could not hold the tears. "I have never—" A bout of weeping prohibited her from further explanation.

Landon relaxed against the swing and covered her heart with her hand. "Thank the Lord," she breathed.

"How could you?" Allie repeated while dashing at the tears.

"Well, dear," Landon said, shaking her head, "it's not *you* I'm worried about. I just know men, that's all."

"But Frederick is a *gentleman!*" Allie squeaked. "If you'd

just give him a chance! Even Sarah said—" Allie stopped herself from another Sarah quote when Landon leveled a straight stare at her.

"Nobody is *that* much of a gentleman, not for long, anyway," Landon replied.

"But—but—" Allie searched for a way to erase the jaded gleam from her aunt's hardened blue eyes. No words came. Two years ago Landon's wealthy husband abandoned her for a swivel-hipped twenty-year-old. While Landon had gotten her share of the massive fortune, she'd also come away with a cynical opinion of men.

Even though Frederick was all man, he'd promised Allie from the start of their relationship that he was committed to the highest morals. He respected both her and himself enough to keep their relationship pure.

Landon stood and placed gentle hands on Allie's shoulders. "Sugar, I *love* you. I'm sorry I've upset you. And you're right, I should have had more faith in you. It's just that all this is such a shock that I don't even know what I'm saying. And if you think *I'm* shocked, imagine how your father is going to react."

A swell of dread started in Allie's mind and flowed to her feet. Never had she crossed her father. Ever since her mother's death, Allie had craved the approval he bestowed liberally upon her elder sister, Evelyn, and had done her best to elicit his praise. Even though Richard Elton had never doted on Allie as he did Evelyn, he'd also never exposed her to the disapproving glare that Allie's younger sister, Macy, had reaped before she left home.

Macy seemed forever determined to do the exact opposite of what their father mandated—right down to declining college for marrying the son of a germ-ridden family. Never mind that the Groves had a national septic system chain that serviced millions of households and that the Groves were independently wealthy. Septic systems were septic systems, and Richard couldn't imagine a peach queen married to a septic king. Nevertheless, that's exactly what he got, right along with two septic–peachy grandsons—twins, no less, now one year old.

The very idea of a red-faced Richard bearing down upon her the way he had Macy made Allie nauseous. And from the day Macy announced she was marrying Charlie Grove, Allie had vowed not to make the same mistake her sister made.

Why didn't I realize they wouldn't approve of Frederick before now? she fretted. She answered her own question before the other one flitted away: *Because they've all treated him like they thought he was great!*

Allie shook her head at the whole mess. She'd been so in love with Frederick, she had been blind to the inevitable. Her entire life she'd made the choices her family expected and had earned her aunt's praise. When it came to her father, she had at least earned his lack of disdain. Allie fought hot tears as her need for her family's approval stifled her love. Her fingernails ate into her palms. She drew a deep breath.

"I hope you'll do the right thing, Allie." Aunt Landon looped her arm through Allie's and urged her toward the mansion's door. "Remember, your obligations to your family are much more important than what you're feeling for a man you only met a year ago. Men come and go, but we're here forever." Landon rested her arm along Allie's shoulders, squeezed, and looked her niece eye-to-eye. "I'm sure you'd never want to do a thing to jeopardize your relationship with us."

Guilt sliced Allie's soul like a scalpel in the hands of a brain surgeon. Her gaze faltered. "N-no, never," she rasped.

"There's really no need to upset your father with this," Aunt Landon chattered on as if they were discussing an upcoming tea party. "The simplest thing to do is make a phone call and end it as gently as possible. Then you can move forward from there. Trust me, there will be someone else out there you'll fall more deeply in love with than you ever did Frederick. And your new man will have oodles of money and position."

"Frederick will be here later." Allie swallowed. Her lips quivered. She wished the heat would go ahead and sap the life out of her so she would be freed from explaining her plight to the man she desperately loved. "I'll talk to him then."

Two

Frederick Wently pulled his used pickup into the mansion's winding driveway. The regal oaks lining the drive were as steadfast as the mansion's white pillars. The rolling green lawn reminded him of the golf course his father wished he could afford to play on. Instead, he'd purchased a family membership at a has-been golf course on the backside of Atlanta, Georgia. That fine specimen of a facility had as much brown grass as green, with sand traps more like quicksand and golf carts that coughed every time you pressed the accelerator. But the Wentlys had enjoyed years of family bonding on that course that even quicksand and brown grass couldn't compromise.

Last year when Frederick secured the job as grounds manager on the Elton estate, both his parents had been ecstatic. Frederick's dad had even hoped the connection might further his prospects in becoming a senator. But never had Frederick or his parents imagined he'd be proposing to the owner's daughter within a year.

When he met Allie, she'd been dressed in a pair of blue jean cutoffs and a faded work shirt. She was digging in a flowerbed. Frederick thought she was an employee and had shamelessly flirted with her for two days before he realized she was Richard Elton's daughter. Another two days lapsed before Frederick understood she was also his boss. When the estate manager who hired him had explained that Mr. Elton's daughter, Allison, managed the mansion's landscaping, Frederick had imagined a high-heeled, red-lipped blonde who sat on the porch and flung orders at him. He never imagined a brown-eyed, pony-tailed brunette with dirt on her knees who simply introduced herself as Allie.

By the time Frederick realized the Allie he'd met in the tulip bed was actually Allison Elton, she'd done a splendid job of flirting right back. They'd discovered a mutual enjoyment of plants and gardens. But Frederick had learned that while his interest was closer to a hobby and a means to earning an interim income, Allie's love of the outdoors involved a master's degree in horticulture. And while her father allowed her to manage the plantation's yard staff, he refused to allow her to teach junior college, which is what she really wanted to do.

After weeks of Allie's silent invitations for more than just friendship, Frederick decided not to heed his mother's warnings about the difference in their economic backgrounds. He liked Allie for who she was, and he was elated that he saw the same appreciation in her eyes. Even though Frederick respected his mom's opinions, he fully believed that his Allie would never allow material issues to taint her heart. His belief in her had paid off.

Pulling the Ford to a halt, Frederick turned off the engine and picked up the tiny velvet box from the passenger seat. He nudged open the lid with his thumb and examined the one-carat diamond twinkling in the evening's light. Frederick had worked hard and saved to buy the ring. Still he'd wound up with a diamond bigger than he could afford—and a credit card balance he'd be chained to for a year, maybe two.

But Allie's worth it, he thought and couldn't wait until they said "I do" and began their life together. Since he was scheduled to leave for boot camp in six weeks, he hoped to be married within the month. They'd already discussed having a private ceremony with only their parents and a few close friends in attendance. Nothing more. The fact that Allie wasn't interested in plastering the society pages with pomp and finery made him love her all the more.

Frederick shut the box's lid with a snap and a smile. He planned to take Allie out to eat. After a sunset walk in the park, he'd give her the ring. His mind whirled in anticipation of the kiss that would seal their engagement.

Even though Allie's hand was twined with Frederick's, her fingers remained cold. His hand's warmth matched the blazing promise in his eyes. Throughout the evening the promise hung between them. His eyes grew more intense. And Allie had never wanted to hide more than now. No matter what she did, she could not get her hands to warm up. But then, neither would her heart. It was every bit as chilled as her fingers—and then some.

The August sun torched the western horizon in a blaze of orange. Streaks of blue sapphire, gray, and amethyst shot out from the glowing ball like a final glorious statement on the whole day. The park's pond mirrored the sunset while eager ducks zipped to and fro in quest of the morsels tossed by a trio of noisy children.

Frederick led Allie toward an isolated bench near a clump of maples. Along with the scent of earth and bark and leaves, the alcove offered them privacy from most of the park's guests without blocking their view of the pond and the lush greenery surrounding it. Tugging her down with him, Frederick settled onto the wooden park bench and squeezed her hand. He smiled into Allie's eyes. Neither had spoken during the stroll through the park. Words weren't always necessary when you are in love.

Frederick leaned forward and brushed his lips against hers. Overcome with the achingly sweet gesture, Allie held her breath and strained nearer. She closed her eyes, rested her hand on his chest, and invited a deeper kiss. Frederick's intake of air hurled Allie into a new realm of heightened confusion. She loved this man with everything she was, but staying in the relationship meant the betrayal of the family she also loved.

The image of her father's disapproving eyes . . . and of her aunt's disdain . . . made Allie break the kiss.

"Wow!" Frederick exclaimed, his dark eyes sharpened with the anticipation of marital fulfillment. "Now *that's* what I call a kiss!" Gazing at her lips, he moved in for another round.

Allie flattened her hands against his chest and halted his progress. Another kiss like that one would make her forget all about her familial obligations, and Allie just couldn't take the chance.

"Frederick, I—we—I need to tell—to tell you something," she stammered.

"You've already told me more than I expected," he teased and eased away with a mixture of respect and disappointment flitting across his features.

Allie lowered her gaze to the top of his shirt that showed off those muscles Aunt Landon had noticed. But Allie also recognized that the shirt had come from the clearance rack at Walmart, while her simple cotton blouse and short skirt were the weekly feature at Macy's. None of that mattered to Allie, but she knew it mattered to her family. And her family meant everything to her. Her mother's premature death had taught her never to take her relatives for granted . . . and never to do anything against their wishes she might later regret.

"What's the matter, sweet thang?" He chuckled through the endearment and touched the end of her nose.

"It's just that . . ." she fretted and couldn't even fathom the right words.

The children's approaching shrieks mingled with the ducks' demanding squawks. Allie glanced toward the noise. The three boys had apparently lured the ducks far enough out of the water to try to catch them. The ducks, clued into the ploy, scrambled toward the pond while furiously quacking. The smallest boy lunged at the last duck, fell into the edge of the pond, and came out of the deal with a handful of tail feathers and nothing else.

"Ah, man!" he cried as he sat up on the water's edge. "I almost had him."

"Cool!" one of his compadres cheered.

"Would you look at those feathers!" the other child admired.

The violated duck streaked across the pond with enough verbiage to make any sailor blush. That is, if the sailor understood duck.

Allie, overwrought with nerves, snickered. Frederick joined her.

"That kid is drenched, isn't he?" he mused. "Reminds me of me when I was his age. My mom stayed in a stew because I was always tearing my new jeans or getting grass stains on my church clothes."

"I bet you *were* a handful," Allie teased.

He winked. "I was. And by the time I was fifteen Mom taught me how to mend my own clothes. She said my future wife would never forgive her if she didn't show me how to fix what I'd torn."

The word *wife* jolted Allie out of the humorous moment

and sent her plummeting back into the abyss of despair. She gazed at the manicured grass and prayed for an easy way to break his heart.

"Speaking of wife . . ." Frederick said and stood.

Out of the corner of her eye, Allie noticed him reaching into his pants pocket and pulling out a tiny box covered in black velvet. She squeezed her eyes shut and prayed she was hallucinating. If she weren't, this was worse than she'd dreamed.

When he settled back onto the bench, Allie's attention was riveted to him, whether she wanted it to be or not. No microphone could have broadcast his motives any louder than his jubilant expression. Her stomach churned. A nauseous bulge threatened her throat. The park began a slow spin that worsened her dismay.

Frederick lowered himself to one knee, opened the box, and said, "Allie, I know we've already talked about getting married, but this makes it official. Will you marry me?"

She gazed at a diamond that was much larger than anything he could afford. The stone exploded with blue-hued sparkles that spoke of its quality . . . and this man's love. Overwhelmed beyond logic, Allie moaned, clutched her midsection, and hunched forward. "God, help me. Oh dear God, help me. I am going *to die!*" she moaned.

"Allie? You're going pale. Are you *sick?*"

"Oh no!" she wailed and covered her face.

"Allie?"

The pain exploding through her spirit was more intense than anything she'd anticipated. All Allie wanted was to make it stop. She had to get away from the diamond, the man attached to it, and the pure love he offered. She jumped up and blindly raced back in the direction they'd walked. As the tears streamed down her face, she wiped at them and did her best to navigate toward the parking lot. What she would do once she got there was still to be seen. But for now, the urge to run . . . the need for some space must be met.

"Allie!" Frederick's panicked calls followed close behind. "Allie, wait! *Allie!*"

She glanced over her shoulder. When she looked back in front of her, it was too late to dodge the backless park bench inches ahead.

"Watch out!" Frederick yelled.

The bench's concrete edge ate into her leg as she toppled forward and landed in a tumbled heap on the other side. She never thought the pain in her soul could be matched by any physical pain until arrows of agony screamed up her left leg. Allie coughed out a protest through her tears. Her lower leg was turned at an odd angle that could only mean one thing: She'd broken it.

Three

Forty minutes later Frederick paced the emergency room waiting area and could only imagine what being here for a life-threatening cause would be like. Allie had broken her leg, and he was on the verge of despair. If her life were in question, Frederick probably would have been facedown on the floor. So far Allie's family hadn't arrived. He'd called Landon Russ as soon as Allie was admitted, and he expected her family to be here any minute.

For now, the only other occupants included a leathery-skinned old man and a young mother with a screaming toddler on her lap. Frederick had no idea who either was waiting on, but he could have done without the screaming. The noise raked his taut nerves as severely as the hospital's antiseptic smell. His sense of guilt heightened. Frederick couldn't get away from feeling that he was to blame for Allie's accident.

Frederick also couldn't stop the haunting reality that her running had everything to do with the ring and proposal and nothing to do with an onslaught of illness. Never had he been so sure of anything in his life. After all, they'd talked of marriage several times, and Allie had seemed ecstatic about the idea and as sure of her love for him as any Juliet had ever been. As his concern mounted, so did his confusion . . . and the horrible conviction that he should have never been so sure of Allie.

He stopped beside a drink machine, pulled out his bill-fold, and retrieved two dollars. After inserting the money, he grabbed the Coca-Cola and indulged in a mammoth gulp. The second the Coke fizzed down his throat, the hospital doors sighed open and Landon Russ stormed the waiting room like a mama bear on the trail of the one who'd harmed her cub. As usual she looked like an over-made magazine girl in high heels and a dress designed for someone fifteen years younger.

Stepping forward, Frederick braced himself for the conde-scending gaze he expected of all the Eltons and their ilk. So far in their acquaintance, Landon had been outwardly warm and friendly, but her eyes reflected a chill that never failed to remind Frederick what side of town he came from.

When Landon spotted Frederick, she veered toward him and didn't give him time to utter a hello. "Tell me what hap-pened!" she demanded. "Did you hit her or push her or—"

"*No!*" Frederick boomed and liked Landon Russ even less.

The baby stopped screaming. Frederick glanced toward the old gentleman. Sure enough, his attention was on Frederick and Landon; so was the baby's and the mom's, for that mat-ter. As soon as Frederick focused back on Landon, the baby released a shriek that could shatter boulders.

Frederick latched on to Landon's arm and pulled her around the corner, toward the hallway they'd wheeled Allie down. "Listen," he snarled into her face, "I don't know what kind of a cad you think I am, but I've never hit a woman in my life. And I don't plan to start now!" He released her arm.

Landon's stony face showed little reaction. Only her eyes re-vealed her fury and contempt. "So tell me what *really* happened, then!" She brushed his low-income germs from the arm of the short jacket covering the expensive dress.

Frederick lifted his hand and huffed. "It's just like I told you on the phone. We were at the park. She was running and fell over a bench."

"It's not like her to be so careless," Landon stated. "She was on the track team in college, even. Were you chasing her?" Her pointed gaze wouldn't relinquish control, and Frederick decided the best recourse was honesty—complete honesty.

"As a matter of fact, I was," he said.

Landon's eyebrows flexed, and her mouth settled into a satisfied line.

Reaching into his pocket, Frederick pulled out the ring box and juggled the Coke bottle while opening the box. "I had just proposed," he drawled as Landon gaped at the blue-tinged diamond. He reveled in jolting the great Landon Russ. Her eyes huge, she lifted her gaze to his.

"Is that thing real?" she asked.

"Of course," Frederick snapped, and a slow burn started in his stomach.

"How did you afford—"

"Oh! Is the *ring* real?" he mocked. "I thought you were talking about the box. I got the ring out of a vending machine."

Landon's jaw tightened.

Frederick hoped his sarcasm hid his doubts and pain. "I'd barely proposed when she went pale," he continued like a reporter. "She started running across the park like a maniac. So yes, I was chasing her, but not because I was trying to hurt her. I was just . . . I was just following her, I guess." He snapped shut the box and placed it back into his pocket. "Because I was confused and, well, I think any man would have done the same."

Landon shifted back, hardened her features, and crossed her arms. "Did Allie expect the ring?"

"Nope."

"Then I know why she was running."

"Oh?" Frederick's heart thudded.

"Because she was going to break up with you tonight," Landon said as if she were reciting a grocery list.

Frederick refused to flinch.

"But before she got the chance, you offered a ring and popped the question." Every word held the finality of truth. "You know Allie. She wouldn't hurt a fly. I'm sure it so overwhelmed her that she just wanted to run."

Frederick gazed past Landon to the nurses' station. A klatch of employees intent on this file or that medication never registered his presence. Allie's words when she saw the ring bombarded his mind: *"God, help me. Oh dear God, help me. I am going to die!"* An elevator's ding sounded like the bell announcing the right answer on a game show. And Frederick felt as if he were being hit in the gut.

"I guess it all makes sense, then," he said and managed a half-smile that he hoped was nonchalant. Never had nonchalant cost so much. After downing a hard swallow of Coke, he allowed himself the luxury of a wince and hoped Landon attributed the reaction to the carbonated beverage and not the agony ripping his soul.

"You know, Frederick," Landon said and placed her hand on his forearm, "Allie comes from one of the wealthiest families in Georgia. It's always better to marry within your . . ."

Her gaze faltered.

"I see," Frederick said and couldn't stop the bitter taint in his words. He gazed down at Landon's perfectly sculptured nails and stepped away from her touch.

She adjusted her purse's shoulder strap and looked him in the eyes again. "Since you've been so honest with me, I'll do the same. Allie and I had already discussed these issues this afternoon. And she came to her own conclusions." Landon shrugged.

"With help from you, I daresay." Frederick's words were void of the tremor starting in his legs.

Landon narrowed her eyes. "Allie's family means the world to her. More than any—any—" She flipped her wrist as if Frederick were an afterthought dish on a second-rate menu. "She'd *never* do anything against our advice."

"I see," Frederick said again and decided he'd been played for a fool. Whatever Allie felt for him, it was nothing compared to her loyalty and love for her family.

You were right, Mom, he thought. *I should have listened to you.*

"You know," Landon purred and crossed her arms, "I'm sure this is all very upsetting for you." She touched his arm and leaned closer, but her hard eyes didn't match her feigned concern. "If you don't feel comfortable staying, I know Allie would understand."

Tempted to scrub at the place she'd touched him, Frederick gazed at the top of his discount boots. Landon Russ's heels probably cost more than three pairs—no, *ten*—of his shoes. The price of his whole wardrobe probably didn't even touch two of Allie's high-class suits. But none of that had mattered in their relationship . . . or so he'd thought.

His family had never taught him to value others more because of money. Neither had they suggested they were less valuable because they lived on a policeman's salary. Nevertheless, Frederick had never felt so unworthy . . . like a dirty street urchin who dared touch the hem of the queen's gown.

Landon's pointed suggestion that he leave Allie's life posed itself as the only choice. Walking away would be so much neater than having to face Allie and hash through all the reasons he wasn't good enough for her.

I've been living a Cinderella fairy tale, Frederick concluded. *Only this time Cinderella is a guy and there is no happily ever after.*

Without another word, he turned and stomped across the waiting room. When he neared the exit, he chose the manual door over the automatic one and slammed his fist against the metal bar. The glass door banged open. Frederick's hand protested the abuse as profoundly as his heart protested his stepping out of Allie Elton's life.

Four

Allie clutched the banister and tried to ignore the whispering pain in her left shin as she descended the steps. Every winter her shin reminded her of the ten-year-old ache in her heart, an ache that began at that Atlanta park. Try as she might, Allie couldn't forget that day . . . or the last glance she'd caught of Frederick Wently as the ER team rushed her down the hallway.

Aunt Landon said she explained everything to Frederick and that he preferred for Allie not to contact him. To underscore Landon's claim, Frederick had never returned to his grounds manager position. Allie accepted the inevitable. She was left to sort out her broken heart alone. The only thing that brought her comfort was knowing she'd done what her family expected.

But just about the time she thought she'd completely forgotten Frederick, winter would set in. With it came the vague reminder in her shin, which prompted her to relive the season of her life when she'd lost her heart . . . and the day she'd chosen her family over Frederick. Unfortunately, on lonely winter nights, her family's approval did little to keep her warm. Ten long years had underscored this reality.

Today was an icy February afternoon—a dreary day perfect for dragging out old memories and wallowing in what-if's.

The low-lying clouds and the promised cold preceding the predicted ice storm seeped into her heart, chilling it to the core. Allie took the final step off the mansion's winding staircase and grimaced with the last dash of pain that pummeled her nerves. She glanced at her wristwatch and realized that once again she had perfectly met her family's expectations. Aunt Landon told her to wait until three fifteen before entering the library where "the talk" was happening. It was exactly three fourteen.

Her low-heeled boots tapping the marble floor, Allie strode toward the library's closed door. As a child she'd thought the teak doors must have been cut from a giant's forest. Now she recognized the carved doors as the works of art they were . . . along with everything else in this house. Allie placed her hand on the doorknob and turned to gaze across the foyer, crowned by a crystal chandelier, circa 1840.

She never imagined leaving this home would catapult her into the sad longing that pulsated through her like a haunting dirge. But the finery wasn't what held her heart. The memories did. This was the home to which she was born . . . and the home in which her mom drew her last breath. Turning the knob, Allie silently eased open the door and braced herself for whatever she was about to step into.

"*Rent the plantation?*" Richard Elton boomed. "Landon, are you crazy?"

Allie stopped. Her fingers tightened on the doorknob. Her focus riveted upon her red-faced father. Her knees weakened, and she held her breath.

Two years ago, Allie recognized that her elder sister Evelyn's flamboyant spending could become a problem. Last year she suspected that the problem was upon them. Within the prior month, her father's creditors had forced him to realize that no one—not even the peach king of the south—could function as if funds were unlimited.

A week ago Allie and Aunt Landon began to piece together a plan that would get the family out of debt and restore them to solvency. Or, rather, a plan sought them out. Aunt Landon had informed her it was the only sensible option. While Landon enjoyed her own wealth, she was also an astute businesswoman who understood the necessities of wise money management, no matter how wealthy a person was. In order to ensure her lifelong financial independence, she had chosen a spacious, one-story home with only three domestic employees instead of a fully staffed mansion.

"Who would ever think of such a stupid plan as *renting out* the plantation?" Evelyn stated from the sofa. Even in surprised mode she carefully pronounced every word—just as she'd learned to do in her collegiate theater training. Evelyn slipped her socked feet from her loafers and tucked them under her. She took a long sip from her mug. Sometimes Allie wondered if every day was a new drama for Evelyn and nothing more.

"Well, the opportunity seems to have fallen into your lap," Landon explained.

Richard jumped to his feet and turned on the fireplace like a general invading new territory. He grabbed the poker's gold-plated handle and jabbed at the crackling flames. The scent of burning oak filled the room with the cozy suggestion that all was well in the Elton home.

Allie stepped into the softly lit room and shut the door with a thump and click. Poker still in hand, her father twisted to face her. Evelyn shifted and turned to look at Allie. Landon, claiming the recliner across from the couch, followed suit.

"Allie, there you are." Landon tugged at her cowl-necked sweater. "I was just telling your father about the offer."

"Allie?" Evelyn exclaimed, her dark eyes flashing in the firelight. "What does *she* have to do with this?"

"Nothing," Landon replied. "Other than the fact that she knows about it and thinks it's a good idea."

"Oh?" Richard lifted his groomed brows. Now in his late fifties, Allie's father was every bit as handsome as he had been in his thirties. Those who knew him well said he'd changed little. His twenty-year-old portrait over the fireplace captured the strong jaw, straight nose, and prominent eyebrows that age had only improved—and maybe a regular regimen of Botox.

"Allie also knows about this budget." Landon lifted a portfolio. "She thinks it's the best plan."

"Budget!" Evelyn's voice erupted as she jolted forward. Hot cocoa sloshed from her mug and beaded on her angora sweater. She glared at Allie and spewed, "Don't just *stand* there! *Do* something! Get me a towel! Anything! Can't you see I've got a mess?"

"Here. Use this cloth from the service tray." Landon laid the proposed budget on Richard's vacated chair and bent over the silver service set. She lifted the urn full of hot water and tugged the cloth from beneath it.

Allie hurried forward and gathered up the teaspoons, extra mugs, and urn of cocoa mix. Aunt Landon said a modest, "Thanks, Allie," while she handed the cloth to Evelyn, who'd never bothered to express gratitude in her whole life and wasn't going to start today.

With the sweater catastrophe at an end, Evelyn tossed the cloth onto the coffee table, which was carved as intricately as the doors, the mantel, and scores of other fine pieces throughout the home. She plunked her mug on the end table, flipped her straight blonde hair away from her face, and rested her arms on the low-backed settee on which she sat.

As usual, Allie felt like a forgotten mouse in the face of Evelyn's beauty. Evelyn had captured the stage in college and the society pages in her twenties. Now, at the age of thirty-seven, she was every bit as breathtaking as she'd been at twenty-seven, and the society editors still loved her. So did her father.

Allie wondered if her dad might have loved her more if she'd been gorgeous instead of mildly attractive. She touched her hair, cropped in what her hairdresser claimed was a high-fashion stack. Evelyn could make straight and simple look like royalty, while Allie could spend hours at the hairdresser and not even come close.

After an intense glaring session, Evelyn finally scoffed, "Whoever heard of an Elton living on a budget?"

Allie exchanged a furtive glance with her aunt and settled in the straight-backed chair near the recliner. She lightly stroked her wool slacks and focused on the dancing fire.

"Either you will go on a budget and rent the plantation or you will lose everything. It's that simple," Landon explained.

Richard released the fireplace poker back into its holder with the grate and grind of ash-covered metal. He picked up the budget like an actor ready to read for a starring role. His turtleneck sweater and year-round tan heightened the effect.

Her spine stiff, Allie prayed her father wouldn't toss the budget into the flames and scorn wisdom.

"And who do you propose is going to rent our plantation?" Richard asked, never taking his gaze from the financial strategy.

"One of your key customers has approached me—

"Approached *you*?" Richard boomed again and glowered at Landon as if she were Benedict Arnold's twin sister. "Why didn't they approach *me?*"

Allie's shoulders hunched. Evelyn mimicked her father's aloof expression.

Landon never blinked. "Well, I just happened to be at a party, and we were talking. He halfheartedly said to let him know if you ever decided to lease the place. He loves the house, and having the peach orchards under his own management would cut out a purchasing step and up his profits."

"Are you going to tell me who it is?" Richard demanded.

"Of course," Landon replied and dusted a piece of lint from her pants. "It's Cosby Enterprises."

"Cosby?" Evelyn mocked. "That sorry excuse for a cannery? Can they afford to lease all this?" She lifted both arms.

"Apparently so," Landon said. "They seem to have amassed quite a fortune."

Allie studied her father, who flipped to page two of the proposed budget. Eyes narrowed, he examined the print while Landon continued.

"Peaches are the Cosby specialty," she said. "Their offer to lease this place is generous. They'd take on the financial burden of running the whole operation. That would allow you to apply all profits toward your debts. If you follow this plan, your debts should be cleared in four years. You'd use the fifth year to save. The sixth year you could move back home. As long as you stay on your budget, you should be fine."

"Cosby," Richard grunted with a bitter grimace. "Who are they, anyway, but blue collars who got lucky?" He tossed the budget to the coffee table, locked his fingers behind his back, and gazed toward the ten-foot ceiling.

Landon cast an uncertain gaze to Allie, who fumbled with nothing and prayed her father wouldn't throw away this opportunity. Renting the plantation was by far better than losing it altogether.

Evelyn lowered her arms from the low-backed couch and reached for her cocoa mug. After a short sip, she mused, "Aren't the Cosbys somehow related to that yardman who used to work here years ago? They're the ones who recommended him for the position, if I recall. What was his name, anyway? Frank? Freddie? Fremont?"

"Frederick, I believe," Aunt Landon supplied, and Allie felt her concerned glance. "Frederick Wently. He's Sophia Cosby's brother."

Allie held her breath.

"Ah yes, I remember him," Richard said. "Believe it or not, their father wound up winning a place in the state senate. Who'd ever have imagined? I guess they haven't done bad for *blue collars*." He frowned.

"I think I even remember seeing Frederick on the national news," Evelyn continued. "Didn't he win some kind of medal for bravery in the Afghanistan war?"

Allie's stomach churned. *Yes*, she thought, *he did win a medal.* She'd created a scrapbook dedicated to his honor. For several months, he'd become an American icon and was even featured in *People* magazine. The fact that his father had miraculously won and maintained a spot in the state senate had heightened Frederick's appeal to the media. Shortly after Frederick joined the Air Force, Fred Sr. had rallied a strong financial backing from middle-income families across Georgia and defeated a long-seated, wealthy senator. All those clippings were in Allie's scrapbook, as well.

She gazed toward the beveled glass window cloaked in the latest in decor. The ivory gauze hanging from an iron curtain rod blurred with the bleak light seeping through ice-laden clouds. Bits of sleet pelted the window like the haunting memories stabbing her heart.

Oh, Lord, she silently prayed, *if you ever give me a second chance with Frederick . . .*

"Cosby," Richard mumbled. "Whoever heard of an Elton bowing to a Cosby? They have no . . . no ancestry at all. Our family—we can be traced through the Revolution—to English noblemen."

"Who says we have to bow out, anyway?" Evelyn added and set her mug back on the end table. "If things are that desperate, why can't we just cut back? I'd be willing to give up . . ." her gaze slid around the room, "to give up redecorating for a season or two."

Allie, impressed with even that concession, nearly applauded her sister.

"And I guess I could go without a totally new wardrobe every season . . . maybe half of one." Evelyn waved her hand, and the three-carat diamond on her right hand sparkled like stardust. "Maybe I could even sell a few pieces of jewelry." Her lips drooping, she lowered her hand and eyed the ring that had been custom ordered from Tiffany's. "Anything but having to leave the mansion." She raised her gaze to her father, and her perfectly made-up eyes took on the pleading of an eight-year-old.

The last time Allie remembered Evelyn looking so bleak was three years ago—the day she fully realized her pursuit of Brent Everson was for nothing. He was the only thing in life that had been denied her. She'd been a compulsive shopper ever since his marriage to their cousin, Chrissy Elton.

"I'm afraid it's going to take more than just selling a few pieces of jewelry and cutting back on the wardrobe." Landon's realistic tone rang with the chill of truth.

Richard's mouth turned down at the corners. A line formed

between his brows. He shot a half-defeated glance toward Evelyn, who hung her head and rubbed her temple.

Allie decided now was a good time to make the one suggestion she had considered from the start of this crisis. Even before she spoke, she knew what her father's reaction would be. And she prayed the mere mention of the *J* word would catapult him to embrace the budget.

"Well, I guess we all could get jobs." Allie's voice barely rose above a whisper.

"Jobs!" The word reverberated around the room.

"Are you nuts!" Evelyn shrieked and lunged forward.

Allie shrank into her chair and didn't say more. For years she had dreamed of taking a job teaching junior college—whether the family needed the money or not. But her father persisted in refusing.

"Lowering ourselves to—to mere jobs," Richard sneered, "is not an option under any circumstance!" He stomped his foot and picked up the budget.

Landon and Allie exchanged a knowing glance while Landon offered a discreet thumbs-up.

"I guess it could be worse," he mumbled while flipping the pages. "At least the Cosbys have made something of themselves. Even though they lack class, they do have *some* money. I guess having a father in the senate speaks something for Sophia Cosby." Richard glanced toward Allie. "Weren't you and her brother friends at one point?"

The question was so unexpected, Allie gripped the chair's arm and swayed with the impact.

"Yes, they were." Landon's casual claim gave Allie time to regain a semblance of composure. "Do you remember him, Allie?" Her aunt's bland observation indicated nothing of the history that existed between her and Frederick. Indeed,

Landon and Allie hadn't even discussed him since that day at the hospital.

Allie nodded and wondered if her aunt really thought she might have ever forgotten Frederick Wently. If the truth were known, she hadn't dated another man. No matter how she tried, no one lived up to Frederick. No one.

"What is your opinion of the family, then?" Landon continued.

"Excuse me?" Allie croaked.

"Wouldn't you agree the Cosbys would be reputable lessees?" Landon widened her eyes and pointedly stared at Allie.

"Oh, of course," Allie agreed. *How ironic*, she thought, but as usual kept the remark to herself. Aunt Landon now wanted Allie to recommend a branch of the very family she once rejected as not good enough. Now Frederick Wently's sister was wealthier than the Eltons. For all Allie knew, Frederick might be, too.

As the conversation continued, Allie once again stared toward the gray sky now hammering the countryside with sleet. Longingly she wondered where Frederick was . . . what his life was like . . . if he'd ever married.

Five

A week later Frederick Wently went through the routine external checks on the Beechcraft King Air 200, then pulled down the airstair door and prepared to climb into the plane for his regular flight. The thrill of piloting a sleek plane through the sky came close to the love of a woman. Today he'd fly from his home in Charlotte, North Carolina, to Atlanta, Georgia.

A few years ago his brother-in-law, Darren, sold his private airport to the county. They'd gained FAA approval and had built a hangar that held twenty planes. Now the airport featured a daily flight for VIPs and dignitaries, with Frederick as star pilot.

When Darren offered to plunk down the million dollars to purchase the seven-passenger plane, Frederick had been ecstatic. It was like owning his own aircraft, only better. Frederick got full use of the plane with no financial obligations. On top of that, Darren allowed him to pocket half the profit from the passenger fares. All Frederick had to do was agree to be Darren's pilot-on-call.

Frederick had developed quite a clientele and a reputation for safety and dependability. Sometimes the flights involved business. Other times Frederick piloted people for pleasure appointments, such as banquets, campaigns, and cruises down the Mississippi. In the last couple of years, he'd shuttled people into scores of major cities across the United States.

The medical discharge he received from the Air Force had included a significant retirement package. That, plus the money he'd saved, enabled him to continue the pursuit of his first love at his own pace.

Well, maybe not my first *love,* he grudgingly admitted. With an icy February wind biting his face, he decided not to think about his first love. Thoughts of Allie Elton usually resulted in unquenchable longing tainted by anger and a bitterness he couldn't shake no matter how hard he tried. Even after all these years, Frederick possessed word-for-word recall of that final conversation with Landon Russ. The memory was enough to make him want to break Allie's heart as she'd broken his. But that was vengeful and anything but holy.

We're not going there today, he told himself, just as he'd told himself many times over the years.

Frederick concentrated on persuading his aching back to cooperate during the climb into the plane. The mid-morning sun belied the frigid temperature that ensured this to be the coldest winter in two decades. Thankfully, the ice storm that had frozen the southeast last week melted when the thermometer crept to a whoppin' thirty-five for two days. But Old Man Winter was back with a vengeance, and this morning's thermometer read 20. Frederick pulled his hooded parka closer and estimated the temperature now at 28.

His complaining spine validated the claim. The Silver Star award the media wouldn't stop crowing about involved an emergency airplane landing and a land mine. The explosion had caused a spinal injury that surgery had corrected. On cold days, his spine reminded him of the whole ordeal. But no pain had ever stopped Frederick from pursuing his dreams. He wouldn't let a complaining spine stop him now.

He grabbed the handle on the plane's side and pulled himself into the aircraft. Frederick relished the exquisite leather seats and plush carpet, part of the reason the Beechcraft was called the Cadillac of the sky. The carpet freshener's brisk smell attested to the cleaning crew's recent presence. That would have been Frederick himself—yesterday. After a check of the pyramid cooler behind the copilot's seat, he affirmed that they were out of bottled beverages. Darren was supposed to be bringing some ice for the cooler; Frederick decided to call him to pick up some drinks, as well.

After unzipping his parka, he slipped it off and tossed it into the seat behind the pilot's hatch. He whipped out his cell phone, pressed the speed-dial number, and waited for Darren Cosby to answer. During the sixth ring, his brother-in-law's unceremonious "Yo" sounded over the line. "Sorry for the delay there. I was on the phone. I've got some good news, but it can wait until I get there."

"Well, I've got some bad news," Frederick rapped out. "We're out of Cokes, water, and even . . . are you sitting down?"

"Yeeeaaaaahhhhh," Darren's drawl was laced with suspicion.

"There's no chocolate milk, man!" Frederick bellowed and slapped his forehead. "How will you ever survive!"

"Go ahead, mock me, why don't you! At least my addiction has vitamin D in it. What did Coca-Cola ever do for anybody but give them stomach ulcers? That stuff will eat your gut like battery acid."

"Now you're getting nosy and downright annoying," Frederick retorted. "Just stop at the store and get us some chocolate milk and a case of Coke. Maybe we can survive all the way to

Atlanta. Who knows, I might even convert you to a grown-up beverage."

"Oooo! That was a low blow."

Snickering, Frederick lowered himself into the pilot's seat and spotted a black BMW whizzing down the airport's long drive. "Hey! Is that you I see already?"

"None other," Darren admitted. "And don't worry. I've already got the drinks. I even brought an extra cooler this time. That baby icebox only holds six bottles. We'll have those downed before we leave the runway."

"Get outta here," Frederick chided and hung up without bothering to say good-bye.

By the time Darren parked his car and walked to the plane, Frederick had already called to alter his flight plan for an earlier arrival. He'd also fired up the engine, received clearance delivery, and called the tower for clearance to taxi to the runway.

Darren had a business appointment in Atlanta, and the man was on the verge of a heart attack because he was afraid he'd be late.

Frederick planned a surprise visit with his friend Jim Bennington while Darren did his thing. Jim, a devoted doctor, had been instrumental in Frederick's walking. Early on, he'd pushed Frederick just enough until he'd taken his first step. One step led to another, and another, and then victory.

Jim now lived in Atlanta and wasn't doing well since his fiancée's sudden death due to an aneurysm in the brain. The poor guy was on depression medication and barely able to work. Frederick planned to pry him from his home, take him to the Bass Pro Shop, and get him to agree to a fishing trip next month.

The sound of footsteps on the plane's steps meant takeoff

would be soon . . . and thirty minutes earlier than planned. "Yoo-hoo, brother, dear!" a familiar female voice chimed.

Frederick's eyes widened, and he swiveled to look over his shoulder. Sure enough, his elder sister, Sophia, was climbing into the plane wearing a smile bigger than Dallas and a full-length fox coat that matched her fiery red hair.

"Ah, man," Frederick complained, "what are *you* doing here? I thought Darren and I were gonna be bachin' it!"

"False alarm," Darren announced as he stepped into the aircraft. He held a small cooler and a briefcase. His sandy hair was windblown, his cheeks were rosy, and his gray eyes were alive with expectation.

"You could have at least *warned* me. I'd have never mentioned the Coke. You know she'll tell Mom, and then I'll get my lecture of the week about how—"

"You should drink more water!" Sophia held up a six-pack of bottled water, broke one out of the plastic, and extended it to him. "The Cokes are off-limits until you drink this. You're going to fry your brain with all that acid."

Frederick grimaced at the water but took it anyway. "It could be worse. I could be an alcoholic or something," he mumbled.

"Don't start those diversionary tactics with me," Sophia retorted, and her brown eyes were every bit as stern as his mother's. "Just because you're not an alcoholic or a drug addict doesn't mean it's okay to be a Coke-aholic."

He glanced toward his brother-in-law, who'd set down the cooler and was shrugging out of his wool coat. "You might be able to reduce him to chocolate milk and bean sprouts, but it's going to take a whole lot more to get me to conform." Frederick pulled himself from off the pilot's seat, nudged Darren out of the way, and whipped open the cooler. Frederick dropped the water inside and pulled a Coke from the ice. After shooting Darren a defiant smile, he said, "Take a lesson," then snapped shut the lid.

"You're both hopeless," Sophia said. "And just for the record, I haven't reduced Darren to chocolate milk. The guy married me drinking the awful stuff."

"That's okay," Frederick chided, "we'll still be alive and kickin' when you die at fifty from an overdose of sea kelp and tofu."

Darren draped his jacket over one of the passenger seats and laughed out loud until Sophia's fake scowl ended his mirth.

"I know henpecked when I see it," Frederick commented.

"Actually, somebody the other day asked me if I was henpecked," Darren said and leaned closer to his wife with a flirtatious grin, "and I said, 'I wish!'"

"You wish," Sophia said over a gurgling laugh. "I bet you do," she taunted and smacked her lips against his.

"Oh brother." Frederick slid back into the pilot's seat. "When are you guys going to adopt six kids and get over the honeymoon?" he complained. When they didn't bother to answer, Frederick refrained from another backward glance. Those two had been married seventeen years, and somebody forgot to tell them they weren't supposed to be so happy together. At least not in front of people whose marital prospects had been shattered.

Frowning, Frederick unscrewed the Coke lid, downed a generous swallow, and relished the cold burn. Even at 28 degrees, he needed a Coke to fully function—and the colder the better.

The bump and clank of the stairs indicated that Darren had stopped romancing his wife long enough to close and secure the airstair door. Darren was the only person Frederick allowed that privilege. With all other passengers, he insisted upon the door duties himself.

Darren folded his stocky frame into the copilot's seat. Frederick glanced toward him and said, "You're going to ride up here? I thought you'd be in the back with Sophia."

"Nope. She's at the end of a mystery novel and has banished me up here. She says she's on the verge of figuring out who-done-it, and she's got to finish the book or die." Darren rubbed his hands against his ribbed sweater, cupped them together, and blew into them.

"Well, I don't fly dead people, so I guess it's a good thing you're up here."

Darren clicked his seat belt and chuckled. "I agree."

"So what's so hot in Atlanta?" Frederick asked and shot a glance to his brother-in-law.

"Nothing, if this weather's anything to go by," Darren said.

"You know what I mean, man." Frederick released the plane's brake.

"Actually, that's the good news I was going to tell you. I just got the call. Looks like Sophia and I will be moving there."

"Oh really?" Frederick raised his brows and enjoyed the warmth filling the cockpit.

"Yep. I made a halfhearted offer to one of our suppliers to lease his mansion and the acres of peach orchards with it. Believe it or not they've taken me up on my offer. We were flying in today to just look over the place and get better acquainted, but it looks like the owner is willing if I am."

"Wow!" Frederick said. "I guess that'll cut out a step in buying your peaches, huh?"

"Exact-a-mundo!" Darren nodded. "It will also give Sophia the bigger house she wants. Then maybe when the lease is up, we'll build our own. Of course, we're going to keep our house here in Charlotte as a weekender. As a matter of fact, we were wondering if you might like to live there. We could cut you a really good deal—as in free rent. It would sort of be like glorified house-sitting."

"I thought people got paid to do that," Frederick quipped and snapped his seat belt.

"Don't push your luck." Darren punched his upper arm.

"Yeow!" Frederick rubbed his arm and scowled at his brother-in-law. "Do you have to get so violent?"

"So what do you say?" Darren questioned through a chuckle.

"Sounds like a plan to me." Frederick nodded. "It'll save me a chunk of money every month. My landlord *loves* that townhouse I'm renting—if the price is anything to go by."

"Good. And our move doesn't have to affect your flying at all. I'm keeping the Beechcraft at the airport here. You can keep your schedule as usual." Darren's sly smile hinted that there'd be many flights between Atlanta and Charlotte.

"That's convenient for you, isn't it?" Frederick teased.

"You catch on fast!"

As the plane coasted forward, Frederick applied the accelerator and pointed the aircraft's nose toward the runway. A thought niggling at the back of his mind soon grew into a full-blown "what if?" that wouldn't be quieted.

No, it can't be, he scolded himself. *Allie Elton's family would never consider leasing their place. It's been in the family since Noah.*

While the plane rolled toward the runway, Frederick decided there was only one way to prove himself right. He'd just ask Darren. "Where is this new place, anyway?"

"It's called Georgia Gold Plantation. The house is named Elton Mansion. Been around since before the Civil War."

Frederick's fingers dug into the yoke, and the stop at the runway's opening jerked him against his seat belt.

"Watch it!" Darren bleated. "You're going to rattle my brains out."

"Sorry," Frederick mumbled and shoved aside the latest bit of information for later consideration. The task at hand demanded that he focus on the details necessary for a safe flight. After doing the run-up checking of all engines and systems, he turned his head and asked, "Sophia, you buckled up?"

"You got it, Captain!"

Frederick picked up his mouthpiece and called the tower for permission to take off. Soon the plane was lifting off the runway with the ease and grace of an eagle. But the pilot had never been so tense.

"Hey, man," Darren said, "you want to go with us today to look over the mansion and help us give the final handshake?"

"No, I don't think so," Frederick growled and scowled straight into the blue horizon. "I was planning on visiting a friend. I'm not dressed for that kind of a trip anyway." He glanced down at his wind suit. At least he'd graduated to top-of-the-line Nikes in his old age, but even that probably wasn't good enough for the Eltons.

No matter what he was wearing, the last thing Frederick needed was risking an encounter with Allie Elton . . . or whatever her last name was these days. *Heaven help me if I had to be polite to her husband,* Frederick grumbled to himself while wondering whatever had possessed the Eltons to lease out their operation.

Probably something rich people do for entertainment, he caustically thought. As the plane gained altitude, Frederick gained a sour attitude that he wallowed in without remorse.

Ten minutes later, Darren's voice seemed to float from

another time zone. "Are you okay? You've got a mean face on. Whatzup? We're not, like, going to crash or anything, are we?"

Frederick managed a tense grin that felt about as sincere as a disgruntled crocodile's. The engine's hum had never been surer. The day couldn't have been more perfect for a safe flight.

"Oh ye of little faith." His attempt at a teasing lilt came out more like a snarl. "The flight is fine," Frederick added and tried to soften his tone. "I've just got something else on my mind," he mumbled and glanced toward the west.

"Oh," Darren replied.

Feeling his brother-in-law's scrutiny, Frederick decided to be honest. "I used to work there—at the plantation—actually," he admitted and tapped his finger against the yoke.

"Really?"

"Yep." He checked his gauges. As the plane reached its final altitude, he shot a glance toward Darren, who was twisting in his seat.

"Hey, Sophia! Did you know Frederick used to work at Elton Mansion?" he hollered.

Frederick rubbed his forehead and stifled a moan. He set the plane on automatic pilot and grabbed his Coke.

"No!" Sophia replied. "Oh, wait a minute. Now I remember. He *did* work as a yard manager for a mansion years ago. Yes, we'd been married about seven years. I remember Mom was worried—" She stopped.

Frederick guzzled his soda and lowered the bottle. "Go ahead and say it," he blandly encouraged. "Mom was worried I was getting in over my head with a woman who lived there."

"Well, that obviously didn't happen," Sophia replied, and Frederick didn't bother to correct her. He'd also never bothered to tell his mother that he'd bought a ring the size of a Ping-Pong ball and proposed. As far as his parents were concerned, the relationship with Allie Elton had just fizzled. Frederick had been far too hurt to explain the turn of events to anyone, even to his family or a store clerk. So he secured the ring in a safety deposit box, where it remained today, and locked the pain in his heart.

"You need to go with us, then!" Sophia insisted.

"Don't think so," Frederick replied.

Darren's scrutiny was still on—all the way on. Frederick felt it. No telling what the guy was thinking. Darren Cosby had a sharp mind that needed only a few clues to piece together the whole picture. Frederick wondered how long he would take to figure out the whole sad, sorry saga.

"Yes, you need to go!" Sophia repeated. This time, she was closer—so close her Giorgio perfume wafted into the cockpit. Frederick had regretted buying her that stuff ever since she unwrapped it last Christmas. She'd sprayed herself down and had reeked ever since.

Frederick glanced up and back to see his sister standing in the aisle behind his seat. Hands on her hips, all she needed was a whip to finish her dictator stance. Her snug black pants and dark gray sweater nicely rounded out the effect.

"I never gave you permission to get up," he snapped.

"I don't *need* your permission. This is *my* airplane," she shot back. "I know when it's safe to get up."

"Suit yourself," he drawled, "but the tower says there's going to be some turbulence. You might wind up with a knot on that hard head of yours before it's over. Consider yourself warned."

Normally Frederick didn't let his bossy sister sway him much. Of course, his stubbornness kept her exasperated beyond all reason. And that alone was enough to fuel Frederick's resolve. While he sensed her glare, a stronger emotion emerged. Even though thoughts of facing Allie were laced with pain, Frederick was overtaken with a curiosity he could not deny. After all these years, he wondered what she was like . . . if she'd changed . . . and yes, if she'd ever married.

"Okay, I'll go with you," he blurted. After another swallow of Coke, he placed the bottle back in its holder and decided he'd just call Jim.

"You mean I win? Just like that?" Sophia snapped her fingers.

"He must be going soft," Darren mused. "Or there's more here than meets the eye."

Frederick pretended a deep interest in a bank of clouds building in the south, the source of the turbulence.

"Well, I guess we'll just have to see," Sophia drawled like a star detective. "I *do* have trouble believing Frederick would go soft."

"If he does, you'll have him drinking eight bottles of water a day and asking for more," Darren said.

Frederick heard him—sort of—but was too engrossed with the dynamics of the coming meeting to form a retort.

Allie's probably not even living there now, he told himself and wiped his dampening palm on his pants.

The plane hit a few bumps, and Frederick glanced back at his sister, who was heading straight for her seat. The snap of her seat belt assured him she'd detected the first signs of the predicted turbulence. And Frederick wished securing his safety for the pending visit was as simple as buckling up.

Six

Allie checked her appearance in the mirror and sighed. The Cosbys were due in thirty minutes, and she couldn't remember when or why she'd left off wearing most cosmetics. She stood in her Victorian bathroom, peering into a basketful of mismatched leftovers from yesteryear. All that was in her new cosmetic drawer was a powder compact, a flesh-toned lipstick, brown mascara, and a barely-there blusher she usually forgot to apply. As for perfume, she did well to remember a scented hand lotion.

Even though the pending visit involved Frederick's sister—not Frederick himself—Allie wanted to look her best. She scrounged through the basket and pulled out a brown eyeliner, a red lipstick the same shade as her top, and a blusher to match. She was on the verge of application when she pondered the message more cosmetics would send to her family.

Sophia Cosby and her husband had no clue that Allie had long sported the bland brunette look. But her family knew and would wonder why she'd decided to go for a more dramatic appeal. From there it wouldn't take Aunt Landon long to piece together Allie's continued interest in Frederick. Then she might begin her decade-old lecture anew.

Even though the Cosbys were now wealthy and Frederick was a decorated war hero, Allie doubted that would matter

to Landon when it came to matrimony between the families.
And it certainly didn't matter to her father. As far as he was
concerned, the Eltons were still bluebloods and the Cosby
clan was nothing more than lucky blue collars.

Allie dropped the cosmetics back into the basket and applied a slather of Sweet Pea hand lotion. She fluffed her hair
and examined her short stack in the mirror. At least her hair
was still shiny, the red highlights as glossy as ever. No gray
in sight, either. She turned from the bathroom, snapped off
the light, and walked across her bedroom suite. Her haven
encompassed most of the third floor and was nearly as big
as her sister Macy's guest cottage, where she, her father, and
Evelyn were scheduled to move within the month.

Like a connoisseur of great treasures, Allie paused near
the elevated bed and stroked the carved post. They were
taking only their personal possessions and linens with them
since Macy's cottage was already furnished. And Allie knew
that when she returned, her haven would never be the same.

Her gaze trailed to a photo sitting on her nightstand. She
and Sarah Hamilton went to Switzerland last year and had the
time of their lives. They'd been outside a spectacular, snow-
crested chalet with a view of the mountains that wouldn't stop
when the photo was taken. The snapshot had captured Sarah's
strength, her dignity, her determination. No one would guess
that the cute African-American woman had overcome strong
economic odds to become a sought-after children's surgeon.

What Sarah didn't know was that Allie had secretively sup-
plemented her college tuition. She'd posed as an unnamed
benefactor who wanted to help economically challenged students. Allie had delved into her trust fund and paid much of
Sarah's fees while modestly assisting two others in order to
keep her cover. Sarah never suspected.

Now Sarah's sheer tenacity, shining from the photo, urged Allie to do for herself what she had done for her friend. She'd been a financial lifeline for Sarah. For herself, she must be an emotional lifeline and pull herself out of the doldrums.

Another photo on the nightstand came into focus. Allie's mom had been such a source of strength, and Allie never could say she'd stopped missing her. Everyone said Allie had her eyes and her smile. And now that smile appeared to hold a courageous edge that said, "I'm behind you one hundred percent." Allie balled her fist, straightened her spine, and willed herself to stop the melancholic nonsense. Her mother would expect nothing less.

We aren't leaving forever, she reasoned. *Just for a few years.* Allie hurried toward the hallway before the sentimentals sucked her under. She planned to read in the library until Aunt Landon and the Cosbys arrived. Then she'd be available with her father and Aunt Landon to interact with the potential leasers.

Evelyn had conveniently scheduled a lunch appointment for today. And for once, Allie truly felt sorry for her. While the move was tugging at Allie's heart, it seemed to be tearing Evelyn to pieces. By the time Allie descended the curved stairway and her pumps tapped along the marble entryway, the doorbell chimed. She checked her watch and decided this must be Landon. Out of habit, Allie waited for the doorman to open the door, and then remembered there was no doorman. As part of the immediate application of the new budget, the staff had been carved to a bare minimum.

Allie hurried forward, turned the brass knob, and opened the massive door. Ready with a familiar greeting and a smile, her face stiffened before she uttered a word. This wasn't Landon. It was Frederick Wently. Allie also received the vague impression of a redhead in a fox coat and a stocky man with sandy hair and a warm smile.

Then there was Frederick. Frederick again. And again. Allie couldn't stop looking at him. No matter how many times she glanced away, her gaze was drawn back to him and him alone.

The years had been good to him. While he lacked the fresh-faced look of a twenty-five-year-old, the slight crow's feet around his eyes and the touch of gray at his temples gave him a mature appeal that quickened Allie's pulse. His haunted brown eyes spoke of years lived and heartaches endured. And Allie wondered if some of those heartaches involved Afghanistan . . . and maybe a beautiful middle-Eastern woman.

"Allie?" he questioned.

"Y-yes," she stammered and barely registered the freezing air bathing her face. "Won't you—won't you come in?" She opened the door wider and stopped herself from checking Frederick's left hand for a gold band. She didn't even want to know. Or, rather, dreaded knowing.

The trio stepped into the foyer, and the redhead said, "Oh, this is divine!" while scanning the room with an awe-struck gaze.

Allie shut the door, secured the lock, and turned toward the guests.

"Hi, I'm Darren Cosby." The sandy-haired man extended his hand, and Allie noted the tailor-made class of his wool coat.

"Nice to meet you. I'm Allie Elton." Allie placed her hand in his for a brief handshake.

"This is Sophia, my wife."

"Hello," Sophia said and gripped Allie's hand for an ecstatic squeeze rather than a shake. Sophia's red hair and translucent skin probably turned as many heads as Evelyn did. But like

Frederick, her shining brown eyes were her most striking feature.

"And it looks like you and Frederick have already met?" Darren asked. He cast a cautious glance toward his brother-in-law.

"Good to see you, Allie," Frederick said, but his lips barely moved through the greeting. And his expression wasn't half as inviting as his sister's.

A slow tremor attacked her knees. Allie looked past him, mumbled something about nothing, and inserted her perspiring hands into her blazer pockets. As she debated what to do next, the doorknob rattled. The doorbell's chime followed and rescued her from the necessity of making a decision.

"Excuse me," she said. "That's most likely Aunt Landon. I locked her out, I guess." Her assumption was correct.

Landon, dressed in a full-length mink, conquered the room with the grace and style of a dozen Southern belles.

"Aunt Landon," Allie said as she once again closed the door, "I know you know the Cosbys. And you probably remember Frederick?" She wondered if her comments sounded as breathless to everyone else as they did to her.

"You're early!" Landon chimed with the warmth of a long-lost relative. She extended her hand to each of the Cosbys and finished with Frederick. "Great to see you again," she said. If his presence surprised her, no one would have guessed.

Frederick's mild smile spoke nothing. Allie wondered how the animated man she once knew had evolved into this masked stranger.

"Well, hello there, Cosby!" Richard Elton's call from the stairway gained everyone's attention.

"Mr. Elton!" Darren replied. "Good to see you!"

The family patriarch stood at the top of the stairs, observing the group beneath him, his blue eyes contrasting with his ever-present tan. One of the luxuries he had refused to relinquish on the budget quest was his tan. After they left the mansion, Richard would no longer have access to his personal tanning bed, and he planned to immediately join a spa.

"So glad you're interested in leasing the place." Richard descended the steps, his turtleneck sweater and easy-swing blazer giving him the appeal of a yacht captain, never surer of himself . . . or his vessel. "I've been absolutely *dying* for some freedom," he added.

"I can imagine," Darren replied. "You've spent your whole life here."

"Yes." Richard approached from the stairway, extended his hand, and graciously greeted each visitor. No one would ever suspect that he viewed them as lessers or that he was on the verge of bankruptcy. "My daughters and I will be doing some traveling abroad—some sightseeing."

Sightseeing? Allie thought. *Since when is moving into Macy's guesthouse considered sightseeing?* Her sister lived an hour and a half south in Macon, Georgia. She and her husband had graciously offered Richard and his daughters their guest cottage rent-free for as many years as they wanted.

Landon's smile and nod held just the right air. Affirmative, but not eager. Pleasant, but not revealing.

And Allie was as mesmerized by her aunt's act as her father's.

"Your offer came at a perfect time," Richard continued with the story he and Landon and Evelyn had concocted last week. This way no one but the Eltons' trusted accountant and the immediate family would know they were forced to lease the property or lose all. They'd made a pact to tell no one, not even their closest friends, including Evelyn's sidekick, Penny Clayton.

While the whole Elton family regularly attended church, at times Allie wondered if she was the only one who took a relationship with God seriously. None of the family seemed to mind spinning whatever falsehood necessary to save face. While Allie thought it unwise to broadcast her family's financial crises, she would never resort to lying for a cover.

Soon the visitors were shedding their coats, and Allie and Aunt Landon agreed to hang them in the closet beneath the stairway. Somehow the fate of Frederick's parka landed with Allie. Keeping her head down, she accepted the coat and refused to give in to the urge to bury her face in it and absorb Frederick's warmth . . . and his scent. He'd always gone for a sporty men's cologne—nothing too heavy or fancy, but just right. And Allie picked up the faint smell of something similar to what she remembered from all those years ago.

While her father chatted up the Cosbys, Allie clutched Frederick's coat and planned to hang up Sophia's fox number first.

When Landon finished with her mink and Darren's overcoat, she pivoted and mumbled, "So what do you think?"

"About?" Allie blinked.

"The Cosbys," Landon insisted, her blue eyes wide. "Have they said they're for sure going to lease the place or not?" Landon dusted at the front of her thigh-length sweater and continued to demonstrate her acting skills. No one would ever guess that she was doing any more than telling Allie there were six extra hangers in the closet.

"They got here only two minutes before you." Allie stepped toward the narrow closet and prepared to hang the fur. "But Mrs. Cosby seemed impressed with the place."

"Who wouldn't?" Landon replied and meandered toward the chattering klatch.

After hanging up Sophia's coat, Allie stole a glimpse of the group as they walked across the foyer. No one noticed her, and the stairway was swiftly blocking their view. Allie clutched Frederick's coat and buried her face in its soft folds. She breathed deeply as his warmth and scent enveloped her senses. The years rolled back and Allie relived their first kiss . . . and their last. A shiver wracked her body. She lifted her head and stifled a moan. Reluctantly Allie placed the parka on a padded hanger and longingly stroked the sleeve one last time before the door clicked shut.

When she released the knob, Allie's spirits plummeted, and only one option remained for her: Escape!

She tiptoed alongside the stairway until she could once again see the group. Richard was leading the Cosbys into the formal dining area and explaining that the furniture would be staying as part of the lease agreement. Landon followed close behind with Frederick at her side.

Allie ached anew with the thought of her family's heirlooms being rented, even though there was no way around the plan. The presence of Frederick coupled with relinquishing her home was too much for one day. She planned to brew some decaf coffee in the single-serve machine in her suite. Then she'd crawl into the corner recliner, try to fathom a reason for Frederick's presence, and round it all off with a good cry.

This has to be some sort of cruel twist of fate, she thought.

As Allie crept up the stairs, she ignored the twinge of pain in her leg and snatched a final glance of Frederick stepping into the dining room. From the way he greeted her earlier, he barely even remembered her name. No telling how many women he'd snared since their near-miss engagement. Allie was certain he'd had his share falling at his feet. A decorated war hero was enough to attract dozens of women. Add tall and handsome and muscular to that formula, and the women probably spanned the hundreds.

Allie's decision not to check for a gold band seemed ridiculous now. She wanted to know. She needed to know. She gripped the banister and debated if she should spy around the dining room doorway just long enough to see his left ring finger. By the time she'd lectured herself out of the deed, the front door burst open and Evelyn invaded the room with none other than Penny Clayton in her wake. "I've got some *wonderful* news!" Evelyn pronounced as if the whole household were awaiting her proclamation.

Allie pressed her fingertips against her temple and thought, *Oh no, not Penny Clayton. Not today of all days.*

Evelyn's attention rested upon Allie. "Where's Dad?" she asked, shrugging out of her leather coat.

"He's in the dining room." Allie pointed toward the right and eyed the bleach-blond, green-eyed woman following Evelyn. She reminded Allie of a chihuahua—bug eyes, a pointed nose, and enough nervous energy for three women. "The Cosbys are here," Allie added.

"Guess what?" Evelyn continued. "Penny's going to Atlantic Beach with us." She beamed toward her friend, who ecstatically shook her hands and said, "Can't wait! Can't wait!"

"Atlantic Beach?" Allie squinted. "As in Florida?"

"Yes." Evelyn shut the door and dropped her leather jacket on the solid brass coat-tree mere feet away. She fluffed her hair and adjusted her short-waisted sweater. "Remember, I bought year-round time in that time-share condominium last year?"

"No, I don't," Allie replied. "I didn't know anything about that."

Evelyn waved her hand. "Maybe I never told you, then," she said.

Penny draped her long denim coat near Evelyn's. The willowy widow claimed to be thirty-eight, but the feathery facial lines indicated she was closer to forty-five.

"And I guess Dad didn't tell you we decided to go to Atlantic Beach instead of Macy's, either, did he?"

"Uh, no."

"Well, last night we decided we're going to Atlantic Beach for a while, and *you* can go on to Macon to visit Macy."

Allie remained silent as the news settled around her shoulders like a yoke of stone.

"Macy texted Dad yesterday. She's sick again. You might know it." Evelyn rolled her eyes. "And you *know* how I don't handle sick well."

"Of course," Allie responded and gazed down at the glossy wooden stairs. Idly she pondered if her family would ever see fit to consult with her about the plans they made for her. An unexpected restlessness troubled the waters of her soul, stirring a latent longing to be her own woman, even if for only one day.

Without another glance at Allie, Evelyn grabbed Penny's arm and propelled her toward the dining room. The sound of gleeful greetings accompanied the entrance of the two women, and Allie recommitted herself to her room's solitude and the cry. The last time she visited Macy in her sick mode, Allie had waited on her hand and foot for two weeks.

Oh well, she thought, *it will at least be good to see my nephews. And maybe this Atlantic Beach trip won't be so bad after all. If Dad and Evelyn decide to stay there awhile, I'll just go visit them if Macy gets too bossy.*

Then she thought of Macy's sisters-in-law, Louise and Helena Grove. Since Macy and Charlie lived on the Grove estate, Macy's sisters-in-law were forever at her home and would

therefore be a regular part of Allie's life. She frowned. While
Helena was definitely a flirt, Louise came across more like
a hussy. She attached herself to anything wearing pants and
didn't mind dragging home every stray male who looked her
way. How the young woman had avoided getting abducted was
anybody's guess. Her father was too interested in indulging
her to offer correction, and her mother was too enamored
with Macy's twin sons to worry about why her twenty-year-
old daughter was out until two in the morning.

Maybe I can be a good influence on both those girls, Allie reflected, and she decided to make a point of trying to get Louise
and Helena to church regularly. Hopefully she could steer
Louise toward a wholesome crowd of young adults. *If I can
at least make a difference in their lives, maybe that will be God's
way of bringing something good out of this upheaval.*

Sighing, Allie turned and began the long trudge up the
stairway again. Only this time, the sound of Frederick's voice
stopped her.

Seven

"Excuse me. Allie?" Frederick questioned and wasn't sure what he'd say next. He had missed Allie in the group about the time Evelyn arrived. Before he could stop himself, he retraced his steps and spotted her heading upstairs.

Allie halted and slowly pivoted to face him. "Yes?"

"I know there's a restroom around here somewhere, but I seem to have forgotten. . . ." He gazed across the mammoth foyer and couldn't decide whether his request was a stroke of genius or just plain stupid. After half a second deliberation, Frederick tossed aside the genius option and settled for stupid. Surely anyone with half a brain could see through such a line and realize he just wanted to talk to Allie again. Why he wanted to torment himself so was anybody's guess. *I'm a glutton for punishment,* he told himself. *End of discussion.*

"The restroom?" she asked and a slight line formed between her brows.

"Yes." He dug his fingers against the pocket of his wind suit. "You know, the place with the, um, toilet." *This is getting more stupid by the minute!* He tried a smile but figured he gave her the disgruntled look instead.

"Oh! The restroom," Allie replied as if she really needed the explanation. "It's right by the library." She pointed with her left hand—the hand that held no wedding band.

Frederick stared at her fingers a full five seconds and locked his knees. "Uh, right. Um, thanks." He cut another glance at her face, figured he better leave before he started hyperventilating, and walked back toward the dining room.

"No. It's *that* way," Allie said.

Frederick stopped and glanced over his shoulder. Allie was still pointing to the left with her ringless hand.

"What is?" He wrinkled his brow.

"The—the restroom," she said. "You know, the place with the toilet." Her taut lips barely turned up at the corners.

"Oh, right." Frederick mumbled and strode across the foyer like a man on a mission.

Once he stepped into the brass and tile restroom and shut the door, he pointed his index finger at his temple as if he were pulling the trigger on a gun. He looked at himself in the mirror, whispered, "I know there's a restroom around here somewhere," and then scowled.

I couldn't have been more obvious if I'd used a lame pickup line, he decided and recalled all the soldiers-on-the-make in the Air Force. "Haven't I seen you somewhere before?" Frederick mocked.

He lowered the lid on the toilet, plopped onto it, rested his forearms on his knees, and stared at the white tile. *I must have been stark raving mad to come here,* he thought.

The bathroom was as opulent as everything else in this mansion—right down to the gold-plated Kleenex box and the crystal candle holder in which burned a votive that smelled like peach cobbler. He picked up the crystal piece and plunked it back down. A drop of wax splashed out and seared his finger. Frederick winced and rubbed the drying wax from his skin.

Nothing had changed. Not even the scent of the candles

the Eltons used. And certainly not the cold gleam in Landon Russ's eyes.

No matter how warm and friendly she was, Frederick recognized what Landon couldn't hide. Not with him, anyway. She still thought she and the Eltons were several rungs higher on the value ladder than he and his family. Except this time there was a thread of desperation mixed with the chill.

"That's odd," Frederick whispered. He rested his forearms on his knees again and linked his fingers. The issue remained an enigma until he recalled Allie opening the front door . . . and hanging up the coats. In his memories, there had always been a doorman to perform those duties. Darren and Sophia even had a doorman these days.

Why not the Eltons? Why not now?

A shocking thought plunged into Frederick's mind and left him blinking. *What if they're broke and they* have *to lease this place?*

"Oh man!" he whispered and stood. Frederick placed his thumb and index finger above his temples and squeezed.

That would explain a lot of things, he thought. *Like why Allie looked so . . . so pale.* He barely even recognized her at the door. The Allie he remembered was bright and pretty with long hair and rosy cheeks. This Allie was almost colorless and her hair was cropped short. While the haircut definitely became her, Frederick ached for the old Allie's vivacious gleam.

He thought of that famous scene from *Gone with the Wind* when Scarlett O'Hara visited Rhett Butler. She'd told him how wonderful everything was at Tara, and he believed her—until he realized her hands were calloused because she'd been working like a field hand.

Frederick crossed his arms, tilted his head back, and closed his eyes. Richard had strongly indicated he was leasing the place for leisure purposes only. Landon supported his claim. But Allie said nothing.

Maybe that's because they're lying just like Scarlett lied to Rhett, Frederick thought. *And maybe Allie refused to participate.*

Frederick opened his eyes. "She always detested lying," he murmured and idly wondered if Allie's ringless hands were calloused. If so, she was being served a massive helping of poetic justice.

But even if the Eltons were broke, Landon still clung to her skewed value scale, which meant Frederick still wasn't good enough for Allie.

Some things never change, he thought and could have whacked himself for coming here. The only good it had accomplished was the stirring of sweet, old memories and the resurrection of hard, ageless pain.

An hour later, Allie sat in her corner recliner, her eyes swollen, her box of tissue exhausted. A mountain of wadded Kleenex rested on the lampstand next to a mug full of coffee, cold and untouched. She stroked the last page of the scrapbook and reread the final keepsake article about Frederick. She'd stumbled across the interview in the *New York Times* and cherished it as much as the *People* magazine cover story.

None of the stories mentioned a wife. And Allie had noted during their conversation about the bathroom that Frederick still wore no wedding ring. The knowledge made the pain more poignant.

He was as handsome now as he had been in all his war hero photos, and even more than when they first fell in love. Allie picked up the last tired tissue from her lap and pressed it against her burning eyes. She retrieved the mug of cold coffee, sipped the acrid liquid, grimaced, and scooted to the edge of the recliner.

Still clutching the scrapbook, Allie stood and padded into her bathroom in her stockinged feet. She dumped the coffee down the marble sink and set the empty mug on the counter-top. Allie didn't even want to look at her red-eyed self, so she kept her gaze away from the mirror and firmly on the hardwood floor.

I probably look more like a bug-eyed chihuahua right now than Penny does, she thought as she walked toward the windows, which were draped in sage-colored cotton. Allie leaned against the wall and gazed out the window. Landon's red Jaguar was sitting in the circular drive; so was a black Cadillac decked in gold trim.

She cradled the scrapbook against her chest and pondered the acres and acres of land that were as much a part of her heritage as her bloodline. The perfectly manicured lawn had become an expression of Allie's spirit. Even in the dead of winter, she and the grounds manager created a horticulture masterpiece with evergreens and annuals.

Allie rested her temple against the window frame and placed her chin on the scrapbook. Her attention settled upon the clouds darkening the southern horizon, and she couldn't re-member a time she'd ever been so desolate . . . so lonely—except for those weeks after Frederick stepped out of her life.

"But even then I still had my home," she whispered.

Detecting a movement out of the corner of her eye, Allie glanced toward it. The Cosbys and Frederick strolled toward the black Cadillac. An animated Sophia hung on her husband's arm and gestured across the lawn while Darren looked over his shoulder at the mansion. Frederick walked to the driver's door and paused as the Cosbys opened the back door and crawled inside. Without warning, Frederick peered toward the third floor, at the window where Allie stood.

Allie's fingers tightened around the scrapbook, and Frederick's gaze met hers for a second before she jerked away from the window. Her pulse pounding, Allie leaned against the wall, closed her eyes, and decided this must be the most wretched day in her life. A knock on her bedroom door only increased her heart's drumming.

"Allie?" Aunt Landon's concerned call jolted her. Her fingers flexed against the scrapbook. No one knew of Allie's memory book. No one.

"Just a minute," she garbled out and lunged toward the ornate wardrobe near the matching bed. Thankfully, she'd left the door ajar when she removed the scrapbook. All that remained was turning the key in the built-in storage cabinet and opening it. She shoved the scrapbook beneath her mother's antique quilts and Sarah Hamilton's last Christmas present: an autographed copy of *Robert Frost's Complete Works*. Her hands trembling, she relocked the cabinet, used the same key to secure the wardrobe, then pocketed the key.

Rubbing her eyes, Allie opened her bedroom door and allowed her aunt to enter.

"Wonderful news!" Landon exclaimed. "The deal is settled! The Cosbys are moving in in two weeks."

Head bent, Allie snapped her door closed and sighed. The days of hanging on were finished. Now was the time to accept what was best for their family.

"Allie!" Landon exclaimed. "Look at you. You've been crying. Are you all right?" Her forehead wrinkled. "Now, that's a dumb question. If you were all right, you wouldn't be crying, now, would you?"

Allie bit her lip and walked toward the antique sideboard

that served as her snack center. She turned off the coffeepot emitting the smell of stale brew and gazed at the floor.

Aunt Landon's gentle touch on her arm meant more to her than it ever had. "Are you finally realizing you're going to be leaving here, sugar, or is it . . . uh, *him?*"

"A little of both I think," Allie admitted.

"Surely not after all these years," Landon commented.

Allie shrugged, looked her aunt in the eyes, and then stared past her. "I can't help but wonder if I should have—should have—"

"Don't even say it, Allie," Landon scolded. "You're still so young. The right man will come along—someone who's perfect for you."

Unable to curb the sarcasm, Allie said, "You mean someone who has as much money as we do?" She raised her hand and then rested her fingers on the sideboard.

Aunt Landon covered Allie's hand with hers and squeezed. "It's not just about *money*," she insisted. "It's about pedigree and social standing." She placed her fingers under Allie's chin and tugged upward. Allie complied and gazed into her aunt's determined eyes. "You just can't mix a thoroughbred with a . . . a commoner. It would never work. I know what I'm talking about, Allie. I was much younger once and had to make choices myself. I married a man with money—someone of my own kind—"

"And he left you," Allie blurted before she thought to stop herself.

Aunt Landon lowered her hand and winced.

"Oh, I'm so sorry," Allie rushed and grasped Landon's shoulder. "I'd never do a thing to hurt you! I don't know what possessed me."

"It's quite all right, dear." Landon tugged Allie's hand from her shoulder and gripped it. "You did nothing but speak the truth. He *did* leave me. But when he left, I was blessed with half of everything he owned. Had I married a poor man, there are no guarantees that he would have stayed with me any longer, now, are there? And if he left he might have taken half of my inheritance."

"But if the poor man loved you . . ."

"I thought the rich man loved me," Landon crooned. "Take a lesson from your dear ol' aunt. If you ever *do* get married, it needs to be with your head first." She slyly winked. "If your heart tags along, then that's fine. If it doesn't, you've lost nothing and gained everything."

Allie picked up a granola bar from her snack basket, fumbled with the wrapper, and wondered if Aunt Landon and Penny Clayton had read the same marriage manual. This time Allie had the good sense to maintain her silence. Aunt Landon would probably never forgive Allie for comparing her with the scheming divorcée.

But the fact was, Penny's interest in Evelyn appeared to be fueled by her attraction for Richard Elton—or rather, his fortune. Allie wondered if Penny would be half as interested in Evelyn's friendship if she knew the pending move was for necessity, not for leisure.

Eight

One month later, Frederick sat at a quaint roadside park on the hood of the Mustang he'd rented in Atlanta, Georgia. He peered down the highway at the twin brick pillars that marked the opening to Grove Acres. Frederick swatted at a fly that was interested in his Coke and then guzzled the soda until his eyes stung. He plunked the bottle onto the hood, propped his boot on the front bumper, and rested his elbow on his knee.

Frederick squinted against the sunshine and wished he felt as carefree as the March breeze that harassed the evergreens and oaks and nipped at his jacket. After an unbearable winter, spring swept in early and with it came Frederick's current bout of temporary insanity. At least, that's the best diagnosis he could come up with. There was no other explanation for why he'd driven to Macon to see Allie Elton after his visit with his friend Jim Bennington in Atlanta.

Before Frederick left the Elton Mansion a month ago, he'd picked up enough details to learn that Evelyn, her father, and the blonde woman named Penny were all traveling to Atlantic Beach while Allie was going to stay with her sister, Macy, in Macon. He remembered enough from when he and Allie were together a decade ago to recall some of the details of Macy and her husband's lives—enough that a search on the internet revealed their address. After that, he needed only to pull up Google Maps to get driving directions from Jim's house, whom he'd been visiting for a few days.

Thankfully, Frederick had regained his senses when he was driving into Grove Acres. That's when he'd turned around and pulled into this roadside park to contemplate exactly what he thought he was up to. One month ago when he spotted Allie looking at him from that third-story window, a tiny hope had sprouted in Frederick's soul—the hope that she'd been watching for him just as he'd watched for her during the rest of his visit that day. That hope had fueled longing. A month later, the longing bred the plan that took over his psyche and drove him to action.

By some miracle, Frederick had gotten Jim to agree to the fishing trip. They'd been hard at it for three days and his swollen index finger proved it—right where that catfish finned him. This morning Frederick told Jim he needed to pay a visit to an old friend. Jim had awakened to a "bad day," which meant he was overtaken with memories of his deceased fiancée, so he'd mentioned needing some time alone anyway when Frederick said he was driving to Macon.

"I'm setting myself up for heartache," Frederick mumbled toward a crumbling stone column that held a historic marker. He began to argue himself into getting into the vehicle, driving to the airport, and flying back to Charlotte where he was safe. *Nothing has changed*, he reminded himself and downed the last of the Coke to the tune of an annoyingly cheerful mockingbird. *Allie is still an Elton. I'm still just somebody who used to be the yardman.* Clenching his jaw, Frederick screwed the lid onto the bottle, slid to the pebbled drive, and winced when he straightened his spine. Even with the warmer weather, his back was committed to complaining.

An unexpected surge of old resentment erupted within Frederick as violently as that land mine had exploded in Afghanistan. While Frederick had used his body as a shield for his crew, there was no one to shield his heart from the agonizing memories of Allie's rejection. After his emergency surgery, he'd floated in and out of consciousness and recalled bits of conversation regarding his future. One doctor predicted that the shrapnel in his spine would ensure Frederick would never walk again. During those desolate hours, Frederick could think of no one but his Lord and his Allie. Daily he begged God to allow her to miraculously appear.

She never did.

Presently, he wondered if she'd have attended his funeral if the emergency plane landing or land mine had killed him. *Probably not,* he grunted and kicked at the vehicle's tire. His spine kicked back. Frederick grabbed his lower back and sucked in a breath. *No more sitting on car hoods!*

He opened the car door and tossed the empty Coke bottle into the passenger seat. With a final glance toward Grove Acres, Frederick decided he was worse than a fool. *I'm a tormented idiot. I'm still in love with her, and I'm bitter—all at the same time. I'm a mixed-up mess.*

The rev of an engine that started as a distant roar hummed closer from around the road's curve. He glanced toward the noise and hoped the driver slowed enough before taking the curve. These Georgia hillsides, while nothing compared to the Rockies, could still pose a threat to a reckless driver. After his experiences in Afghanistan, Frederick had turned into a granny driver himself. At least, that's what Sophia called him. So let it be. Frederick had kissed death. He was taking no more chances.

He frowned toward a fiery red Corvette—a convertible, no

less—as it sped around the curve with the shriek of tires and the thump and grind of heavy metal music. The driver's long blond hair blew in carefree ribbons as the vehicle whizzed by. Frederick must have caught her eye, for she darted a swift glance toward him. Her racy sunglasses and red lips gave Frederick the blurred impression of young, beautiful, and rash. He scowled after her and resisted the urge to follow and give her a "big brother" lecture on safe driving.

Shrugging, Frederick opened the car door and decided to get himself and his aching spine back into his airplane and all the way home. But the scream of brakes, the skid of tires sent a jolting shock along his nerves. Believing his predictions were fulfilled, he whirled toward the Corvette and pulled his cell phone from his pocket. Fully prepared to dial 9-1-1, he realized the Corvette was still in one piece and backing out of the Grove Acres drive. The convertible then lurched forward with a screech, a fishtail, and a line of smoke in its wake.

Frederick huffed, placed his hand on his hip, and wished for five minutes of the young woman's time. Somebody needed to tell her to have some respect for her own life and his heart. The way it thudded, Frederick was amazed he hadn't had a heart attack. He rammed the cell phone back into his pocket.

When the Corvette swerved into the roadside park and skidded to a halt mere feet from his rental car, Frederick stumbled backward and rammed into the Mustang's side-view mirror. A shower of gravel pelted his shins as his car door slammed. Frederick's back raged. Hot tingles shot into his thighs. And cold sweat dotted his upper lip and forehead.

The woman switched off the music and called, "Hi there!" with a Southern twang every bit as sassy as her red-lipped grin.

Frederick glared at her. "Are you crazy?!" he croaked. *Or drunk?* he added to himself.

She took off her glasses, tossed them on the passenger seat, threw back her head, and laughed. "Crazy! I like that! Maybe I am a little crazy!" After turning off the Corvette's engine, she opened the door, stepped out, and slammed the door. The woman placed her hand on her hip, shifted for a sensuous pose, and shot him a flirtatious smile that made Frederick want to add another paragraph to his lecture. She couldn't have been more than twenty and had no business stopping on the side of the road to talk to a strange man—especially not while wearing those low-cut jeans and cropped sweater. If she were his kid sister, he'd have sentenced her to house arrest for a month for this behavior.

Her smile fading, she crossed her arms and leaned closer. Her high heels crunched along the rocky drive as she neared. Distracted by what she might try next, Frederick shoved the ache in his spine to second in importance.

"Haven't I seen you somewhere before?" she asked.

While there was no trace of alcohol on her, he picked up the scent of some light perfume that an innocent thirteen-year-old might wear.

How ironic, he thought and wondered if the woman didn't realize he would recognize a pick-up line when he heard one. Scores of women had identified him after the media turned him into a hero, but that had been several years ago. Presently, Frederick wasn't in the market for a pick-up, especially not by someone nearly young enough to be his daughter.

"I don't think we've met," he said and fumbled to reopen the Mustang's door. "I need to be going—"

"No!" She laid her hand on his arm. "I thought you looked familiar when I passed. Now I *know* you do!"

Her blue eyes intense, she inched closer and studied his face. Despite his desire to escape, an unexpected memory

nibbled the back of his mind. The sharp eyes were what triggered the recollection. He recalled a time in his distant past
when an obnoxious child of the female variety had followed
him around, chatted his ears off, and pelted him with enough
questions to exasperate a stone monument. Even when Frederick had turned his back on her to dig in a flowerbed, he'd
felt her gaze on him like a vulture zoned in on its prey.

A cloak of certainty settled upon her features. "Did you ever
work at a place called Elton Mansion in Atlanta?" she asked.

"Yes," Frederick admitted and nearly groaned. Images of
the precocious ten-year-old who'd spent her whole spring
break harassing him evolved into the young woman standing
before him. The woman's lips were redder than the girl's.
Her hair was longer. And she was all grown up. But Frederick would recognize the devil-may-dare tilt of her chin in a
crowd of a thousand.

"Oh my goodness! You're Frederick Wently, aren't you?"
she oozed and clung to his arm like an awestruck fan.

"And you're Louise," he stated as her name plunked into
his mind.

"Yes. Louise Grove." She giggled. "I was ten the last time
I saw you. It was my spring break. I was visiting Elton Mansion with my sister-in-law. She grew up there. Remember?"

"Yes," Frederick admitted.

"Her name's Macy. Macy Grove."

He nodded and thought, *I remember well.*

"Did you know I had the *biggest* crush on you that week?"
Her eyes went gooey.

"I would have never guessed," Frederick drawled and
backed away from her clutch. While he couldn't deny that
Louise's admiration was flattering, he detested the thought
of taking advantage of the situation. Not very many years

ago, Louise Grove was only ten, and he'd been twenty-five. Frederick couldn't think past that—except for the fact that she probably didn't look the same in jeans and a midriff sweater so tight he wondered how she breathed. Like a protective uncle, Frederick thought about taking off his jacket and insisting Louise cover herself until she could put on something decent.

"Oh! I just had the most wonderful idea!" Louise squealed and bounced up and down. "You've *got* to come home with me for a while. You've just *got* to! I can show you off to my sister and parents. They'd never believe my catch of the day!"

"Your catch of the day?" Frederick wrinkled his forehead.

She waved her hand and laughed. "It's just a family joke. They say I go out fishing for guys and bring home a new catch every day."

"And they don't mind that?"

"Heavens no," she said and fluffed her wind-tossed hair. "They just take it all in stride. I change boyfriends like you change socks. It's all just a part of who I am. But now with you . . ." She grabbed his arm and cut him a sly wink. "I might keep you for a long, long time."

Frederick lifted his hands and stumbled to the car's rear bumper. "Now wait a minute," he protested. "I never committed to anything. I was just sitting here finishing my Coke when—"

"When I drove by and saw you. And aren't you the most handsome thang I've seen since I was ten and I saw you the first time. Now come on, darlin'! You've *got* to come home with me and let me show you off." She crooked her finger at him.

"Louise, it's been very nice to see you again, but . . ." Frederick hedged and couldn't fathom what Allie would think if he showed up at Grove Acres with her kid sister-in-law hanging on him.

Wait a minute! he thought. Frederick narrowed his eyes and gazed past the blonde. *This would be the perfect cover.* His mind spun with the possibilities. Frederick could see Allie again under the assumption that he'd bumped into Louise, they remembered each other, and she invited him home for a visit. If Allie was jealous, that would give Frederick a good indicator that she was still interested in him. If she didn't care that he was with another woman, then Frederick could once and for all put himself out of his misery, go back to Charlotte, and get on with his life.

Of course, if Allie did care for him, Frederick still had to deal with a few small obstacles such as latent bitterness, unforgiveness, and lack of trust before he could even begin to renew a healthy relationship with her. There was also still the issue of the royal Elton status in the face of his mere mortality.

It's too much to overcome, he reasoned and wondered why he was even here. The blustery March wind reminded him of his temporary insanity and cooled the sweat Louise's near miss had worked him into. As the perspiration evaporated, the logical advantages of showing up at the Groveses' estate trickled through the insanity. Frederick was thirty-five. He still wasn't married and hadn't been able to develop a long-term relationship with any woman because of Allie.

I cannot spend the rest of my life like this, he thought. *Maybe this will be a way to get her out of my blood once and for all. If she rejects me again—and she most likely will—maybe I'll have enough sense to forget her and find a wife!*

Louise came into focus again. Her lips were moving, but Frederick had no idea what she was saying. If Frederick was the pick of the week, Louise would be his ticket into Allie's life. Next week Louise would move on to another catch of the day and no harm would be done.

Finally Louise frowned at him like a spoiled child. She stomped her spike heel and said, "You haven't been listening to a word I said!"

"Huh?"

"I said if you don't come with me, I'm going to scream" Louise replicated the same singsong voice she'd used when she was ten and wanted Frederick to push her around in the wheelbarrow full of peat moss.

Frederick crossed his arms. "I'll cut you a deal. I'll come for a visit if you promise you won't tell anyone you saw me at this park." *That way Allie won't find out I was already this close and suspect I drove to Macon just to see her,* he silently added.

Louise shrugged. "Okay, deal," she said with a nonplused expression. "I'll just tell them I bumped into you at the gas station or something."

"No, don't lie," Frederick admonished. "We can just say you, uh, ran into me. It's pretty much the truth." He eyed the skid marks Louise's tires had left in the gravel mere feet from his rental car.

"No prob." She waved away the whole issue. "I'll say whatever floats your boat as long as you come home with me."

"Deal." Frederick extended his hand for a shake and thought better of it when she wrapped both hands around his and lifted it to her lips. Before Frederick could extract his hand, she'd covered his knuckles in red lipstick.

"You're even more yummy than you were ten years ago!" she exclaimed through a high-pitched giggle.

Frederick jerked his hand from her grasp, rubbed his other palm across the red smudges, and recalled the saucy kiss she'd placed on his cheek when she was ten. "You don't need to be kissing on total strangers," he said, his elder brother tone in full swing.

He was on the verge of branching into a sermon about her wardrobe and driving when Louise declared, "But you're not a stranger! You're an old, old friend."

"Hold that thought," he admonished. "I'm a *friend*. A *family friend*. And yes, I am old! Another couple of years, and I'd be old enough to be your father."

"Oh pooh! You're not *that* old! You can't be. You're my catch of the day." She smiled and wiggled her fingers for a momentary good-bye before swaying toward her sports car.

Frederick plopped into the driver's seat of his car, gripped the leather-covered steering wheel, and watched Louise get into the Corvette and replace her sunglasses. The whole time he debated the level of wisdom involved in this scheme. On a scale of 1 to 10, with 10 the highest, he ranked the plan a 1, 2, 3, 4, 5, 6, 7, and 8—depending on which way he looked at it.

"Not only am I a tormented idiot," he mumbled, "I'm as confused as all get-out." By the time Louise was barreling out of the roadside park, Frederick was praying that God would either deliver him or miraculously bring something good out of the next few hours.

Nine

"Allie? Alllllllieeeeeeee!" Macy's strong voice floated through her home's open windows to the rose bed where Allie worked.

Allie laid aside her miniature spade, rocked back on her heels, eyed the new rosebuds, and sighed. After lunch Macy had been stricken with "the worst headache of the century" and just *had* to lie down. Of course, that was only *after* Allie asked her to help with the rosebushes and to pick up her own sons from school this afternoon. Since Allie's Mercedes was being serviced, she assumed Macy would agree to pick up Barry and Bart and give Allie a break. No deal. Macy had simply insisted Allie use her Town Car to pick up the twins.

"Out here, Macy!" Allie stood and dusted her gloved hands against each other. "Right where I said I'd be," she grumbled under her breath and slipped off the gloves. Allie tilted her face toward the sky, arched her back, and enjoyed a good stretch. March had come in like a heavy-breathing monster. A fresh gust of wind whipped Allie's hair in all directions and shoved at the rosebush's limbs. Frowning, Allie pushed one of the climbing rose shoots back through the trellis behind it.

"You guys need to stay put," she admonished.

"There you are," Macy said as she rounded the brick home's corner. Her dark hair mussed, she yawned and covered her mouth with her fingers. "You're still out here?" she questioned. "How can you *work* so long?"

Allie checked her watch and noted one thirty. "It's only been a couple of hours."

"That's *forever!*" Macy glanced around the flowerbed. "And I can't tell you've done a thing."

Allie cleared her throat and eyed the twenty-one rosebushes that decorated the house's west garden that separated Macy's home from the guesthouse. "Well, I've dug around half the roses, weeded, fertilized, and sprayed them for fungus and aphids." She pointed toward a collection of bottles and boxes near the brick border. "Other than that," she wryly added, "I haven't done a thing." She shrugged.

"Oh. Well." Macy languidly eyed the roses and toyed with the tie on her lounging pants. "You must be ready for some herbal tea, then. We've got blueberry."

"That sounds wonderful," Allie said, nearly staggered with Macy's offer. Her younger sister hadn't even lifted a finger to help Allie carry her suitcases in when she arrived for her stay last month.

"Good, then," Macy replied. "I'll have some, too." She stroked her temple and turned toward the house. "I'll be in the den when you get it made," she added over her shoulder. "And don't be too long. Remember, Charlie's fishing today. You have to leave at two thirty to pick up the boys from school."

Allie rolled her eyes as she watched her younger sister stroll around the home's corner. *I should have known!* During the last month the old childhood patterns had resumed. Macy put on her "I'm the family baby" face and was perfectly content to allow the next eldest sister to do everything for her. Of course, when their mother died, the whole family had fawned over "the baby" because she was "only twelve." Those years had irrevocably ingrained the patterns.

Atlantic Beach is calling my name, Allie thought. Even being bossed around by Evelyn and watching Penny Clayton make eyes at her father would be a relief compared to acting as Macy's slave. Thankfully, Macy did have a part-time yard-man and full-time maid and cook. Otherwise, Allie would have changed her name to Cinderella and been done with it. While dusting the soil from the knees of her capri pants and the front of her cotton shirt, she resigned herself to the inevitable. Macy was never going to change.

Within fifteen minutes, Allie balanced a tray laden with a crockery teapot and two matching cups and walked down the hallway to the spacious den. Her sister had just finished having the home redecorated, and the champagne-colored carpet gave the whole house a new smell. Macy sat in the corner of the sofa reading the suspense novel she had started that morning. She never looked up. She was already halfway through the thick book. Allie deduced Macy must have read rather than take the nap she vowed she needed to relieve the headache.

With Macy's head slightly bent, her lips pursed in concentration, her hair now swept into a ponytail, Allie caught a glimpse of the little girl she once had been. Allie's heart softened; her irritation vanished. Even with all her faults, Macy was still her sister, and Allie would die for her.

"Here you are, dear," she said as she slid the tray onto the coffee table. "Blueberry." Allie poured the two cups full of tea.

Macy never responded.

Allie stirred a packet of sweetener into her tea, picked up the cup and saucer, and settled on the cream-colored settee near the window. As was the whole house, this room was decked in the latest fashion. Everything intricately matched, from the cinnamon-colored walls to the same shade in the floral drapes to the replication of the settee's coloring in the wool rug. Amazingly, Macy's illnesses never stopped her from ordering new drapes and furniture when the urge struck.

Sipping her sweet tea, Allie stared beyond the home's wrap-around porch to the lane that twined through scenic woods, past the Grove's mansion, and ultimately to the highway. While the last month hadn't been perfect, country life had been therapeutic for Allie. She'd found a special rock near the creek where she spent an hour a day in prayer, meditation, and Scripture reading. On that rock Allie had poured her heart out to God and found an inexplicable peace about leaving her home behind.

Frederick Wently was a different matter altogether. Regardless of how often she prayed for God to ease the memories his recent visit had awakened, there was no relief. If anything, Allie was more haunted than ever by the what-ifs. And the last kiss they shared blazed through her mind with the potency of only hours gone by, rather than years. She gulped her tea and winced against the hot liquid as it hit the back of her throat.

A flash of white near the wood's edge snared Allie's attention, and she welcomed the sight of a doe bounding through the trees, her white tail twitching as she fled. Allie had a grain trough behind her house that attracted many deer, and she thought she recognized the doe. She abandoned the disturbing thoughts of Frederick in favor of the doe's beauty. Atlantic Beach . . . the sand and the sea . . . didn't hold half the appeal as the deer, her rock, the stream, and the whippoorwills that serenaded her at sundown.

The deer disappeared through the woods and stirred a covey of quail in its wake. As the birds flurried in all directions, another movement gained Allie's focus. A group of people strolled down the tree-lined lane. Allie immediately recognized Macy's svelte sisters-in-law and pleasingly plump mother-in-law. In the middle of the animated trio sauntered a man who strongly resembled . . .

"Frederick!" Allie exclaimed, and her cup clattered against her saucer as she leaned forward. "But it can't be!"

Deciding all her pining was making her hallucinate, Allie closed her eyes, shook her head, and reminded herself that her brother-in-law, Charlie, was tall and had dark hair. He had gone fishing after lunch in the family lake behind the Grove mansion. His walking back home with his mother and sisters was something he'd done scores of times—especially when Martha Grove wanted to invite Macy to dinner.

In the midst of the closed-eyed reasoning, Allie reminded herself that the man she saw didn't walk or look like Charlie in the least. In the face of that logic, she convinced herself that her aching heart was superimposing Frederick's image upon Charlie . . . just as it had filled her dreams with images of Frederick every night since he'd arrived at Elton Mansion with the Cosbys.

Certain of her verdict, Allie opened her eyes, fully expecting Charlie Grove. What she saw was Frederick Wently. She blinked hard. Frederick again. She looked away, and darted her gaze back to the man. And again he was Frederick.

Allie could deny the truth no longer. Frederick Wently was walking toward the house with Louise hanging on one arm and Helena on the other. And the way Martha was ogling him, she was as smitten as her daughters.

"It *is* Frederick!" Allie croaked and scrambled to stand. Her teacup tilted and jostled a puddle of purplish-brown liquid into the saucer. Somehow she managed to plunk the teacup back onto the tray without losing a drop. She looked down at her soiled work clothes and smoothed her hands over her hair. Allie touched her face and figured she probably looked like a shiny-nosed wench.

Her attention shifted to Macy, still riveted to her book.

A slow tremble assaulted Allie's knees. "Macy, there's—there's a man coming," she rasped and shook her sister's arm.

"What?" Macy's distant focus shifted to Allie.

"Your mom and sisters are coming with a man," Allie stated.

"With a man?" Macy shrieked and looked down at her lounging pants. She twisted toward the window and leaned forward. "Oh my word!" Macy stroked her ponytail. "You're right! I need to change and fix my hair." She jumped up and dashed toward the hallway before Allie had the chance to breathe. "Let them in, will you? Tell them I'll be right down!"

"But—but—" Allie helplessly watched as Macy disappeared down the hallway. She'd have loved to slip to the guesthouse to freshen up before having to face Frederick. The last time she saw him she hadn't exactly been supermodel material, but at least she hadn't been dirt-smeared and windblown.

A lump formed in her throat. Her eyes stung. She looked heavenward. "Help!" Allie begged before hustling toward the brass-trimmed mirror hanging near the fireplace. One glimpse and she groaned. Forget sneaking to the guesthouse to freshen up. As bad as she looked, she needed to disappear for good. Dirt streaked her chin. Her nose and cheeks were sun-bitten, her hair, wind-licked. After shoving desperate hands through her hair in a sad attempt at finger combing, Allie rubbed at the dirt on her chin. The smudge refused to budge.

Frantically, she zoomed to her teacup, snatched a paper napkin from the tray, and dunked it into the hot tea. Back at the mirror, she sponged the dirt away and prayed there was no purple left to deal with. Thankfully, the dirt vanished and her chin remained purple-less.

The doorbell rang. Allie jumped and dropped the napkin. She kicked it into the corner and scurried from the den toward the entryway. When she was ten feet from the front door, Allie stopped, closed her eyes, took a deep breath, and willed herself to emit a calm persona. By the time she turned the knob, Allie was committed to feigning complete composure.

Ten

Anytime Allie was with Louise, she always came away feeling like she'd been hit by a tornado. Today was no different. The second the door opened, Louise stormed the home with Helena in her wake.

"Look who we've got with us!" Louise crowed.

"He's Louise's catch of the day," Helena exclaimed. With both her arms draped through Frederick's, the nineteen-year-old gazed up at him like he was a trophy. "And mine, too," she added, and Allie wondered if Helena had completely forgotten she had a steady boyfriend.

"I do believe he's the best one yet," Martha confirmed. The matron's green muumuu swayed as she waddled inside. Allie closed the door, made brief eye contact with Frederick, and did nothing to acknowledge their acquaintance.

"We brought him over to see if you and Macy remember him." Louise, still hanging on to Frederick, rested her hand along his upper arm. "His name's Frederick Wently. He used to work at Elton Mansion," she continued through a giggle. "I bumped into him today and just *had* to bring him home with me. Isn't this the smallest world *ever*!"

Allie twined her fingers behind her back and trained her focus upon Louise. Her proprietal attitude toward Frederick sent a white hot burst through Allie. She had never even been tempted to be jealous of Macy's sisters-in-law. Instead, she'd viewed herself as their spiritual big sister and had nearly convinced them to attend church with her. But now, with one in a miniskirt and the other in a pair of low-rise jeans—neither of which would look good on Allie's size-twelve hips—she was stricken with the difference in her appearance and theirs. And she felt about as spiritual as a bullfrog.

If that wasn't enough, Frederick looked far too satisfied about being the catch of the day.

"Good to see you again, Allie." He tossed her a distracted smile before glancing toward the ladies on his arms.

Allie didn't bother to respond. She was too busy trying to control her temper. In her opinion, a thirty-five-year-old man had no business whatsoever being the "special guest" of a twenty-year-old woman. *She's almost young enough to be his daughter!* Allie fumed and was tempted to whack Frederick.

"So do you remember him?" Martha prompted. "He says he used to be the grounds manager at your place."

Allie eyed Martha and offered a polite smile. "Of course I remember him," she choked out. "We worked together some."

"Yes, and I had the *biggest crush* on him the year I spent spring break there with Macy." Louise's adoring gaze suggested the crush was back in full force.

The memories were starting to trickle into Allie's mind. Until now, she had totally forgotten about the week Louise had visited the mansion. Allie recalled both she and Frederick growing annoyed at Louise's perpetual presence and nonstop chatter.

Right now Frederick looked anything *but* annoyed.

I wonder why? Allie sarcastically thought and suspected that this must be some cruel twist of fate. She'd gone ten years without even a glimpse of Frederick. Now he was popping into her life at every turn. Seeing him alone was hard enough, much less accompanied by beautiful females.

Martha gazed around the foyer. Her short, gray hair and rotund figure were the antithesis of her daughters' high-fashion, pencil-thin images. And Allie was hard-pressed to find any family resemblance between the ruddy-faced matron and her offspring. But at least Martha didn't make Allie feel dowdy. She resisted the urge to rub at the dirt stains on her capris.

"Where's Macy?" Martha questioned.

"She's changing," Allie answered and saw this as an opportunity for escape. "I'll go check on her. You guys make yourselves comfortable in the living room." She pointed toward the formal room that housed a baby grand piano and a wall full of collector's sculptures.

"Is there a place I can hang my jacket?" Frederick asked and broke contact with his fan club long enough to shrug out of it.

"I'll hang it up for you," Allie offered, and took the jacket with the same eagerness she'd accepted his parka a month ago. Even in the throes of irritation, she couldn't stop the anticipation. Her fingers sank into the jacket's warmth, and a delightful shiver laced her body.

"Thanks." Frederick smiled, and his brown eyes were every bit as inviting now as they'd been when she first met him. Allie remembered that day well. She hadn't been much older than Louise and Helena were now. And while her reaction to him had been every bit as strong as theirs, Allie had maintained her composure.

The longer she looked at Frederick, the more Allie recognized something in his eyes that hadn't been present a decade ago. Something angry. Something bitter. Something far from inviting. A shock teetered along Allie's nerves, and she looked at the floor.

"We'll just wait in here, then," Martha exclaimed. "Come on, kids." She waved them toward the living room and looked over her shoulder at Allie. "I came to tell Macy about the big sale at Dillard's and to invite y'all to dinner tonight. We'll have a big time now!" Martha pointed to Frederick's back and offered an exaggerated wink.

Allie's face went so stiff she couldn't respond.

As the four guests strolled into the living room, she rushed up the stairs that led to Macy and Charlie's suite. Once she arrived on the landing, Allie leaned against the wall, closed her eyes, bit her bottom lip, and forced the tears back into the well from whence they'd erupted.

Her heart pounding in her throat, Allie finally gained control of her emotions. When she opened her eyes, Macy was standing three feet away, studying her. Allie jumped and covered her heart with her hand.

"Oh my goodness," she breathed. "I didn't know you were there."

"Are you okay?" Macy asked.

"Yes, fine," Allie eked out. "I was just coming up to get you. That's all."

"You look pale, Allie." Macy's soft gray eyes sharpened as she leaned closer. "Are you sure you're—"

"I'm fine!" Allie snapped.

Macy started.

"Sorry." Allie's eye twitched. "I think I need to go lie down for a while." She strode toward the other end of the hallway where a narrow staircase led down to the kitchen. All the while she felt Macy's scrutiny.

"But what about the boys? You've got to leave in thirty minutes to pick them up."

Allie stopped and thought, *They're your kids. Why don't you pick them up?* Instead she quietly said "I won't forget" over her shoulder and continued her journey.

She hurried out of the kitchen, hustled past the rose garden, and raced toward the quaint guesthouse. The pine house was a perfect fit for the woods surrounding it and appeared to be at one with the terrain more than Macy's Victorian-styled home. Allie trotted around the picnic table in the yard, thumped up the porch steps, and swept into the spacious living room. The home's warm plaids, soft leather, and the cheerful smell of apple potpourri belied Allie's agitated spirit. She was anything *but* warm and soft and cheerful.

The door banged shut behind her. Allie wadded up the warm jacket and shoved her face into the folds. When she detected the weak scent of feminine perfume, she lifted her face and stared, horrified, at the piece of clothing.

"Oh no!" she yelped and threw it on the straight-backed chair near the front door. A set of car keys flopped out of the pocket and clinked to the hardwood floor. Allie knew she had no choice. As much as she wanted to avoid seeing Frederick with his fan club, she would have to take the jacket back to him.

She scooped up the keys, grabbed the jacket, and shoved the keys back into the pocket. But when she removed her hand, a dainty slip of paper fell out of the pocket and landed face up. The plump scrawl, clearly feminine, beckoned Allie to read the message. Every scrap of Allie's propriety insisted she shouldn't. But when she picked up the filigreed paper, she spotted the imprint of a pair of red lips near an extravagant signature. The lips plus the weak scent of sweet perfume created a lure too great. Allie possessed no power to stop herself from absorbing every syllable:

> *To My Hero,*
> *I enjoyed last night so much.*

Allie's mouth fell open, and she continued to the next line.

Can't wait until tonight.

She gasped, and the note trembled.

I love you more than ever.

"She loves him!" Allie whispered.

Never let me go!

"And he's holding on to someone else right now!" she moaned.

Glancing toward Macy's house, she thought of *two* some-ones—aged nineteen and twenty! Bile rising in her throat, Allie digested the final line.

Your biggest fan, Annie

"Annie? Who's Annie?" Allie squawked and examined the lip imprint. Whoever she was, she liked lipstick every bit as red as Louise's. Allie was also stricken with how closely *her* name resembled Frederick's girlfriend's . . . or one of his girlfriend's.

"I wonder how many Annies and Allies and Abbies the man has these days?" she asked and couldn't believe how easily he had taken up with Louise and Helena. If she added their ages together, the sum wasn't much more than Frederick's age.

Allie gripped her midsection, dropped onto the sofa, and groaned against the nausea. All these years she had kept Frederick on the same pedestal as the man who'd bent on one knee to propose in the park. He'd been a gentleman—a true gentleman—who respected her and respected women enough not to philander. Frederick Wently had been Allie's hero then.

But that was before he joined the Air Force, Allie reminded herself. *And before he turned into a national hero.* She'd heard enough stories about wild soldiers and their parties to understand that many opportunities must have posed themselves for Frederick to stray from his standards. She also knew that some of the strongest men had at times fallen. . . . Even David, Israel's most beloved king, had yielded to temptation.

Too sick to look at the lip-imprinted note again, Allie replaced it in the jacket pocket and determined to once and for all end the Frederick chapter in her heart. There was no doubt he'd turned into a ladies' man.

But as soon as the note left her fingers, Allie was overcome with a burning need to know if more incriminating evidence might be in his other pocket. Like a wife who's certain her husband is cheating, Allie dug into the other pocket but found nothing. That's when she noticed a zipped pocket hidden inside the jacket. Her fingers unsteady, Allie unzipped the pocket. She was about to explore it, too, when her scruples troubled her anew.

"This isn't right." She paused on the pocket's threshold. "I have no right. . . ."

A faint squeal from her front yard sent Allie into a stiff-spined trance. Upon the heels of another scream, she hurried to the window near the love seat and peeked through the blinds. The scene before her validated her every assumption.

Louise stood on top of the picnic table, of all places. Hands on hips, she threw her head back and laughed into the wind while Frederick reached for her. His half-smile mingled with a hint of concern as he appeared to be coaxing Louise down.

Allie eyed the young lady's spike heels and wondered how she had mounted the picnic table without breaking her neck.

With no warning, Louise reached forward and fell toward Frederick, who was forced to catch her or let her hit the ground. Staggering backward, Frederick struggled to maintain his footing until he stumbled over a great tree root protruding from the earth. Yelling, he crashed to the ground with Louise in the tangle of his arms and legs. His muffled bellow mingled with Louise's delighted squeals, which ended when she planted her lips against his.

Huffing, Allie released the blinds and stomped her foot. This was even worse than if Frederick had waltzed into her life with a wife!

Forgetting her own scruples and everyone else's, Allie invaded the hidden pocket. This time her search was productive. Her fingers encircled a cylindrical case that proved to be a gold tube of lipstick. Another dive produced a small bottle of perfume with *Giorgio* scrawled across the front. Allie pulled off the top and sniffed. As she suspected, the scent matched the note's smell. She replaced the cap and dropped the fragrance back into the pocket. Next Allie removed the lipstick lid, twisted up the color, and found exactly what she suspected—the same shade that was on the note. The bottom of the tube read "Hot Lips Red."

"Oh brother!" she fumed and couldn't believe she'd actually sat in her room a month ago and cried over Frederick Wently and that pathetic scrapbook she'd created in his honor. *I have been a fool!* she thought and wondered if perhaps he'd *always* been a ladies' man and she'd just been too young and too in love to see it.

Then Allie recalled his tender kisses and the gentle respect with which he'd treated her. Her eyes stung. She swallowed and prayed this was all a dreadful mistake—that even if he couldn't be *her* Frederick, at least he hadn't turned into *everyone's* Frederick. Hot Lips Red came into focus and proved the only argument she needed.

Allie covered her eyes and retreated to that corner in her heart once more . . . the corner in which she'd mourned for her lost hero. The mourning began anew.

The sounds of footsteps on the porch steps mingled with Louise's animated chatter. Allie jumped, dropped the lipstick lid, and helplessly watched as it rolled behind the love seat. Her eyes wide, she gaped at the tube of lipstick. When a knock pounded the door, she twisted the lipstick down.

"Hello, people! Anybody home?" Louise called with a renewed round of door thumps. Knowing she couldn't put the lipstick back into the pocket without a lid, Allie was left with only one choice. She bent and shoved the tube under the love seat, then zipped the jacket pocket. If Annie missed her lipstick, then that was just too bad!

Whoever heard of Hot Lips Red, anyway? There's nothing more disgusting! she decided and draped the jacket back on the chair.

Assuming the most bland expression she could muster, Allie opened the front door. The first thing she noticed was that Frederick now wore lipstick himself. It was the exact shade of Louise's blurred red and was smack in the middle of his forehead in the shape of Louise's lips. That's when Allie knew there was indeed something more disgusting than Hot Lips Red—red lips on Frederick.

Eleven

Until Allie opened the front door, Frederick prayed she hadn't seen that ridiculous episode in the front yard. After he'd extracted himself from Louise's lip-lock, he'd examined the home's windows and detected no signs of Allie's spying. Once he hobbled up the steps despite his aching back, Frederick had rubbed his lips free of red and held his breath until Allie opened the door. With her disinterested gaze sweeping both him and Louise, Frederick was certain she'd missed the whole ordeal—except, for some reason, her gaze lingered on his forehead.

"You stole Frederick's jacket!" Louise teased before he had the chance to even say hello.

"Well, I didn't believe you were actually *stealing* my jacket," Frederick explained at the same time Allie said, "I just wasn't thinking."

"When you said you were gonna hang it up, we didn't know you meant over *here*! I spotted you out the window and came after you." Louise pushed past Allie and stormed the guesthouse. "Come on in," she called over her shoulder.

Frederick cast a questioning glance toward Allie, who retrieved his jacket from a chair and extended it without a word. "I decided to come back to the guesthouse," she explained, her face stiff. "I wasn't thinking," she repeated as Frederick accepted the coat. "I didn't realize I had it. I just looked down and there it was." She glanced at his forehead again and held the door wider.

He stepped inside while Allie closed the door and was tempted to touch his forehead but decided not to give in to the impulse. Frederick didn't want to indicate that he was tuned in to the direction of Allie's focus and tried to convince himself he was imagining her distraction.

Next he wondered at Louise's boldness of inviting herself and him into Allie's quarters. But that fit everything about Louise. She was more than a mere woman. She was a *force*! From the second Frederick stepped into the Grove mansion, he felt he'd lost all control of his person. He was now Louise's property, and suspected that Helena might be vying for joint ownership, even though Louise had hinted that her sister had a boyfriend.

What a problem to have, he thought and remembered a time twenty years ago when he'd have given anything to have two pretty women fighting over him. Of course, he'd been fifteen at the time, a little girl crazy, and a lot scrawny. Not many girls fought over him those days. Now that they *were* fighting over him, Frederick couldn't have cared less. All he was interested in was Allie.

So far she seemed about as interested in him as the Beechcraft's landing gear. Already Frederick suspected that his roadside brainstorm was failing with Allie and backfiring on him. Allie had been so eager to get away from him she'd accidentally carried his jacket with her. And she didn't seem to care one flip that Louise and Helena had filed for joint custody of him.

As far as his side of things, Frederick was battling simultaneous attacks of the old longing and leftover bitterness. The stab of pain in his lower back only ushered in the memory of those early days after the injury . . . of his yearning for Allie . . . of his realization that she wasn't coming. Ever. As a result, he wanted to embrace Allie one second and yell at her at the next. Her being oblivious to him now added to his anger. And Frederick was beginning to see that Allie had gouged him out of her life and probably never gave him another thought.

"So what do you think?" Louise asked and gazed around the cozy room.

"I don't understand," Frederick mumbled. His attention sliding to Allie, he realized he'd voiced his thoughts, which in no way answered Louise's question.

Meanwhile, Allie hunched her shoulders, crossed her arms, and turned toward the window. Frederick felt as if she were as elusive as a mystical phantom. He didn't know what to do or say and had no clue if he should go or stay.

"I meant what do you think about *the house?*" Louise replied and slapped his arm. "Wake up!" she commanded as if they were long-time friends.

"Oh," Frederick replied and shifted the jacket to the other hand. "The house." A rock fireplace claimed the corner, above which hung a massive painting of a deer in the woods. The leather furniture and pine walls reminded Frederick of a Swiss chalet. The faint scent of apples suggested someone had been cooking. His stomach was too tied in knots to care.

"Very nice," he said with an approving nod and wished the hunting cabin he'd leased in Arkansas was this nice. Or at least had indoor plumbing.

"So now you've seen all three houses—ours, Macy's, and this one." Louise smiled up at him with a coy invitation. "Which do you like the best?"

Frederick placed his thumb in his jeans pocket and said,

"This one, I think," while gazing anywhere but at Allie. "It's just more, I don't know, comfortable, I guess."

Allie looked different today than she had when he saw her a month ago. She was sun-kissed and windblown and reminded him of the first time he'd met her. Allie had been digging in the flowerbed. Her knees were dirty; her nose, red. And her hair was a mess. Then she'd had a ponytail. Now her hair was short.

With Louise chatting about who knew what, Allie walked toward a wide doorway that opened into the kitchen. While his heart trotted after her like an abused pup begging for any scrap of attention, his body stayed put and in the grips of its new owner.

This is crazy! he thought and decided he should leave immediately after dinner and not return. Frederick had his answer. He'd come here to see if she showed any signs of interest in him at all. She had shown none. Not even one hint of jealousy. He had decided that if she showed no interest, he would get on with his life. Maybe look for a wife. He glanced at the babbling Louise.

Someone close to my own age, he reminded himself and shifted his stance. His lower back complained. Too many more Louise attacks and he would be paralyzed for life.

The sound of footsteps on the front porch prompted Louise to tiptoe toward the window. By the time the first knock sounded, Louise was spying through the blinds. "Just like I thought," she whispered. "It's Helena!"

The door burst open. The redhead charged in and slammed the door. Like a general scouting out the scene, she sized up the situation. Her focus landed just above Frederick's eyes and stayed there.

"I knew it!" she fumed. Helena trounced forward, her gaze remaining on Frederick's forehead.

He could resist the urge no more and touched his forehead. Louise giggled. And Frederick examined his fingertips, now tinted in red. *Oh no!* he thought and vaguely recalled Louise ending the lip-lock with a smack on his forehead. Frederick had been so worried about getting his lips clean he'd forgotten about the forehead episode.

Helena stopped only inches away and planted her glossy bronze lips on his cheek. After pulling away she pouted and said, "If Louise gets to kiss you, then so do I!"

Frederick disentangled himself from his latest captor and hustled toward a mirror hanging behind a lamp. His worst fear was founded. The imprint of a pair of red lips marred the center of his forehead. And if that wasn't bad enough, his cheek had now been bronzed. Frederick reached for the tissue box at the end of a bookcase and rubbed himself free of the brands.

Then he turned on his captors, lifted his hands palms outward, and said, "Look, ladies, I'm flattered by all this. Really. But we've got to get something straight here. If I'm going to survive the rest of the evening, I need some space. Okay?"

"See what you've done," Louise said and glared at her sister.

"Me?" Helena laid both hands across her chest.

"Yes, you. Have you forgotten about Craig?"

"What Craig doesn't know won't hurt him," Helena said and flipped her hair over her shoulder.

"Maybe I'll just tell him." Louise crossed her arms.

"You wouldn't dare!" Helena shot back and doubled her fists.

Frederick placed his thumb and index finger at his temples, closed his eyes, and decided he'd been insane when he agreed to be Louise's catch of the day. If he hadn't already promised to stay for dinner, Frederick would have driven back to Atlanta at warp speed to hide at Jim's.

He lowered his hand, opened his eyes, and glanced toward the doorway Allie had gone through, only to discover she was back. She'd gotten rid of the soil-smeared gardening gear and was wearing linen pants and a royal blue top that did nice things for her dark eyes. Again, Allie peered straight at his forehead, then away. And Frederick now understood why she'd looked at his forehead before.

A tiny hope flared within. Maybe—just maybe—she wasn't as disinterested as he'd assumed.

"I've got to go pick up the twins from school," she explained, her keys rattling. "I'll be back soon. Please continue to make yourselves comfortable," she said like a female butler.

"That's okay," Frederick said and walked toward the door. "I just came for my jacket." He pulled his arms into the sleeves and looked back. The sisters followed close behind like a couple of groupies. Frederick didn't know whether to feel sorry for Craig, or pray for a "Craig" for Louise. He knew *he* certainly couldn't be that for her. Even if she hadn't been fifteen years younger, Louise was just too much for him.

He followed Allie out the door and thought of Darren's reaction to his being tackled by a flying blonde. Frederick imagined his brother-in-law's mirth and laughed out loud before he could stop himself.

Allie shot him a silent "what's so funny?" over her shoulder while Louise said, "Let us in on the joke!"

Helena banged the door shut and said, "Yeah!"

"Oh, it's nothing," he mumbled and shoved his hands into his jacket pockets. His fingers encountered a piece of paper next to his keys, and Frederick pulled it out. While scanning the note, he detected a whiff of the Giorgio perfume Sophia always wore. He'd smelled the fragrance when he put on Darren's jacket after landing the plane, and figured every-

DEBRA WHITE SMITH   105

thing Darren owned smelled like Sophia. The coat Frederick brought from Charlotte had been too heavy, so he'd
been glad to find this light jacket that Darren had left in the
plane—Giorgio and all.

Folding the note back up, Frederick rolled his eyes and
thought, *Oh brother.* He slipped the paper back into the
jacket pocket and hobbled down the porch steps. His back
complained with every step, but that didn't keep him from
wondering if Sophia and Darren would *ever* get out of the
honeymoon stage. Even Sophia's nickname, Annie, started
on their honeymoon. Darren had left for Hawaii calling her
Sophia and come back home calling her Annie, a derivative
of her middle name, Anne. Of course, Sophia had pet names
for Darren, as well—some of which Frederick was certain he
was glad he did *not* know.

Frederick winced as he stepped to the ground. He stopped
and gave his back time to tell him he could move on while
the wind whipped around him. He scanned the yard and
spotted Allie striding toward Macy's Victorian-style brick
home. Other than her noticing the lip prints on his forehead,
she didn't act like she cared if Louise and Helena gobbled
him up.

"Are you okay?" Louise asked and bee-bopped to his side.

"Fine," Frederick replied and braced himself against another attack as Helena staked her claim on the other side.
"It's just my back," he explained. "An old injury."

"Oh no, poor thang," Louise crooned and patted his arm.
"And I guess it probably didn't help things when you had to
catch me."

"Well . . ." Frederick left the rest unsaid.

"You need a massage," Louise purred.

"No!" Frederick exclaimed and broke away from her. When

her face crumpled into a hurt frown, he smiled an apology. "Thanks anyway."

With Helena glaring at Louise, Allie turned for a backward glance. Frederick narrowed his eyes and began a train of thought he hoped was based on fact, rather than desperate wishes. Allie had done a remarkable job of projecting indifference—almost too remarkable. But would an indifferent woman "accidentally" carry his jacket with her or care if he had red lip prints on his forehead or even bother to look over her shoulder at him and his groupies?

Frederick squinted against the sun glaring through the trees and tried to make sense of Allie's subtle messages. Either she was more moved by his presence than she was showing, or Frederick was placing meaning where there should be none. As much as he wanted to assume the former, he decided to withhold his verdict until after dinner.

That is, if the leech ladies would give him enough space to think. Frederick glanced at Louise and then Helena. Both of them smiled up at him like they were hungry lionesses and he was a scrumptious side of beef. Frederick smiled back—sort of—and decided that before his "friendship" with these two was over, he'd have a firm chat with both of them about the pitfalls of throwing themselves at older men. Well, any man for that matter.

It's a good thing I'm not a philanderer, he thought and shuddered to think what fate might await the leech ladies if they ever encountered a true playboy. Why their parents didn't put a curb on them was anybody's guess.

Twelve

Allie couldn't get away from Frederick and his fan club soon enough. The longer she was with them, the more nauseated she grew. She scurried toward Macy's house and counted the seconds until she could escape in the Town Car. But the garage door's opening halted Allie. The cream-colored Town Car's backing out of the garage hurled her into an ocean of confusion, until she realized Macy must have decided to pick up the twins herself.

Her mouth dropped open, and she was on the verge of recanting every negative thought she'd had about Macy's irresponsibility, when high-pitched beeping floated from her purse. Allie pulled her phone out and saw it was Macy.

She'd barely placed the phone against her ear when Macy's excited voice came over the line. "Hot news, Allie! Martha says Bloomingdale's is having a big sale." Allie watched the vehicle and weakly smiled at Macy as she madly waved from the driver's seat. "We're going now!"

"But what about the twins?" Allie asked.

"Get Louise or Helena to go get them."

"No!" Allie exclaimed. "Those two drive like maniacs. I'll take one of their cars." She sheepishly glanced over her shoulder in hopes that neither of the sisters heard her. Fortunately they were too enamored with their catch of the day to listen to anything Allie said.

"Good point," Macy said and ended the call with an abrupt "See ya!" Then she wheeled the vehicle around and darted up the paved lane. Allie sighed and watched the Town Car zoom away. Apparently a headache couldn't withstand a big sale. Allie repented about her former urge to recant her calling Macy irresponsible. She wondered how her sister's sons had survived to eleven, and attributed it to their living so close to Charlie's parents. Mr. and Mrs. Grove had played a big role in raising those boys. Although no one would have guessed that with Martha Grove dashing off to Bloomingdale's in a bargain-crazed frenzy.

The afternoon sun warmed Allie's nose and cheeks with the cheerful promise of a delightful spring. Allie looked toward the cloudless horizon and once again pondered Atlantic Beach. Here the wind was scented with fresh foliage and pines. There it smelled of sand and saltwater. Here Allie was nanny and gardener and chief complaint-hearer. There Allie would be free to laze on the beach.

But I'd still have to listen to complaining—mainly Evelyn's. Allie fought the wind for a strip of hair she tucked behind her ear and wished for Elton Mansion and her third-floor haven.

"Something wrong?" Frederick's voice stroked Allie's neck and sent a shiver down her spine.

She turned to face him and tried to remind herself he was a womanizer. When his brown eyes did interesting things to her temperature, she made herself remember that many, many women experienced the same effect. "I was going to take Macy's car to pick up her sons from school." Allie pointed toward the lane. "But she and Martha have decided to hit a sale at Bloomingdale's. My car's being serviced, so—"

"I'll drive you in my rental car," Frederick offered.

"No!" Allie shook her head and nearly ran. "I could never impose—"

"You wouldn't be imposing." Frederick waved aside the very thought. "It's the least I could do. For old time's sake." His carefree smile reminded her of their first date. They'd gone to the park and Frederick pushed her swing so high she felt like she was flying.

"Is there room for me?" Louise purred from close behind.

"Me too," Helena added.

"'Fraid not," Frederick said. "I'm in a Mustang. By the time the kids get into the backseat with their backpacks, there won't be much room left." His tight smile suggested he was a bit tired of his fan club.

Allie's brows twitched, and she wondered if he might be missing Annie and her "Hot Lips Red" kisses. Thoughts of that lipstick sent a worry rippling through Allie, and she wondered if she should consider somehow replacing the tube in the jacket pocket.

"So what do ya say?" Frederick prompted.

Allie checked her watch to see that it was already two thirty. She should be leaving now. Her only other option was asking to borrow either Louise or Helena's Corvettes. Their father had given them identical vehicles for Christmas, and both girls acted like they were race car driver wannabes, although Louise was worse than Helena every day of the week. Chances were high they'd want to drive, and there would barely be room to cram both boys in, let alone another adult. Allie was more ready to chance a ride with her near-miss fiancé than allowing the boys to ride with either of those two road lizard race mavens. At least she wouldn't have to worry about losing her life with Frederick at the wheel. He was a safe driver ten years ago. Allie banked on his being a safe driver now.

"Come on," Frederick teased through a broad grin. "We're probably talking about half an hour in a car, right? You look like you're ready to consult a committee."

"Okay, I'll go with you," Allie replied.

Frederick blinked. "Really?"

"Well, yes. I don't have much of a choice, do I?" She avoided looking at Louise and Helena, who had resumed their places hanging on his arms. She tried staring past Frederick for a few seconds and felt even more awkward than she did when looking into his eyes.

"Good, then," he said. "Let's go!"

"Okay, except . . ." Allie checked her watch. "I really need to hurry now. I try to get there early so I can be one of the first in line. The way things are looking, I'm going to be one of the *last* ones in line—or even worse—late."

Frederick grabbed her hand, broke away from his fan club, and hurried from the yard with Allie trotting to keep up. "See ya tonight," he called over his shoulder.

Allie's brief glimpse of Louise and Helena, wilted and disheartened, would have left her feeling sorry for them under other circumstances. She casually removed her hand from Frederick's and tried not to remember how treasured she'd felt when he held her hand all those years ago.

"I'd run," Frederick explained, "but my back is giving me grief." No sooner had he admitted this than he closed his eyes, clutched at his lower back, and halted.

"Are you going to be okay?" Allie asked and put her hand on his arm. Once she realized what she'd done, she jerked her hand away.

"I'm okay. Really." Frederick's face contorted and he opened his eyes. "It's just a war injury. That's all. They thought I would never walk again, so I guess I should be thankful it's just pain. It's much better than paralysis any day." He tried to smile.

"Look," Allie said, "why don't I go get your car and drive it back here. Do you think you could drive from here?"

"Sure," Frederick replied. "I'll have to. I'm the one on the insurance. I'll just need to take some ibuprofen first. Shouldn't take long. It's in the glove box. You wouldn't happen to have a Coke, would you?"

"Still haven't broken that habit, have you?" she joked.

"You remember?"

Allie looked into the woods and avoided an answer. "Macy's refrigerator is full of Cokes and Dr Peppers and 7 Ups. I don't know why the twins' teeth aren't rotting out. Why don't you get Louise or Helena to get you a Coke while I go for the car." Allie gazed toward the young ladies who were just catching up behind them.

"I'll go," Helena offered and dashed toward Macy's house before Louise had the chance to take one step.

"I'll stay here and help." Louise patted Frederick's shoulder. "Poor baby," she purred.

"I'm fine," Frederick insisted. "I just need time to recover. I'll be good as new tomorrow."

"I should have never jumped at you like that, but I didn't know," Louise said.

Frederick nodded and cut Allie a worried glance that she decided to try to interpret later.

Right now the clock was ticking. The boys would be waiting. "I need your keys," Allie said.

"Right." When Frederick reached into his pocket and extended the keys, the filigree note flittered to the ground—lipstick-side up.

While Allie would have loved to pretend she didn't see the note, she lost the ability to fake indifference this time. Her gaze latched on to the lips and wouldn't falter. Finally Frederick's cowboy boot covered the note. Allie jerked her focus up to him, only to detect more worry mixed with the pain.

"This is my brother-in-law's jacket," he explained. "The note is from my sister to him."

You're lying! Allie thought. *The note is from somebody named Annie. Your sister is Sophia.* Not only was Frederick a womanizer, he was a *lying* womanizer! When she'd known him before, he never lied. Her dismay grew to greater heights.

He slowly bent down and picked up the note and put it in his pocket. He extended the car keys to Allie.

"It's the white Mustang. You can't miss it," he explained.

Allie took the keys, gripped her purse, and ran down the lane.

Thirteen

"Are you enjoying your stay in the guesthouse?" Frederick asked as he steered the Mustang from the country toward the city.

"Yes," Allie replied. Her attention rested out the passenger window, so her subdued answer was barely discernible. Furthermore, she was exerting no effort to even glance at him.

Okay, Frederick thought and shifted in his seat. His back was killing him, but he tried not to show it.

"Mind if I listen to some music?" he questioned.

"No, not at all," Allie replied, still not looking at him.

Frederick pressed a button on the radio and welcomed the saxophonist's rendition of "In Christ Alone."

After glancing toward Allie three times in as many minutes, Frederick decided to concentrate on the winding road. When he'd agreed to going home with Louise, he never imagined he'd be in a vehicle alone with Allie within a couple of hours. Frederick lightly tapped the steering wheel with his index finger and racked his brain for something to say.

So what have you been up to the last ten years? he sarcastically thought. *How many more hearts have you broken since mine?* That thought process did nothing but remind him of the old anger. He decided to abandon that vein before he actually blurted something he'd regret.

Even though the invisible wall between them was as dense as stone, Frederick was determined to engage Allie in conversation. He refused to allow this opportunity to pass by. As the music swelled and flowed, Frederick thought of several more questions, all of which would reap a yes or no answer. Finally he stumbled upon a query that would hopefully bring results.

"So . . . how long are you planning on staying with your sister?"

Frederick felt her cautious glance, her hesitancy. "I don't know, really," she admitted.

"Your father and sister are in Atlantic Beach, right?"

"Yes," she replied with a *How did you know that?* edge to her voice.

Frederick decided if he had to answer the unspoken questions to have a conversation, he would. "Mrs. Grove mentioned where they were earlier today," he explained, and didn't tell Allie that he'd also picked up the clue when he visited Elton Mansion with Darren and Sophia. "They seem really glad to have you."

"I'm enjoying my stay," she quietly replied, and Frederick remembered how much he'd loved Allie's soothing personality. She was his opposite, so low-key and gentle, and proved a perfect complement for his goal-oriented traits.

Of course, the Afghanistan experience had taken the edge off all his goals. A jab of pain shot from his spine, and Frederick caught his breath, then moaned. The pain medication had yet to kick in, and it couldn't happen soon enough.

He felt Allie's gaze again. This time it was more than a mere glance.

As they entered the streets of Macon, Frederick spotted a gas station and knew he had no choice but to get out and walk around.

"I need to pull in here for about two minutes," he explained. He slowed and turned on the blinker.

Allie remained silent as he parked the vehicle.

"Want anything?" he asked. "I'm going to get a bottle of Coke. That microscopic can wouldn't fill up an eyedropper." He pointed to the empty eight-ounce can in the console's beverage holder.

"Yes. A bottle of water would be nice," she replied and shifted in her seat. "If you don't mind, the twins will want something if we have drinks in front of them."

"Of course," Frederick said and shot her a glance.

This time she was looking at him. And Frederick was hit with the impact of the royal blue top and doleful brown eyes that held questions and a hint of accusation. He didn't need an explanation for the accusation. Her expression had implied that she hadn't believed him about Sophia's note. No telling what she was thinking.

"Know what the twins like?" he asked. Frederick turned off the engine and decided to deal with the note issue later, when his back wasn't hurting.

"Anything with sugar and fizz. They're charter members of 'Future Addicts of America.'" Her witty remark was accompanied by a smile so faint, Frederick wondered if he'd imagined it. If his back hadn't graduated to a state of pure agony, he would have replied with a flirtatious remark. But his spine would have no part of it.

Frederick opened the door, gripped the top of the car, and pulled himself out of the vehicle. He closed his eyes, clamped his teeth together, and pressed his fingers into his back. Once the pain subsided, he closed the door and tried to step forward, but to no avail. Frederick held on to the vehicle's roof while his legs refused cooperation.

"*Stupid Louise,*" he groaned and wished he hadn't called her stupid, but she was the one responsible for this agony. If she hadn't tackled him in Allie's front yard . . .

The passenger door opened and Allie got out and peered at him over the top of the car. "Are you okay?" she asked, her eyes round.

"Yeah," Frederick breathed and gritted his teeth. He offered her the disgruntled crocodile grimace and said, "It's just the price I pay for being in the war. I'll be okay." He took one step, then another.

"I can go get the drinks if you like," Allie rushed.

"No." He shook his head but didn't look at her. Frederick directed all his focus and energy on remaining on his feet. "I need to walk," he panted. "It works out the kinks."

⌇⌇⌇⌇⌇⟋⟍

Brent Everson sat across the street from Macon Christian Academy as he'd done every day for the last week. The Dairy Queen parking lot proved the perfect place to spy on the middle Elton heiress. He scanned the diminishing line of cars for Allie's blue Mercedes but didn't spot her. Brent checked his watch and frowned. She'd been early everywhere she went ever since he'd begun "Project Allie Elton." He looked back at the cars and carefully noted a Honda, a Ford pickup, a Chevy van, and a Mustang, last in line.

Brent sipped his DQ shake, narrowed his eyes, and decided he must have somehow missed Allie today. *No huge loss,* he surmised. After only a week of studying her, Brent had already learned quite a bit. The clues he'd gained coupled with the information Penny Clayton was providing was giving Brent major insights into her character.

Allie Elton was a no-nonsense kind of lady who was methodical to a fault. According to Penny's findings, her sister Evelyn said she even color-coded her closets. The woman despised empty flirtation and had never really dated that much. While she was attractive, she was a long way from being gorgeous and miles removed from the kind of woman Brent usually found appealing. Therefore, he knew he couldn't approach her flippantly or without careful research. The persona he presented must be that of a man who would seriously attract her. So far Brent had deduced that the kind of man who would snag Allie's attention was his absolute opposite.

The woman was a church hound. Attended three times a week. She didn't party at all, and she was so uptight about morals Brent wondered if she even believed in sex *after* marriage. The best Brent could tell, the most exciting thing she did was read Robert Frost. Yawn. If that wasn't enough, she didn't drink, smoke, or chew, and she wasn't about to start going with men who did. The smoking and chewing wasn't an issue with Brent. Living without alcohol posed the problem.

Brent set his empty shake cup in the Rolls-Royce's cup holder, reached toward the glove compartment, clicked it open, and pulled out a small flask of rum. He always liked to chase his ice cream with a little heat. The nip proved exactly the ticket to steadying his nerves. But as the liquid burned into his stomach, he lectured himself about backing off until Allie was wearing his wedding band. Once that happened, Brent would only be good enough to keep her . . . and her money.

He chuckled under his breath. *Shouldn't be a problem*, he thought. *I'm the king of sneaky*. His first wife, Richard Elton's niece, never suspected Brent's long line of mistresses or his penchant for gambling. He frowned as regret nibbled at him. Now that Chrissy was dead, Brent was sorry he'd cheated on her . . . sort of. Just not enough to discontinue the relationship with Penny Clayton, the mistress who'd been in his life when Chrissy died.

Last year when Brent received news of his wife's killer-bee attack, he had been with Penny. At that point, he and Penny had only been an item for a few weeks. Now, Brent couldn't say he was in love with her or ever would be. Furthermore, their relationship hadn't stopped him from enjoying a few flings. But Brent could say he and Penny thought too much alike to be without each other. They were both too practical to let anything like love or the lack of it stop them from pursuing their goals. Their pact was simple. They would each try to enable the other to marry into the Elton clan. If only one succeeded, they both would benefit. If both succeeded, they would have twice the money.

Brent relished another nip of rum, replaced the lid, and stashed the flask back in the glove compartment.

When he glanced toward the school again, he noticed Allie getting out of the white Mustang's passenger side. He frowned, leaned forward, and fumbled for the miniature binoculars lying in the passenger seat. While Allie greeted her fair nephews, Brent examined the guy behind the wheel. He was a dark-haired cat with the kind of chiseled features many women found appealing. He looked like he should be dressed in a flannel shirt and holding an ax in one of those outdoorsy spreads so many advertisers loved.

"Great," Brent mumbled and pondered his own appearance. While many women found blond hair and pale green eyes highly appealing, especially when coupled with silver-tongued flattery, Brent was a long way from brandishing an ax. And the closest thing he owned to a flannel shirt was the Ralph Lauren ribbed sweater he now wore.

"I couldn't be an outdoorsman even if I tried," he worried.

Brent lowered the binoculars and watched as Allie hustled the twins into the Mustang's backseat. She settled into the car. Brent lifted the binoculars and studied the competition's body language. The driver barely glanced toward Allie and didn't exactly look like he was enamored with this little chore.

"He almost looks like he's in pain or something." Brent focused on Allie. She clicked on her seat belt and gazed straight ahead, as if the hunk of a driver weren't present.

"Hmm." Brent tossed the binoculars back into the passenger seat and decided not to worry about the driver. At least not yet. Not until he talked with Penny. If she didn't have the scoop on the outdoorsman, she could get it. Allie's body language didn't suggest he was anyone who'd romantically interest her. The driver appeared to hold the same opinion of Allie.

Probably just a cousin or something, Brent decided and began to brainstorm ways to casually enter Allie's life. The timing must be perfect; Brent's cover complete. She need never know that the Rolls was one of his last luxury items or that his gambling had eaten up all the wealth from his previous marriage.

Fourteen

Three weeks later Allie sat on her back porch with her friend Sarah Hamilton. The two had done next to nothing for two days except get new haircuts. Now they were doing nothing again except sipping tea and watching the wildlife in Allie's backyard. Sarah had a few days off from her pediatric practice. Her husband, owner of an upscale sporting goods store, had taken a skiing trip to Colorado with a group of his friends. That left Sarah with nothing to do, so she'd driven to Macon.

Allie lazily watched a doe eating from the grain box near the woods. After a morning shower, the early afternoon was turning into a delightful spring experience. The smell of fresh rain still lingered in the air, and Allie tilted her head back and absorbed the April sunshine that warmed the earth. In the distance, the blue-black clouds and rumble of thunder suggested another shower might be on the way.

She opened her eyes, looked toward Sarah, admired her new hairstyle, and only hoped hers looked as good. Their cuts were supposed to be similar, but Allie's lacked the body Sarah's had. "You look like Diana Ross with that 'do," Allie said and sipped her warm cinnamon tea. "You remember her hairstyle when she was singing in the '60s."

"I can be Diana Ross any day." Sarah touched the back of her bobbed hair, then started singing "Stop, in the Name of

Love" at the top of her voice. With every beat she moved her neck and shoulders for the whole Diana Ross experience.

Allie giggled and finally said, "Stop! Stop! It's just not the same!"

Sarah fell back against the lawn chair and laughed. "You don't look half bad, either. Now we just need to get you some war paint. I wish you'd let Louise talk you into going to her Mary Kay party today. It would have been my treat." Sarah checked her watch. "It's still not too late."

"You're a hypocrite. You know that, don't you?" Allie teased. "You never wear makeup. And look at you. You look like a model—or at the *very least*, Diana Ross."

"No, I don't, and you know it, girl." Sarah waved her hand. "I'm just not pale like you are. You white women need more . . . I don't know . . . *something*. So what do you do? You go lie on the beach for hours trying to get browner . . . like us!" Sarah lifted her hand as if she were the Queen of Sheba. She certainly had the royal look with a ruby-colored sundress complementing her dark, smooth skin.

"That's a low blow," Allie shot back with a sassy grin and eyed her pale legs where her shorts stopped. "You and I both know I've never worried about getting a tan." Sarah always lovingly harassed her because of their racial differences, but the two adored each other. Her lifelong friend was one of the few people Allie could really relax around, and she was always happy to engage in Sarah's witty banter.

"Really, Allie, I love you to *death*," Sarah said as she leaned forward. "And I'd never say a word to hurt your feelings. But if I were you, I'd *get* a tan or some makeup or something. With that Frederick Wently on the loose again, it wouldn't hurt to spruce up a little." She wiggled her eyebrows and then winked.

Allie waved her hand in an attempt at nonchalance. "Like I already said, he's after Louise."

"Oh . . . so that's why he watched you all during dinner last night," Sarah responded.

Peering into her cup, Allie didn't move. She'd possessed no idea that Frederick even noticed her last night. As always, she thought he was too engrossed with Louise. He and his friend Jim Bennington had driven down yesterday for a long weekend in Macon. Frederick had claimed that Jim, who was suffering from depression, needed to get out of Atlanta. But Allie and everyone else in the family suspected Frederick's motive lay completely with Louise.

Nonetheless, Allie and Sarah had been roped into the dinner outing. They'd spent yesterday evening talking to Jim about his fiancée's death while they ate steaks and baked potatoes. As usual, Helena and Louise had sandwiched Frederick between themselves. But before the evening was over, Sarah and Jim were talking medicine, and Allie was left to stare out the window at nothing and relive the last few weeks.

Neither she nor Frederick had said much after they picked up the boys from school. On the way back home, the twins had been so intrigued by this new man and the cool Mustang that they dominated the conversation. Frederick's strained features during the return trip had bespoken his pain, and Allie truly felt sorry for him.

She knew the story behind the pain. He'd sacrificed himself trying to protect his crew in Afghanistan. But Allie hadn't realized the injury still caused him so much trouble. After all, he was the outward picture of health. On the drive back home, Allie's respect for his sacrifice had grown as swiftly as her pity for his pain. But later that day, when Louise had draped herself on his arm and Frederick looked like a satisfied tomcat, Allie's concern had ceased to exist.

Ever since then, Allie and Frederick had been in each other's company off and on—especially evenings like last night at the restaurant or tonight when Martha Grove invited everyone to dinner at her place. Usually neither she nor Frederick spoke to the other. At times Allie even dreamed up some believable excuse to get out of having to watch Louise monopolize him. Other times, like last night, she accepted the inevitable and attended whatever outing had been arranged.

"You and Frederick once had it bad for each other. I can't believe it's not still there." Sarah's unassuming voice cut through Allie's distraction, and she received the impression that perhaps Sarah had said a few other things she'd missed.

Allie glanced at her friend, whose sharp stare made her squirm.

If the truth were known, Allie had been enormously tempted to go to that Mary Kay party today, but she didn't want anyone—including Frederick—to think she was fixing herself up to snare his interest. The new hairdo was enough for now.

"You know, I think he's turned into a womanizer," Allie admitted and swirled the liquid in her cup.

"I'd have to disagree," Sarah said. "He doesn't strike me that way. Seems more like the strong Christian type to me."

Allie recalled the music they'd listened to on the way to pick up the twins from school. The combination of Christian music and chasing women didn't logically coexist, but then, who said the pursuit of sin had to be logical?

"And I'm not convinced he's even a little bit interested in Louise," Sarah continued as if she were the sage of the century.

Allie glanced at her friend. As suspected, Sarah's head was

tilted at that certain angle that usually meant the woman was right. Nevertheless, Allie clung to her assumptions. After all, she'd seen the lip print on the note.

"But even if he were a womanizer," Sarah continued, "if he repented and changed, why couldn't you forgive him? God would."

The question left Allie squirming to the point that she was ready for a major subject change. "Why don't you just stick to terrifying helpless children with IV needles and stop trying to play matchmaker," she responded with a wicked grin.

"Now who's throwing the low blows?" Sarah teased.

The rev of a sports car neared her house, and Allie sat up straight. She'd learned to recognize that sound early in her stay at the guesthouse. She'd also learned to be on the alert, especially when in the front yard. Louise or Helena was out in one of the Corvettes, and Allie wouldn't put it past either of them to crash through her front yard. When the vehicle roared closer and stopped, Allie knew they were about to have a visit from one of the perky sisters.

"My guess is that's either Louise or Helena," Allie mumbled. "Wonder what they want?"

"It's probably the Mary Kay draft," Sarah said and wiggled her brows again.

Allie stood and entered her back door. She didn't understand Sarah's remark until she was halfway through her kitchen. By the time she opened the front door, Louise was climbing the porch steps and Allie figured Sarah must be right.

"Where are you?" Louise chimed. "We've been waiting on you."

"On me?" Allie asked.

"Yes, for the Mary Kay party, silly. Remember?" Louise

tilted her head to one side and her cloud of loose ringlets attractively shifted with her move. "I invited you and your friend last night."

"But we never said we'd—"

"We'll be right there." Sarah's strong voice boomed from behind Allie and left no room for argument.

"Great!" Louise exclaimed and clapped. "That will make a perfect dozen—which will get me my free prize." Louise flounced back down the stairs in her high heels and miniskirt before Allie had time to conjure a rejection.

Allie wondered why Louise cared about some free gift. Her father had enough money to wallpaper her bedroom in hundred-dollar bills. She could *buy* anything she wanted.

She turned to Sarah, who now looked like the Queen of Sheba having a victory gloat. "Okay, I'll go," she agreed. "But if you're pulling me into this, Diana Ross, then you're getting fully painted, too."

"Of course." Sarah's grin couldn't have been broader. "That's the whole point. We're going to have a big girlfriend party. And don't tell me you don't really want to do this, Allie Elton," Sarah challenged. "I've known you too long not to see through your act. You're more interested in Frederick Wently than you want anyone to know."

The next evening Allie stood in front of her dresser and examined the woman before her. Whoever she was, she certainly was an improvement over the old Allie, all thanks to Mary Kay and Sarah Hamilton. The truth be known, Allie had wanted a full makeover ever since Frederick visited Elton Mansion with his sister and brother-in-law. But she'd been reluctant because she didn't want anyone to suspect that Frederick was the motivating factor. Presently, she was nearly too ashamed to admit it to herself.

Despite what Sarah said, Frederick was clearly on the scene for Louise. Allie was beginning to think watching him fall in love with a woman fifteen years younger must be God's way of repaying her for breaking his heart ten years ago. That, coupled with the fact that he'd become a lying womanizer, was too painful for words. Of course, Sarah didn't agree with this verdict, but Allie wasn't ready to toss aside evidence in preference for Sarah's conclusions . . . or the fact that he still chose Christian music.

Still, something deep inside drove Allie to at least give Frederick a glimpse of the woman he'd nearly married. Allie never considered herself drop-dead gorgeous; however, when she took some time with her appearance, she looked ten times better than the "pale-faced old maid" she was becoming.

The Mary Kay party couldn't have gone better. From the start, Louise, Macy, Helena, Martha, and Sarah encouraged Allie to buy the whole setup and use it. When Allie agreed, Sarah insisted on paying for the spread. Sarah was the only person Allie had told of the Eltons' financial hardship. Even though Allie still could have afforded the indulgence, Sarah flipped out her credit card and wouldn't take no for an answer.

Now all the ladies except Sarah thought Allie's new look was *their* idea. No one suspected that Allie's motivation stemmed from Frederick's presence. No one except Sarah, that is. Finally Allie grudgingly admitted the truth before Sarah left for home this morning.

Allie pulled at her bangs and coaxed them into final position before pumping a light mist of hairspray on them. The melon smell tickled her nose and left a stiff residue on her forehead. Allie set the bottle aside, stepped back, and stared at her reflection. Yesterday's haircut had added some volume to her hair, while the raspberry-red lipstick lent color to her face and proved a nice balance for the brown eyeshadow and pink blusher.

"I look good," Allie said with a surge of self-assurance she hadn't felt in many, many years—not since the last time Frederick was in her life. "This is so weird," she admitted.

Slipping out of her house robe, Allie began to really look forward to tonight's barbeque and games. The last Allie heard, Louise was hyped on teaching Frederick how to play spoons, and Helena was vowing to be as big a part of teaching him as Louise.

"Poor Craig," Allie mumbled as she slipped on the new sundress that perfectly matched her lipstick. Helena had continued to go out with Craig, and Allie doubted he'd be pleased with the blazing flirtation happening behind his back.

This all sounds like something from Maury Povich. Allie imagined herself sitting across from Maury, and the famous talk show host saying, "*So, as I understand this, you broke up with Frederick Wently ten years ago because your Aunt Landon wanted you to marry someone with more money.*"

"*Yes, Maury, that's right.*"

"*And now this Frederick is back in your life. The two of you are barely speaking and haven't even brought up the past at all?*"

"*No. Not at all.*"

"*Instead, he's now interested in your sister's sister-in-law, who's fifteen years younger.*"

"*That's right.*"

"*And the other sister-in-law is trying to steal Frederick from her sister—despite the fact that she has a steady boyfriend.*"

Allie smoothed out her dress and reached for the wide belt

lying atop the bed's brocade comforter. "You've got it right, Maury," she said out loud.

"That's weird." Maury's voice bounced around Allie's mind.

She chuckled. "Yes, very weird," Allie replied and pivoted to examine her appearance as she looped the low-slung belt just above her hips. "Not bad for thirty-five," she asserted and decided Aunt Landon didn't need to know the motivation for her makeover.

The grapevine was swift. Allie's father and sister learned— probably from Macy—that Frederick was around these days. Aunt Landon had been next. Her email warning Allie of the pitfalls of reuniting with Frederick arrived ten days ago. She'd also made vague references to her will that Allie understood all too well. No one but Allie knew that she was Landon's sole heir. Her aunt's hints about disinheritance underscored the seriousness of her conviction regarding a match between Allie and Frederick. Even though the email rankled, Allie assured Landon that Frederick and Louise were together; then she chatted about the wonderful way the roses were responding to their new fertilizer.

Allie finished buckling the belt, checked her watch, and prided herself in running a few minutes behind. She didn't want to give Frederick the idea that any of this dressing up was for him or that she was eager to see him again. He was probably already at the Groveses', flipping burgers by now.

The very thought of him sent a shiver through Allie. She gripped the side of the oak dresser as the matching bed seemed to tilt. *I'm still so in love with him,* she admitted and tried to remind herself that Frederick was a playboy who was after a woman nearly young enough to be his daughter. *But Sarah's right. I'd forgive him,* she pined and voiced the pivotal point she'd arrived at this morning. She'd realized that God's love and forgiveness were available for Frederick, and that the least she could do was offer the same. All he had to do was ask.

Allie frowned and huffed. "Stop it!" she demanded and slipped on the spike pumps she'd bought to complete her outfit. *And if you don't, Oprah's going to be camping on the front porch.* She headed down the narrow hallway and into the kitchen, her heels tapping along the Italian tile. Allie paused at the breakfast bar long enough to pick up her keys and purse.

But before she walked to the door, a gold tube lying on the kitchen counter caught her attention. She picked up the tube of Hot Lips Red and stared at it. Allie hadn't felt right about throwing it away, but she didn't want the ever-present reminder of Frederick's girlfriend's lips around, either. On impulse, Allie dropped the lipstick into her purse and decided to figure out why later.

She decided to take her car to the Groveses' rather than walk the quarter of a mile in the killer heels. When she pulled the Mercedes into the Groveses driveway, Allie was glad she was the last one to join the party. She saw that Charlie, Macy, and the twins had already driven over. They'd called twenty minutes before Allie left to ask if she wanted to ride with them. That just left Frederick. His extended-cab truck confirmed his presence. After several shuttle flights in and out of Atlanta and Macon, Frederick had driven his pickup down for an extended visit with his Atlanta friend, Jim.

Allie didn't even want to think about the family upheaval it would cause if Frederick and she *did* get back together. Aunt Landon would probably start popping nitroglycerine pills to stop a heart attack, and no telling *what* Allie's father would do. She imagined the eruption and didn't cringe half as much as she might have five years ago. As far as Aunt Landon's nitroglycerine, Allie shrugged and put the car in park. Maybe popping nitro pills would give Aunt Landon something to do for a change.

The facts were that Allie was thirty-five, still single, and had no prospects in sight. Her love for Frederick hadn't waned. If anything, it had increased to the point of unbearable proportions and doubled daily—despite Annie and her "Hot Lips Red." And she decided that if by some miracle Frederick was willing to put his womanizing ways behind him and even hinted that he wanted a reconciliation, then Allie wouldn't discourage him.

And the family . . . well, the family could just deal with it. This was her life, not theirs. Even if it meant Aunt Landon's ultimate disinheritance, Allie decided the loss was worth being happy for the rest of her life. Even though she still received an allowance every month, Allie's family was nearly broke now. She was surviving just fine. If it came to it, she and Frederick could survive without a fortune together.

"Why am I even thinking this way?" Allie groaned and turned off the ignition. *He's after Louise. End of discussion.*

She grabbed her handbag and got out. As Allie walked through the April evening, fragrant with freshly bloomed irises and azaleas, she eyed the pillared mansion. The six o'clock sun highlighted the white paint against brick the color of cinnamon, and Allie pondered the similarities of this newer home with Elton Mansion. While the Grove house was a replica of an old plantation home, Elton Mansion was the real deal.

She sighed for the home that had been her haven since birth, but talked herself out of a melancholic droop. Allie decided to do the best she could to enjoy the evening given the present set of circumstances. She'd focus on Barry and Bart, pretend Frederick wasn't present, and pray no one noticed that his every glance sent her into a quivering fit. But if *he* noticed and made a move, Allie decided once and for all she would not discourage him.

While Louise was way more beautiful and twenty-year-old fresh, Allie embraced the fact that she possessed a composure and wisdom that came with age. Even though the old Frederick had enjoyed it when Allie looked pretty, he had valued character and solid morals over external appeal. Despite the fact that Frederick had given no indication that he wanted to resurrect their former relationship, an inexplicable hope insisted that his old value system was still alive . . . or at least available for resurrection.

She trotted up the mansion's steps, paused in front of the massive door, rang the doorbell, and waited. Allie fully expected to be greeted by one of the mansion's employees, but when the door swung inward, Frederick stood on the other side. He was dressed as he'd often dressed years ago—in a pair of worn blue jeans, a black T-shirt, and cowboy boots. And the effect was much the same tonight as it had been all those years ago. Allie's fingers tightened around her purse strap, and she hung on for dear life as the rush and flow of adrenaline roared through her.

Fifteen

Frederick had only just arrived at the Groveses' mansion when the doorbell rang. He'd spotted Allie's vehicle winding toward the home seconds before he stepped inside, so when she rang the bell, he had eagerly offered to open the door and fully expected her on the other side. But what he hadn't expected was the transformed beauty who stood before him like an angel beamed down on the shaft of sunlight she stood in.

Wow! he thought, then heard himself say it before adding, "You look great!"

"Thanks," she demurely replied. "We had a Mary Kay party."

"All hail Mary Kay!" A surge of bravado encouraged Frederick to up the warmth of his broad grin.

When Allie's pink cheeks grew pinker and she studied his feet, Frederick received more encouragement than he'd gleaned in three weeks. The only thing that kept him coming back all these weeks was the subtle clues and discreet glances that indicated Allie might not be immune to him. Her otherwise disinterested persona usually left Frederick in a tailspin of doubt. He never knew if she really was allowing a few clues to slip out or if he was a desperate man reading something into nothing.

But now no one could deny that Allie truly appreciated his

appreciation. Frederick's hopes soared to an all-time high. Add to that the fact that merely being in her presence had awakened his love to a frenzied fit. The flood of love had swept aside any resentment over the past in a deluge that left Frederick breathless. In his case, love really had covered a multitude of sins. He'd come to realize that Allie had been young and impressionable all those years ago. But the woman before him now seemed to better know her own mind. If only her mind were focused upon him.

Now nothing stood in the way of reawakening their former relationship. At least, nothing on his side. Whether or not Allie still allowed Landon Russ's blueblood prejudices to affect her remained unseen. Furthermore, Frederick still suspected she hadn't believed him three weeks ago when he told her that note with lipstick on it had been from Sophia to Darren. Her eyes had screamed doubt, and Frederick couldn't even imagine what she must be thinking about him.

"I guess I should come in," Allie hedged with a shy grin that left Frederick's knees weak.

"Oh! Yes! Of course!" Frederick burst and felt like the fool of the century. Thankfully the Groves had been too focused on making the acquaintance of Frederick's guests to notice his and Allie's front door interaction.

As Allie stepped inside the foyer and he closed the door, the Groves and his guests paused in their greetings to look toward the latest arrival. "Allie, I know you've already met my sister and brother-in-law," Frederick said, and motioned toward the Cosbys. "They surprised Jim and me with a visit this afternoon, and Mrs. Grove said it was fine for them to crash the party."

"Of course! Of course!" Martha enthused. "The more the merrier!" Her face beaming, she wore a flowy red dress that heightened her color.

"That's what she kept saying when we were having children," Charlie Sr. drawled and stroked his handlebar mustache.

The group burst into laughter.

Frederick had long since decided that all Mr. Grove needed was to replace his casual slacks and shirt with a uniform from World War I and he could have posed as a soldier from the past.

Allie exchanged brief handshakes with Sophia and Darren and smiled toward Jim, whom she'd met last night. He stood on the edge of the group near Louise and Helena and had exchanged his perpetual sad-eyed expression for one of near panic. Frederick was nearly overcome with more laughter.

Poor Jim. The thirty-year-old doctor was still mourning the death of his fiancée and hadn't even looked at another woman in months. Now he'd been attacked by two sirens dressed in hip huggers. But that was exactly what Frederick had hoped for. Whether Jim was ready or not, or interested or not, Frederick was playing matchmaker. And he prayed that Louise would target her nurturing tendencies toward Jim and no longer him.

"Allie, you just met Jim last night," Frederick said.

"Nice to see you again, Jim." Allie extended her hand for a brief shake. Her soft greeting and encouraging smile was met with a relieved sagging of Jim's shoulders.

He latched on to Allie's hand and held on a little too long for Frederick's peace of mind. While the dull depression never left Jim's eyes, his face relaxed and he fell in beside Allie as the group moved toward the back of the house with the Groves in the lead.

Frederick frowned. As he had last night, Frederick brought Jim as a therapeutic measure, but he hadn't envisioned Allie being the one to give the therapy. Frederick decided to try to run interference on what looked like swift bonding before it went too far. In his estimation, Jim needed someone lively and young and unpredictable. That someone was Louise Grove. If Jim did go for lively and young and unpredictable, that would get Louise out of Frederick's hair. So while his motives weren't pure, they did involve his concern for his friend's well-being.

Jim's latest diagnosis was clinical depression. Since Felicity's death, the guy had worked only part-time, had barely eaten, and Frederick had to insist that he iron his shorts and polo shirt tonight. Even though Jim resisted coming to the party to the point of nearly kicking and screaming, Frederick had stayed determined. He'd even texted Louise this morning and encouraged her to give "poor Jim" extra attention.

Frederick had then embarked upon a fervent fit of prayer that Louise would begin to genuinely experience feelings for "poor Jim." While she looked nothing like the doctor's former fiancée, she certainly had Felicity's sanguine personality type, which perfectly complemented Jim's melancholic–phlegmatic tendencies.

"Macy and Charlie Jr. are already out back," Martha called over her shoulder as she opened the French doors leading to the huge backyard.

"We promised the twins we'd play football with them," Helena admitted. The two sisters erupted onto the deck and bounded away.

"Hey, guys!" Louise hollered. "Where's your football?"

Frederick exited the house last and closed the door behind him as the evening air cooled his face and arms. In the distance, whippoorwills serenaded the countryside and predicted the nearing night. While their calls usually held a cheerful resonance, their singing stroked a despondent chord within

Frederick. The jovial conversation floating from the grill and the delightful shrieks from the football game did nothing to lift his sinking spirits.

This whole "Jim plan" was backfiring.

In silent desperation, Frederick watched as Jim gravitated toward Allie, who showed every sign of being completely tuned in to the man. The force of their instant kinship was so great, Frederick was nearly knocked over by it. Their bond must have started last night at the restaurant.

How did I miss it? Frederick pondered and recalled Jim's talking more to Allie's doctor friend, Sarah, than he had to Allie.

While Charlie Jr., Darren, and Sophia joined the Groves in preparing the burgers and hot dogs, Frederick plopped into a lawn chair beside Macy and blindly stared across the acres of rolling Georgia hills.

The smell of grilling meat lost appeal. Frederick gripped the chair's armrests and considered yanking himself bald.

"I could really use another soda," Macy hinted.

Frederick gazed at her for three seconds before her words penetrated his desperation. He'd noticed early in his relationship with the Grove clan that no one expected much of Macy. Occasionally he had detected a thread of frustration in Allie's eyes over the issue, especially when Macy assumed her sister should take more responsibility with her sons.

"Do you want one?" She raised her brows and lifted her hair off her neck.

"Yes, as a matter of fact, I do," Frederick said and was pleasantly surprised at Macy's offer. "My blood turned into Coca-Cola years ago. I have to keep it up now or I'll die," he joked.

"Good," Macy said with a weak smile. "That's the way I feel about Diet Dr Pepper. When you get your Coke, would you bring me back a Diet Dr Pepper?" She gestured toward the outdoor service bar that featured a refrigerator, ice machine, and microwave. A roof shielded the open-walled structure from the elements.

"I'd do it myself," Macy touched her temple, "but I haven't felt well today. One of my headaches, you know."

"Sure," Frederick said through a chuckle. *I guess I fell for that one, didn't I?* he thought. As he stood, Frederick glanced over the designer dress Macy bought last week on an eight-hour shopping spree. He'd been around that evening, and Macy had bragged to the rafters about all her purchases. *Too bad she can't get that enthusiastic about anything else—like parenting her own sons, for instance.*

He walked toward the refrigerator laden with sodas and eyed the touch football game underway on the lawn. The football had splashed into the Olympic-sized pool, and the boys' father had just been drafted to retrieve the ball with a net on a pole. Then Charlie Jr. joined the game. When Louise spotted Frederick looking their way, she bounded toward him. Knowing what was coming, Frederick made swift work of retrieving the sodas. He gave Macy hers and was guzzling his Coke by the time Louise was dragging him toward the other players.

"We need another guy to even out the teams," Louise chattered.

"I'm no good!" Frederick protested. "I'm in cowboy boots."

"So take them off!" Louise insisted. She lifted her bare toes and pointed toward a pair of spike heels lying near the deck. "We did."

"But what about my back?" Frederick yowled.

"We'll let you be quarterback. You don't even have to run. Besides, it's just touch football." She winked and slung her hair over her shoulder in a gesture more suited for a seductive model than a backyard football maven. And Frederick decided the "big brother" lecture must come soon. Maybe tonight. And maybe if he started acting more like a big brother or a father figure with Louise, she'd quit thinking of him so romantically.

Nevertheless, Frederick determined to use this opportunity to hopefully divert Allie's attention from Jim. "Help!" he playfully called toward the group near the grill. "I'm being kidnapped."

"Ah, poor baby," Sophia crooned while the rest of the group knowingly laughed.

Frederick darted a glance toward Allie in hopes that his teasing might stir at least a hint of jealousy, but she was so intent upon what "poor Jim" was saying, she never even registered Frederick's antics.

Sixteen

Five minutes later, Jim dismissed himself for a trip to the men's room, and Allie retrieved a bottled water from the fridge. When she raised from the task, she smelled a familiar perfume—the same fragrance she'd smelled on Sophia when she greeted her earlier. For some reason, the scent was strangely familiar and troubled Allie somewhat. Thoughtfully, Allie turned and nearly bumped into Sophia Cosby.

"Oh, excuse me," Sophia oozed and gripped Allie's hand. "I came in here to chat with you for a few minutes." She glanced over her shoulder and then looked Allie square in the eyes. "I know we haven't known each other that long, but I wanted to tell you how much I appreciate . . ."

As she began to talk, Allie was so distracted by the combination of her perfume and her full, red lips she barely registered what Sophia was saying . . . something to do with Jim Bennington and how grateful she was for Allie's taking an interest in him. Not long into Sophia's spiel, Allie fully recalled what perfume the redhead wore and where she'd smelled the scent before.

It was Giorgio.

It was in Frederick's jacket.

And it was accompanied by that tube of red lipstick—the exact shade of Sophia's lips now.

There had also been a fragrant note saying how much the writer enjoyed the previous evening.

But Sophia is Frederick's sister! Allie thought and tried to collect her thoughts in the whirl of confusion that followed.

"Here you are, Annie dear," Darren said as he slipped into the service bar and draped a familiar jacket across his wife's shoulders.

"Oh, thanks so much," Sophia said while her husband pecked her cheek and patted her shoulders. "I don't know what I was thinking when I wore this sundress. It was perfect earlier today, but now with the night coming on, it's getting too cool."

"Can't have my lady cool," Darren crooned.

Sophia's deep-throated chuckle hinted at marital bliss, and Darren headed back to the grill with a sassy wink for his wife.

The combination of the bottled water's chilling her fingers and the wisp of a spring breeze sent a shiver through Allie. She stared at the familiar jacket. "I thought that was Frederick's jacket," she blurted.

"Oh no. It's Darren's." Sophia waved her hand, and her fingers sparkled five carats' worth.

Allie set her bottled water on the counter, crossed her arms, and hunched her shoulders against a stronger puff of wind. The seashell windchimes hanging nearby merrily clanked, and Allie wished she could feel as cheerful about some of the assumptions she'd made about Frederick.

"Did Darren just call you Annie?" she questioned while her heart sank.

"Yes." Sophia nodded and slipped her arms into the jacket. "Anne's my middle name. He's called me Annie since our honeymoon. Just one of those married people things, ya know," she said with a secretive grin while tugging the jacket tighter around her.

"Oh." Allie gripped the counter and silently stared at Frederick's sister. If the jacket belonged to Darren, then the note and the perfume and the Hot Lips Red all must have been Sophia's. Frederick *had* told her the note was from his sister to her husband.

And I didn't believe him! Allie admonished herself and had never felt so judgmental in her life. *Sarah was right! Frederick's* not *a womanizer!*

"Are you okay?" Sophia questioned and leaned closer.

"Uh, yes. Yes, I'm fine. Just fine," Allie replied. She picked up the bottled water, unscrewed the lid, and gulped the liquid until the back of her throat ached and her stomach felt full of ice.

When she lowered the bottle, she couldn't stop the glance toward Frederick. Helena had grabbed him around the midsection in a bear hug that Allie suspected was supposed to be a football move. But it didn't take Einstein to see that Helena was blatantly taking advantage of the situation. Frederick first raised his hands, then tried to disentangle himself from the nineteen-year-old. Just about the time he broke free, Louise made a move and didn't let him go until she'd slipped in a kiss on his cheek. Interestingly enough, Louise and Frederick were on the same team.

Allie expected Frederick to frown or discourage her as he had Helena. He didn't. He just laughed and threw the ball to Barry. Allie looked down at a potted fern and was hit with the force of the situation. Even if Frederick wasn't a lying womanizer, he showed signs of immensely enjoying Louise's company.

But what single man wouldn't? Allie thought. *She's beautiful, vivacious, and very available.* Furthermore, past and present society was full of men who had married younger women.

If Frederick fell in love with Louise, he wouldn't be the first man who'd been snared by a gal fifteen years his junior.

"Allie?" Sophia laid her hand on Allie's arm.

She looked up into a pair of discerning brown eyes that suggested Sophia had already sensed too much.

"Did you and Frederick . . . did you know Frederick before—when he worked at Elton Mansion?"

Allie stiffened and did her best to appear casual. "Of course," she said and didn't even allow herself a blink. "We all did. He was our yard manager."

"Oh." Sophia's gaze faltered and a veil of confusion played on her features.

Allie relaxed and hoped her act had been good enough for long-term convincing. No telling what her expression had shown when she was looking at Frederick.

She groped for a means to change the conversation and Sophia's train of thought and recalled that tube of lipstick in her purse. Now she knew why she'd felt prompted to drop the tube in her bag. "I've got something I think belongs to you," Allie said and hurried toward her leather handbag, sitting next to her chair. When she raised up from digging the Hot Lips Red from her purse, Jim was reclaiming his former seat next to hers.

"Want a bottle of water or something?" Allie asked and held up her bottle before setting it beside her purse.

"Sure." Jim's sad smile spoke of loss and survival.

"Okay. I'll be back shortly," Allie said and hurried toward Sophia as quickly as the high heels would allow. After stepping into the service bar, she held up the tube of lipstick and said, "Recognize this?"

"My lipstick!" Sophia exclaimed. She looked at the label on the bottom, removed the lid, and twisted up the tube. "Yes.

It's mine! I've been missing this for weeks. How did you know it was mine, and where'd you find it?"

"It was . . . uh . . ." Allie hedged and tried to decide how best to relate the story without lying, but no matter how she approached the truth, it incriminated her.

"Oh well, what does it matter?" Sophia said and fished inside the jacket until she unzipped the hidden pocket. "I'm just thrilled to have it back." She dropped the lipstick into the pocket and rezipped it. "This was a seasonal color that's been discontinued. I bought two identical tubes and thought I'd lost this one forever."

"I'm glad I could help," Allie said with a grin she hoped reflected the genuine affection she was beginning to feel for Frederick's sister. "I just promised Jim a bottle of water, so I guess I'd better deliver." Allie opened the refrigerator and retrieved another bottle. As she shut the refrigerator door, the grill sizzled and snapped with the promise of culinary masterpieces. Whether you could call hamburger patties and grilled wienies masterpieces, they were certainly starting to smell like works of art.

"Well, I'll let you get back to poor Jim," Sophia said and patted Allie's arm. "Like I said, I'm so glad you're taking an interest in him. He's been a family friend for *years*. He's like a brother to Frederick and me. His parents were older when he was born. They'd been married years and didn't think they could have any children, then *boom*—there Jim was. Now both his parents are dead. So we're really all the family he's got, and we haven't been able to pull him out of this terrible depression."

"He told me his fiancée passed away nine months ago," Allie said. She had immediately felt a kindred spirit with Jim because she could well relate to the loss of a fiancé, even if it wasn't to death. Allie stole another glimpse of Frederick.

"Yes." Sophia nodded, and her feathery, auburn hair shifted with every move. "That's what started the depression. All he wants to do is sleep and read poetry." Sophia grimaced and Allie hid a grin.

She and Jim had already been comparing notes on some poetry. The two of them had much in common, including their love of Robert Frost.

"Macy, come quick!" Helena's breathless exclamation floated from near the deck.

All chatter on the deck ceased. Allie and Sophia turned toward Helena.

Macy sat straight up in her chair.

"It's Barry! He's throwing up!" Helena exclaimed.

The child's father beat Macy off the deck, but she was close behind. Allie plopped the water on the counter, hustled out of the service bar, and arrived at Barry's side shortly after Macy and Jim Bennington. The next few minutes turned into the bustle and upheaval of getting the skinny preteen into the house, where he was stretched onto the couch and pampered more than any lapdog could ever claim.

But despite Barry's mom, dad, aunt, and grandmother giving him 7 Up, a cold compress, and plenty of encouragement, the boy was ashen. His pulse was racing. And he wanted to go home.

"Probably a virus," Jim said and touched Barry's reddened cheeks. "I've seen several patients this week with the same symptoms. In a matter of minutes, they go from being normal to throwing up and feeling like death warmed over."

"I feel awful." Barry covered his eyes and restlessly stirred.

Allie and Martha exchanged a resigned glance, and Martha stepped aside to place the can of 7 Up on the end table while Allie knelt to Barry's side. She stroked his fair hair. How the twins ranked blond hair and blue eyes when both their parents had dark hair and eyes had always been a source of mystery to Allie and the rest of the family.

"Please take me home," Barry whimpered again.

"That's the best thing, I think," Jim said and stepped near Martha.

"Well, okay," Charlie hesitantly said and looked toward Macy, who sat at her son's feet.

"What are you looking at me for?" Macy snapped.

"He says he wants to go home," Charlie replied and stretched to his full six two height.

"Are you implying I'm the one who should take him?" Macy retorted without ever acknowledging her husband's power move. "Why not you?"

"You know he's going to want you." Charlie crossed his arms, and his knit shirt stretched tightly across broad shoulders. "They always do when they're sick."

"So I get to leave the party while you have a high old time. Is that it?" Macy stood up, doubled her fists, and glared at her husband.

Jim cleared his throat. Allie winced and turned her attention to her shorts-clad nephew. Everything with those two was a power struggle that apparently didn't stop even when their children's welfare was in question.

Barry whimpered and lowered his hand from his eyes. Allie slipped her fingers around his, looked into his confused gaze, and said, "I'll take him home."

The boy's face relaxed. He closed his eyes.

"Aunt Allie will make you a comfortable spot on the couch," Allie crooned. "We'll find you a good movie on TV, and I'll give you some ice chips. Okay?" She stroked his clammy forehead.

The child nodded.

"So it looks like it's all settled, then," Martha said from the end of the couch, her tone laced with disapproval.

"Yes." Allie looked up at her and nodded, only to realize Martha's attention was on her son and daughter-in-law. "I just need to get my purse from the deck." Allie stood and adjusted her belt.

"Are you sure you'll be okay without me?" Macy asked and moved near her son's head.

"Oh brother," Charlie mumbled.

Allie nearly shot him a look as sour as his mother's but stopped herself. Neither Charlie nor Macy had room to criticize the other. If they had been excellent parents, both would have put their own wishes aside and taken their son home. But neither of them could think past themselves long enough to put anyone's needs first, even those of their children. Allie wondered how Charlie and Macy had stayed married, and prayed that if she ever married, it would never deteriorate into such a mess.

Seventeen

Brent Everson settled into a theater chair in the north section of Macon Community Church. He gazed across the mammoth sanctuary filled with seats that wrapped around the auditorium. The building offered the latest in design and high-tech equipment—right down to the overactive air conditioner that left the tips of his ears and nose feeling frostbitten. Brent was glad for the wool blazer he almost didn't wear due to the spring's increasing heat.

He'd been thrilled several weeks ago when he tracked Allie and her family to this large congregation. The huge crowd gave Brent the cover that a small country church would have never offered. Bumping into Allie was by far more "coincidental" at a church with five thousand members than one with fifty. And Brent desperately needed to bump into Allie. After weeks of following and studying her, he was ready to make his move. Or at least, he'd better be. The little bit of money he had left was dwindling, despite the fact that he'd slowed the gambling. He or Penny Clayton needed to marry an Elton within six months. Penny wasn't having much luck currently, so he *must* make a move.

He spotted Allie entering the south door with one nephew at her side. *Wow!* he thought, and couldn't quite believe the change in her appearance. But then, Brent was always a little mystified by what he called the bathroom miracle. He often saw Penny go into the bathroom looking like a flat-haired, pale-faced rat, but when she emerged an hour later, she could almost run for Miss America. Apparently Allie had learned the tricks of the bathroom miracle. She looked ten times better today than she had the last time Brent spied on her.

He slowly grinned and decided that pretending an attraction for Allie might not be as big a chore as he'd originally thought. Of course, that didn't change the fact that she was a Bible-thumping prude—but a pretty Bible-thumping prude was way easier to live with than a bland one.

She meandered down the aisle with the thin kid at her side. He was as tall as Allie and favored her more than he did his own mother. The best Brent could tell, Allie was a better mother to him and his twin than was Macy Grove. Macy and her husband, Charlie, walked behind Allie and looked about as happy as two bad-tempered tigers with their tails tied together.

Brent snickered under his breath. *So much for marital bliss*, he sneered and wondered why Charlie Grove didn't direct his interests elsewhere. The best Brent could tell, neither Charlie nor Macy were having an affair or even an occasional fling.

Probably because of the church thing, he thought and abhorred the thought of living such a life.

He scanned the recessed lights that cast an ethereal glow upon the striking sanctuary and wondered what anybody saw in obeying a long list of do's and don'ts. No matter how pretty you packaged the rules, they still were nothing more than a jail cell. Nevertheless, Brent would do whatever he had to do to get money. If it meant feigning a holy life and attending church until he was ninety, then so be it. But he would never truly embrace the church or its long list of boneheaded rules.

Brent's attention rested upon Allie once more. She and the

Grove clan were claiming an empty row near the back that offered a perfect spy point from Brent's position. And now they were being joined by another group. Brent placed his elbow on the armrest and leaned forward. His legs tensed.

The chiseled-faced outdoorsman was back. After Brent had seen him with Allie at that Christian school, he'd noticed the dude prowling around her more than once. So Brent had clued Penny in to the guy's presence. She found out his name was Frederick Wently, and he once worked at the Elton Mansion years ago. Now Frederick was bringing friends with him.

The redheaded lady and her husband didn't bother Brent. They interested him. . . . Rather, their obvious wealth, as evidenced by their fashionable clothing and the golfball-sized diamonds the woman wore, interested him.

Then there was a sad-faced, moping man who settled beside Allie. Immediately the guy struck up a conversation with Allie. Her relaxed response and receptive expression clanged Brent's alarm system. He'd been worried about the outdoorsman. Perhaps his concerns had been misplaced.

Louise Grove, who research had proven was Macy Grove's sister-in-law, plopped next to Frederick in the seat nearest the aisle. The femme fatale briefly laid her head on Frederick's shoulder and grinned up at him like a cat eyeing gourmet fish.

Brent's eyes widened at such blatant display in church. *Hey, hey, hey,* he thought and decided that a relationship with Allie might have its perks. Louise Grove looked like his kind of woman.

But Frederick Wently ignored Louise and leaned across the sad-faced guy to say something to Allie. Her distracted smile suggested she was more interested in the man sitting next to her than anything Frederick might say.

Checking his watch, Brent noted that church wouldn't start for fifteen minutes. He had originally planned his "chance" meeting with Allie for after the service, but decided even an hour was too long to wait. The way things were going, if Brent didn't move swiftly Allie might no longer be available.

Frederick had never been so frustrated in his life. Every plan he laid was backfiring. The very man he'd hoped would catch Louise's attention hadn't. Instead, Jim had totally snared Allie. When she left the party early last night to take care of her nephew, Frederick actually thought Jim was going to go home with her. And the way Allie acted, she would have been glad of it. But when she drove off, the only man with her was her nephew. Frederick had been left to baby-sit Louise and Helena and watch poor Jim pine.

For the first time since Jim's fiancée's death, Frederick was tired of having to deal with it. He'd been there for Jim through the whole ordeal, held him up during the funeral, even went to grief therapy with the guy. And Frederick had given him all sorts of grace. After all, Jim had kissed his fiancée goodnight on Tuesday, only to find her dead of a brain aneurysm on Wednesday.

While Frederick hadn't lost his fiancée to death, he had lost her. Looking back, he'd grieved the loss of Allie nearly as hard as if she had died. Now she was back in his life—sort of—and that was part of his problem with Jim. Allie appeared to be finding a secure place in Jim's life, as well.

The two of them were now softly laughing over some joke Jim had cracked and Frederick missed. Whatever it was, he was certain depressed people weren't supposed to be funny. If those two were this cozy after only a couple of meetings, Frederick was sure they'd be engaged by next month. And all because of "poor Jim's" depression stirring Allie's caring spirit.

Despite Frederick's compassion for Jim, he was sorely tempted to tell Jim to get over it. He stared straight ahead at the platform full of choir chairs and grudgingly admitted that his exasperation really had nothing to do with Jim's mourning within itself. The problem lay in Allie's response to him. Frederick cut her a glance and was once again taken with how good she looked.

Today she wore a yellow dress with fuchsia flowers emblazoned on it. Her lipstick matched the color of the flowers. Her hair was styled to perfection. And her skin possessed a luminescent quality that made Frederick want to stroke her cheek. He rubbed his thumb against his fingers and imagined how her skin might feel beneath his touch. His gut tightening, Frederick pinched his bottom lip and glared toward the pulpit.

"You aren't listening to a word I'm saying!" Louise's whiny words crashed into Frederick's misery before she slapped at his arm.

"Excuse me?" Frederick turned his attention toward the blonde. As usual, she was dressed in a skirt that slid up to "here," and Frederick was tempted to remove his blazer and cover her legs.

"I was asking how long you're staying in Macon," she said through a pout.

"Oh." Frederick gazed past her and noticed a sandy-haired man in a dark sport coat gazing toward them. The guy casually looked away and then stood. Frederick dismissed him and tried to remember Louise's question. "I guess a few more days. Like I said last night, I was just trying to get Jim out of Atlanta—to give him something to do. So we rented a suite here in Macon. Sophia and Darren decided to join us for a night or two, but they have to be back in Atlanta tomorrow."

"So why don't I go back to Atlanta with you, and you can give me a ride in your airplane?"

"The plane's in Charlotte right now. I drove down in my truck."

"Why couldn't you catch a shuttle flight and go get it?" she challenged. "Maybe I could even visit your place in Charlotte." Louise twined her fingers around his arm and winked at him.

Frederick decided the time had come for his big brother lecture. Today. It had to be today. Before Louise got any more ideas.

"Uh . . ." he hedged and decided to just be honest. "Really, Louise, I normally don't make a habit of having women at my place . . . um . . . *alone.*" He emphasized alone and hoped she would drop the topic. Years ago Frederick had drawn some lines to protect his personal integrity. As the years rocked by and he found no wife, those lines had been harder and harder to respect. But by the grace of God he *had* lived a life above reproach and held no plans to change.

Her lips drooping, Louise looked away. Finally she said, "Well, okay. Maybe you'd just go get the plane and take me for a ride, then."

"Now *that* I might be able to do, especially if everyone else wants to go, as well." Frederick glanced toward the long line of friends and family before his gaze landed on Jim and Allie. For once the two weren't locked in deep conversation. Jim was absently staring across the sanctuary while Allie focused on Frederick.

The mixture of respect and astonishment in her big brown eyes suggested all manner of possibilities. Furthermore, the wall that had been between them all these weeks had vanished. And Frederick couldn't have looked away even if he wanted to. His heart jumped to his throat and began a fierce patter that took his breath. And he knew for a fact that all those tiny clues of her interest had indeed been clues and not his imagination. To further confuse matters, Allie's eyes began to fill with tears.

With no warning, she jumped up, bumped across Bart and his parents, and nearly landed in Sophia and Darren's laps before stumbling into the church aisle and hurrying toward the exit door.

Sophia looked at her brother with a silent *What did you do to her?*

Frederick shrugged and swiveled to watch Allie hit the door and dart into the foyer. Before the swinging door stilled, the man Frederick had seen watching them exited behind Allie. An uneasy instinct sent Frederick to his feet.

"Felicity would have loved this sanctuary," Jim said and looked up at Frederick.

Wrinkling his brow, Frederick peered down at his friend and realized the guy had been so out of it he'd missed Allie's departure.

"Hey, where are you going?" Jim's question confirmed Frederick's assumption.

"I just need to go," Frederick asserted and squeezed past Louise.

"That's not it!" Louise exploded. "You're following *her*. What's the deal with her, anyway?" Louise's shrill question pierced the gathering congregation's low hum. A suspenseful silence settled upon their corner of the sanctuary, and Frederick didn't have to imagine what people must be thinking. Their speculative glances said enough.

While he was tempted to crawl under the carpet, Frederick ignored the curious glances and headed for the exit door Allie had just passed through.

Eighteen

Allie burst into the foyer and blindly raced toward the ladies' room. The warm tears that had blurred her vision trickled to the corners of her mouth and left their salty trace upon her tongue.

When Frederick turned down Louise's blatant invitation, Allie had been stricken anew with the gross misjudgment she'd dealt him. She had lined up a few pieces of incriminating evidence and assumed the worst of Frederick without even giving him a chance. And this morning, she clearly recognized his body language. More than once, he had attempted to put some healthy boundaries between himself and Louise, but she kept ignoring his hints.

After negotiating around a young couple, Allie hit the restroom's door and plunged into the posh lounge. The smell of rose potpourri struck her as strongly as the new rush of emotions. Realizing she'd left her purse and the packet of tissue therein, Allie hurried to the countertop box of tissue. She grabbed a handful, wheeled toward a stall, and nearly plowed over an old lady and her walker.

"I'm sooooo soooooorrrry!" Allie wailed.

"That's okay, sugar," the matron soothed, and looked at Allie like she was bananas. "You don't have to cry about it. You didn't even *touch* me."

"Oh, it's not you I'm upset about!" Allie fretted while the woman stared at her. "It's . . . it's . . ." She waved her hand. "Never mind," Allie mumbled and scurried into a stall.

No sooner had the stall door slammed than the old lady grumbled, "These young women and their problems."

Allie bit her lips together, blotted at the tears, and tried to regain her composure. In the height of emotion, her left leg complained against the new spike heels she'd bought to match her outfit. The building's cold temperature had finally gotten to her old break. Allie examined the tile floor on which she stood. The best she could tell through the tears, the floor was clean. She slipped out of the heels and wiggled her toes against the cool tile. The pain in her leg subsided to a dull twinge.

As always, the pain brought back memories of how the injury occurred. Allie hiccoughed over her tears and remembered the infinite respect and integrity in Frederick's eyes the day he proposed. The respect and integrity were still there. He could have taken Louise up on her offer. Instead, he'd told her he didn't entertain women in his house alone. *He hasn't changed,* Allie thought with a surge of new tears. *He hasn't changed at all.*

She relived that day Louise had jumped from the picnic table into his arms, knocked him down, and kissed him. At the time, Allie had interpreted the incident as something Frederick must have enjoyed. But in the light of her discoveries from last night and Frederick's rejection of Louise's invitation, Allie realized Frederick had very likely been a victim of Louise's tornado tendencies.

Her heart swelled with more love than she thought possible. Allie placed her arm against the stall, rested her forehead on her arm, closed her eyes, and recalled his open admiration from last night. That same blatant attraction had been present only minutes ago, like a force from the past that simply would not go away. And mingled with the attraction was a tinge of pain and a question.

"Oh, God," Allie whispered through a sniffle, "have you put Frederick back into my life for a reason?"

The answer to her prayer came with the memory of her decision from last night—that if Frederick were interested then she would reawaken their relationship, regardless of what her family thought.

"I should have married him ten years ago," she affirmed as a slow anger began to burn against herself and Aunt Landon.

"God, help me," Allie whispered. "Oh, God, help me. Help *us.*"

She lifted her head, lowered her arm, and dabbed at the tears. Allie hadn't been seriously interested in a man since Frederick Wently. And she knew she never would be. He was the standard by which she judged all men; and in her eyes, they all came up lacking. After several seconds of deep breathing, her trembling subsided. Her legs strengthened as did her resolve. She decided that perhaps she could face the world again. Allie stepped back into the fuchsia heels, opened the stall, and nearly bumped into the same lady with her walker.

The woman gawked straight at Allie, then whipped her walker around and scooted toward the exit. Allie watched her go and realized she'd just been eavesdropping. Shaking her head, Allie moved to the mirror.

"Some people need to get a life," she muttered at her reflection, then giggled. *No telling what that poor woman thought,* she mused and assessed the makeup damage her cry had created. Fortunately, her eye makeup was waterproof, so the only evidence of her tears was a few streaks to her blusher. Allie gently smoothed a tissue over the problem areas and dabbed at her eyes again. Other than slight puffiness tinged with red, there was no evidence she'd been crying. She hoped by the service's end even the redness would subside—and certainly by the time she got home. Even if no one else noticed the evidence of her emotion, Mrs. Grove would. That eagle-eyed matron missed little.

She certainly hadn't missed Allie's desire to go to services this morning. Allie had reluctantly offered to stay home with Barry, still in the throes of a stomach virus. But Mrs. Grove had taken one look at Allie and insisted that she and her husband would tend him. Of course, Macy and Charlie never argued with the Groves or offered to stay with their son themselves. They were too hyped about trying the new steakhouse after church. Now Allie was so glad the Groves were stubborn in their insistence to stay behind. If she hadn't been here, she would have missed one of the most important moments of her life.

Allie squared her shoulders. The time had come to face Frederick again. Maybe they could start over. And maybe this time, they could make it last.

Frederick stood near the sanctuary door and watched the ladies' room. He also watched the sandy-haired man in the sport coat. The guy was obviously waiting on Allie. He'd been trotting behind her while she streaked across the foyer. Just about the time he was going to tap her on the shoulder, she'd maneuvered around a young family, and the guy lost the moment. Now he leaned against a pillar, arms crossed, waiting.

Narrowing his eyes, Frederick sized up the man. The guy checked a large gold watch and fidgeted with the clasp as his attention darted around the hall. The assured tilt of his head gave him a cocky edge, and Frederick wanted to wipe the smug expression off the guy's face.

The ladies' room door opened. Allie stepped out and strode back into the foyer. Other than her slightly reddened eyes, no one would guess she'd been crying. And Frederick was as curious as ever for the reason. He sensed her emotion involved him and prayed it was all good.

When the stranger stepped toward her and spoke, Frederick decided not to leave Allie to the snares of what he called a "church wolf." Frederick had long ago realized that many men and women used church merely as a place to hit on the opposite sex. While he saw nothing wrong with a strong singles' group and figured the best place to meet a spouse was at church, Frederick found it hard to swallow when people used the church as a hot spot for picking up dates and nothing more. If this dude wasn't a wolf, Frederick would eat one of his cowboy boots. He moved toward Allie, who was gladly shaking the guy's hand and smiling into his face as if she already knew him. And the church wolf was looking at Allie like he'd like to take her home with him *now*. A fresh shaft of jealousy surged through Frederick. What was the deal with Allie and men these days? First Jim, now this . . . this . . . impostor.

Without acknowledging the man, Frederick neared Allie and said, "Are you okay?"

"Yes, I'm fine." Allie glanced into his eyes, ducked her head, and tucked a strand of short hair behind her ear. Frederick used every ounce of restraint to keep from taking her hand in his. Her eyes hinted that she would have liked nothing more.

"I'm Brent Everson," the stranger said and offered his hand to Frederick. "I don't believe we've met."

"No, we haven't," Frederick said and made himself shake the guy's hand. He looked into the man's eyes and saw everything he expected to see—right down to the self-centered desires.

"Brent is my cousin," Allie explained.

"Well, a used-to-be cousin," Brent supplied and smiled toward Allie. "Like I was just explaining to Allie, I saw her from across the sanctuary and was nearly dead sure that was her. Turned out I was right." He shifted his weight to the left and shifted back to the right.

"I married Allie's cousin," Brent continued. "But she passed away last year." He looked beyond Allie with just the right hint of regret.

Frederick nearly raised his hands and huffed, *What gives with these dead wives or fiancées?*

"I was so sorry when I heard," Allie said and laid her hand on his arm. "That was the saddest funeral I've ever been to in my life."

"It was just such a shock," Brent said, his eyes going red.

Nice theatrics, Frederick thought and wondered if the guy could ever love someone as much as he obviously loved himself.

"I had no idea that killer bees could really *kill* someone," Allie continued.

Frederick swallowed an incredulous snort. "Killer bees?" he blurted.

"Yes. My wife—her name was Chrissy—she loved to garden, much like you, Allie . . ." Brent paused long enough to bathe Allie in an adoring gaze. "Anyway, she was near the woods behind the house one evening and stumbled into a hive of killer bees. They overtook her and," he lowered his head and crossed his arms, "she had an allergic reaction and died."

Frederick eyed Allie, who was just as attentive to "poor Brent" as she had been to "poor Jim."

"It was *just dreadful*," she soothed.

Brent sniffed and squared his shoulders. "But I'm getting better all the time. You know, life must go on."

"Listen, would you like to sit with us?" Allie asked. "I've got a new friend—Frederick's friend, actually—whose fiancée suddenly died about nine months ago. I think the two of you might be able to help each other."

"Sure, I'd love to sit with you," Brent agreed, and the hungry look in his cold, green eyes suggested he barely remembered his wife's name. "It's been so long since we've seen each other; we need to get caught up." He tugged Allie into the crook of his arm and moved toward the sanctuary.

Frederick rubbed the corners of his mouth and watched the two walk away. Allie didn't even have the decency to look back at him. He glared at Brent and decided the time had come to make a move with Allie. Enough with this undercover operation. Frederick should let his heart and intent be known or risk losing her forever.

"Frederick!" Helena's ecstatic voice echoed from near the entryway.

He braced himself for a knock-you-flat hug and a cloud of perfume to go with it while turning toward her. She broke loose from a tall, lanky guy who looked like he could stand beneath a basketball net and dunk the ball flatfooted. His jeans were twice as long as Frederick's, and Frederick tried to imagine the guy folding himself to fit into his airplane. The image left him on the verge of laughter.

"Frederick!" she repeated. "I didn't know you were going to be here this morning!"

"Well, it was a last-minute decision, actually," Frederick explained as the orchestra's first strains of "Lord, I Lift Your Name on High" filtered from the sanctuary.

Helena looked every bit as cute as her sister was gorgeous. For once she wore a demurely cut dress that made her look closer to twenty-nine than nineteen. Her hair was caught up in a twist, and she had the decency to offer Frederick a friendly, sideways hug and nothing more. However, her knock-your-socks-off perfume was as powerful as her hug was discreet. A sixth sense told Frederick the guy approaching must be Craig Hayden.

"Craig," Helena said and turned toward him, "this is my sister's boyfriend, Frederick."

"More like a big brother," Frederick corrected and shook Craig's hand.

"Yeah, right," Helena teased, her glossy lips curving into a knowing smile.

"I've heard a lot about you," Craig said. The sharp-eyed guy looked from Helena to Frederick and back to Helena like a pitbull protecting his favorite bone. Frederick nearly raised his hands palms outward in silent denial of any romantic interest in Helena. Frankly, he was thankful that Helena's boyfriend seemed so attached. Maybe the two of them would get married, and Helena would stop kissing on him.

The orchestra's increased volume suggested the service was within seconds of starting. "I guess we're just in time," Helena said as she grabbed Frederick on one side and Craig on the other.

"We're sitting on the south side," Frederick said. He pointed to the right, suavely disentangled himself from Helena, and motioned for the couple to move ahead of him.

By the time Frederick entered the sanctuary, he suspected that Allie had somehow landed between "poor Jim" and "poor Brent." When he stepped down the aisle, his suspicion was confirmed.

Nineteen

The day couldn't have been longer for Frederick. He watched Brent compete with Jim for Allie's attention all during lunch at the steakhouse while Louise monopolized him. The only person happy about the Louise business was Craig Hayden, who finally decided Frederick might be a potential friend, rather than a rival for Helena's attention.

The good thing that came of lunch was Frederick's learning more about Craig, including that he was a senior who played basketball at the University of Georgia. The guy seemed every bit as stable as Helena was flighty. And Frederick hoped the young woman had the good sense to marry the guy. The best Frederick could tell, he was everything she needed, and he desperately loved her.

After lunch Brent Everson assumed the group was breaking up. No one bothered to tell him differently. While he drove off to wherever he was staying, the rest of the group gravitated back to Grove Acres. They spent the afternoon playing pool and card games. Mrs. Grove asked their cook to prepare sandwiches for the evening meal. Frederick couldn't recall what he ate or who won the games. He was too exhausted trying to keep from being mauled by Louise while doing his best to eavesdrop on Allie and Jim's conversation. The two had remained apart from the group all day. Now they were

taking a moonlit stroll along the landscaped creek that also
ran near Allie's guesthouse.

Frederick stood on the mansion's deck, rested his hands on
the railing, and strained for any signs of Jim and Allie. Deco-
rative street lamps lined a path that looked like a romantic
rendezvous from *Southern Living*. The sound of the creek
played the accompaniment for a hoot owl's lullaby. Frederick
felt like a victim of his own schemes. The moon had never
been fuller or brighter; the balmy evening, laced with the
scent of magnolias, never more perfect for lovers.

Frederick revisited his resolution from this morning. He
had decided to make his move. Tonight would be the night,
even if he had to lock Jim in the bathroom and beg Allie for
a few minutes of her time.

Frederick rested his elbows on the railing and leaned forward. His back threatened to tighten into a kink, and he
jerked upward. He'd learned to heed those little warnings.
Frederick had spent too many days in bed because of foolishly
ignoring the threat of a kink or two. A chilling breeze stirred
the trees into a whispering frenzy, and Frederick rolled down
the sleeves on his shirt and buttoned the cuffs.

Just about the time he'd relaxed again, the patio door
opened. He swiveled toward the house as Louise erupted
onto the deck.

"There you are!" she purred. "I wondered what happened
to you."

His shoulders tensing, Frederick stopped himself from
jumping over the rail and decided this was the perfect opportunity to have their little talk. The time had come for
some unquestionable boundaries.

But Louise stopped halfway across the deck and gazed at the
stars and golden moon. "Is this perfect or *what*?" she oozed

and lifted her hands skyward. Then she scurried toward the service bar, and Frederick strained to see her through the shadows.

When an instrumental melody floated across the deck, Frederick understood Louise's intent. He covered his eyes and decided he needed to be firm. Very firm. Gentlemanly hints were not working here. When he lowered his hand, Louise was sashaying toward him, her sandals slapping against the ground. With a sly smile, she looped her arms around his neck, rested her head on his chest, and began to sway to the music. Her tank top left her shoulders nearly as bare as her short, denim skirt left her legs.

"It's cold out here," Louise said and shivered. "I need a big, strong man to keep me warm."

Lifting his hands, Frederick debated his options while a cloud of her sweet perfume nearly sent him into a sinus attack. Finally he gripped Louise's hands, removed them from his neck, and put some space between them.

"Louise, we've got to talk," he said.

"Who can talk on a night like this?" she gurgled while moon-beams danced in her hair. Frederick couldn't deny that Louise was gorgeous—even more so in the moonlight. But she didn't stand a chance next to Allie and the memories she stirred.

"Listen." He cupped her hands in his and jiggled them for emphasis. "Just listen to me," Frederick admonished like a correcting father.

She blinked as confusion played upon her features.

"You need to understand that you shouldn't throw yourself at men like this." Frederick shook his head from side to side. "There are some men out there who'd take you up on what they see as an offer of . . ." Frederick searched for the best words and finally came out with, "well, you know."

All Louise's confusion was chased away by a veil of joy that brightened her eyes. "You're jealous!" she enthused and hopped up and down. "You saw me talking to Jim earlier and you're jealous!"

"No!" Frederick declared. "No, I'm not!"

Louise lunged forward and wrapped her arms around him for a tight hug. "Oh! You love me! I *knew* you did. I just *knew* it," she rushed. "I can't *wait* until we get married. It's going to be *wonderful!*"

"Get married?" A surge of desperation attacked Frederick. He gripped Louise's shoulders and pushed her away a second time. "Louise, listen!" he barked. "This isn't about marriage or love or . . . or jealousy! I'm trying to tell you I need some space and that you need to be careful! You just don't treat men the way you've treated me without most of them thinking it's an offer! You're lucky I'm not just out for myself, otherwise—"

"You mean you're breaking up with me?" she squeaked.

"No!" Frederick wailed. "How can we break up when we aren't even—" The tears filling her eyes stopped him. Frederick worked his mouth as a hard reality hit him between the eyes: *She really thinks I care for her. But all I've done is use her to get to Allie.*

"Oh man," he groaned and turned back toward the yard. Frederick gripped the handrail and gazed at the dark sky filled with a canvas full of stars. *Now what?* he thought and realized he wasn't much better than the men he was trying to warn her against. While he was afraid someone might take advantage of her physically, Frederick had used her attachment to him as a cover. Both involved selfishly using Louise.

Frederick had rationalized his choice by assuming he'd be another of Louise's "catches of the day" and that she'd get over him as quickly as she had the other "fish" she brought home. *But what if I'm really not just another catch of the day for her?* he worried and didn't even want to look at her.

The sound of sandals clapping against the deck preceded the patio door's slamming. Frederick's shoulders drooped. He'd rather die than hurt a woman, but it looked like that was exactly what he'd done.

He stared toward the creek and wondered if Jim and Allie were *ever* going to finish their walk. Sophia and Darren left an hour ago, and Frederick was ready to go home, too. Thoughts of Louise's hurt glares were enough to drive him away for good . . . if not for Allie's presence.

A hint of soft conversation soon turned into distinguishable voices, and Frederick detected the shadowed figures of his friend and ex-almost-fiancée nearing through the darkness. Worries about Louise vanished as they merged into a yard lamp's glow near a row of weeping willows. Fully expecting them to be holding hands, Frederick rammed his hands into his jeans pockets and stiffened. But the tension was for nothing. The two were several feet apart and not even touching.

Frederick released his breath and rubbed the base of his neck. Before he could even call a greeting to them, the back door opened again. Frederick glanced over his shoulder. Louise stared at him, and even through the shadows he detected the tears. The soft beat of a jazz swing number filled the night with romantic promises that were as ironic as they were sweet.

"Are we still going on the flight with you t-tomorrow?" Louise called, her voice wobbly.

"Yes, of course." Frederick didn't know what else to say or how to communicate the regret swelling his heart. Before Sophia and Darren left for the evening, Louise had once again invited herself for a plane ride. Frederick had included the whole group. He'd already booked a seat on a shuttle flight to Charlotte for early tomorrow morning. By noon he should be landing the Beechcraft at the county airport near Atlanta. Tomorrow afternoon, the gang was all set to drive to the airport, where Frederick would take them for a ride.

Louise's spontaneous smile accompanied her dashing aside her tears. "Good," she said as if she'd won some sort of contest.

Frederick squinted. Before he could even begin to fathom her logic, Jim's voice floated from nearby. "I need to go. I'm not doing well."

Turning from Louise, Frederick focused on his friend, who trudged up the deck's stairs like a sailor who spent a long night on a stormy sea. The owl's lonesome hooting mingled with the music and accented Jim's hollow-eyed desperation.

"He's really not doing well," Allie mouthed from close behind him. She pretended to be slitting her wrists and raised her brows for emphasis.

Frederick cut his gaze back to Jim, who stared straight ahead with a lifeless expression. Even though Jim had never referenced suicide, Frederick had worried about the possibility. After all, Jim had been depressed out of his mind, and depressed people often thought of taking their own lives.

Jim walked toward the house like a zombie. Stunned, Frederick watched him as a tendril of regret twined through his soul. Only this morning he had been aggravated at Jim for monopolizing Allie. Now the poor guy didn't look like he even realized Allie was female, let alone attractive.

Allie moved to Frederick's side. He glanced her way. "You mean suicide?" he queried.

Crossing her arms, she nodded.

Jim paused at the door and twisted toward Frederick. "I'll be waiting," he said softly.

"Uh, sure," Frederick replied and gripped Allie's arm. "Tell me what he said."

"We were talking about Robert Frost," Allie explained. "You know that famous poem, 'Stopping by the Woods on a Snowy Evening'?"

"Yeah, yeah, yeah," Frederick replied and searched his memory until he unearthed bits and pieces of the poem. "What about it?"

"Jim just said he thinks it's about suicide. The poet says he's looking into the forest dark and deep, but he's got miles to go before he sleeps. Jim thinks sleep refers to death and that the writer is tempted to commit suicide. And he said he didn't feel like he had miles to go—that he wished he could *sleep now*." She lifted one hand and drew invisible quotation marks around the last two words.

"Oh man," Frederick said. "I've been afraid of this."

Allie nodded. "I told him all this poetry might be dangerous. He needs to read a funny novel or something to get his mind off his problems. The poetry's just magnifying them."

"Yes, but who'd have thought Robert Frost would—"

"There's more to him than meets the eye."

"Cause of death: Robert Frost," Frederick quipped.

Allie snickered and covered her mouth with her hand. "Sorry," she said through her fingers. "I shouldn't be laughing, but that just struck me funny."

"I guess I shouldn't be so flippant," Frederick replied and tried to remain serious, but a smile shoved its way through anyway.

That's when Frederick realized he was still holding her arm and looking at her eye to eye. A new tune drifted on the night, a saxophonist's rendition of a classic number from the late '70s, "I Honestly Love You." All humor vanished as a haunting memory flashed between them.

When their relationship was new, Frederick had taken Allie to the lake one evening. They'd walked hand-in-hand along the shore until they stopped near a campsite. Somebody had a radio turned to an oldies station, and Olivia Newton-John's fluid voice had serenaded them at sunset. Frederick took Allie in his arms as they swayed to "I Honestly Love You" and relished their budding love. Even now Frederick could smell the water, hear it lapping against the bank, and see the birds' silhouettes against a blazing sun half immersed in the horizon. He could also taste Allie's lips.

Her gaze faltered at the same time Frederick's did. He released her arm and stepped away. "Allie . . ." he hedged and looked toward the house where Jim stood just inside the patio doorway. "I've got to go tonight, but could we talk tomorrow night . . . maybe after the flight? Just you and me?"

"I'd love to . . . talk." Allie's voice broke with a delightfully nervous squeak as she toyed with her sweater's button.

"Good. Make sure you come in your car alone. Don't ride with the family. That way you can stay behind when everyone else leaves, okay?" He raised his brows in a silent invitation he desperately hoped she'd accept.

"Okay," she rasped as his own expectancy bloomed upon her face.

Frederick smiled into her eyes and recalled the soft warmth of their embrace. In that moment, he wasn't worried about Jim—or that Brent character, either, for that matter. All he saw was the reflection of what he and Allie once shared, all sweet and powerful and everlasting.

Deciding to take his chances, Frederick reached for her hand. When she didn't resist, he lifted her fingers to his lips and brushed her knuckles. He caught a faint whiff of lilacs, a refreshing reprieve from Louise's blast-you-batty perfumes.

The kiss, intended to be a chaste promise, left Frederick's pulses pounding. His gaze never left hers. "Here's to tomorrow then." He lowered her hand and stroked her palm with his thumb.

Her eyes wide, Allie mutely nodded. When her fingers trembled, Frederick was tempted to live dangerously and take her into his arms for a real kiss.

"Frederick?" Louise's voice accompanied the patio door's opening again. "I'm worried about Jim. Oh!"

He pivoted toward Louise and released Allie's hand. The blonde looked from him to Allie and back. Deciding not to allow the awkward moment to stretch another second, Frederick hurried forward.

"Yes, I'm worried about Jim, too," he awkwardly stated, sure his voice couldn't be more artificial or strained. "I'm taking him back to the hotel now. Hopefully he's just overtired. I've dragged him all over the place this weekend." Frederick stepped into the house and thought Louise followed.

Twenty

Allie turned toward the backyard, lifted her face to the bejeweled heavens, and silently thanked God that He was answering her prayers. The promise in Frederick's eyes was everything it had been ten years ago. Everything and more. Frederick offered the maturity of a well-traveled man, weathered by war, seasoned by life. And Allie began to think their union would be sweeter because of their long absence from each other.

She rubbed her thumb across the hand he'd kissed and rested her knuckles against her lips. Allie closed her eyes and swayed with the memory of the tingles that had threatened to knock her flat when his lips touched her skin.

"What's the deal with you and Frederick?" Louise's strained question pierced Allie's thoughts.

Startled, she turned toward the young woman. Arms crossed, she peered down at Allie. The blonde's height coupled with her exasperated expression sent Allie back several steps.

"Excuse me?" she queried and considered shrinking from sight. But unexpected strength bolstered Allie and insisted she square her shoulders instead of hunching them.

"Don't think I haven't noticed." Louise narrowed her eyes. "He's always watching you. Then today at church he chased you out of the sanctuary. Now he's out here holding your hand." She placed her fists on her hips.

"Um . . ." Allie hedged and gripped the handrail.

"I'm going to tell you just like I told Helena. He's mine!" Louise pointed her finger at Allie's nose.

Speechless, Allie grappled for the best recourse. Finally she decided the truth was her only option. "Louise, I don't think Frederick *sees* you like that. You're so much younger than he is. Don't you think you'd be better with someone your own age?"

"No!" Louise stomped her foot. "He's the one I want. And *I'm* going to marry him!" she stormed like a five-year-old who's warring for her favorite doll.

"Well, okay," Allie said over an unexpected chuckle. "But does *Frederick* have a choice in this? Because if he does . . ." Amazed at her own confidence, Allie lifted her hands and shrugged.

Louise's face darkened; her eyes sharpened. She glared at Allie like a she-devil declaring war. "Don't think you'll *ever* outdo me, you little pale-faced pipsqueak," she bellowed, then stomped toward the house. When she slammed the French door, she purposefully locked it while directing a final glare toward Allie.

But nothing could dampen the thrill of Frederick's kiss— not even Louise's angry threats. *Heaven help the man she does marry*, Allie thought. Even though she had never been the object of Louise's ire before now, Macy had shared a story or two that exposed Louise's temper in all its glory.

Shaking her head, Allie fished in her gauzy pants pocket for her house key. She had driven home after lunch, changed into the wide-legged pants and a light sweater, and walked back to the Groveses' mansion. Thankfully, Allie had opted not to carry a purse. Instead, she'd slipped her house key and a lip gloss into her deep pocket. Now she didn't need to reenter the mansion in order to retrieve her purse.

With a carefree wave at Louise, she walked down the deck's steps and strolled toward the shortcut between the guesthouse and the mansion. In minutes she'd crossed the narrow bridge that spanned the creek and skipped up her porch's steps.

By the time Allie traipsed inside and entered the bathroom to remove her makeup, she was humming "I Honestly Love You." Allie relived that night she and Frederick had danced at sunset and then shared a kiss that sealed their awakening attraction. It had been their very first kiss, and Allie had been certain she would drown in the delicious waves of pleasure the closeness unfurled.

She opened the storage cabinet, retrieved her skin-care regime, and pushed her hair back with a terry cloth headband. Armed with her eye makeup remover in one hand and a saturated cotton ball in the other, Allie eyed her reflection and contemplated Louise's comments.

"I don't care what she says," Allie told her complexion. "I'm not a pale-faced pipsqueak." She giggled. "Frederick doesn't think so anyway."

Allie closed her eyes and shivered. *I can't wait until tomorrow*, she dreamed and scoffed at the very idea of Louise Grove posing a threat to her and Frederick. "Sorry, Louise," Allie piped and opened her eyes. "Frederick wants someone closer to his age." She winked at her reflection and reveled in the sassy confidence that overtook her. Allie hadn't felt this way in ten years—not since the last time she and Frederick were in love.

Once she finished removing her makeup, Allie planned to retrieve her Frederick Wently scrapbook from her nightstand. And this time she would pore over it like a lovesick teenager, not a mourning widow. The whole prospect sent a delightful rush of goose bumps along her arms.

She lifted the cotton ball to her eye and prepared to swiftly remove all traces of Mary Kay, but a rattling noise in the kitchen stopped her. Allie held her breath and listened. This time the rattling noise was accompanied by scratching. Allie's eyes grew bigger as her heart pattered. After spending her life in Atlanta, Allie never left her doors unlocked—not even in this remote locale. She distinctly remembered double checking the front and back door locks when she got home.

A kitchen cabinet door banged. Allie jumped and squealed.

She dropped the cotton ball into the sink and plopped the eye makeup remover on the cabinet. Her knees quivering, Allie cracked the bathroom door and peered up the hallway toward the kitchen. She'd heard of kitchen thieves before—people who broke into homes and stole food only—and her mind raced with the possibility that the guesthouse had been invaded.

The noise stopped just as quickly as it began, and Allie dared open the bathroom door all the way. She placed one foot into the hallway and stopped when she realized she had no means of self-defense. Allie whirled back into the bathroom and grabbed the hair dryer from the wall shelf. She raised the dryer over her head and edged down the hall. Only when she was halfway to the kitchen did she realize the hair dryer was about as much defense as a water gun. Her palms sweating, she lowered the dryer but still held it with a death grip.

It might not be a baseball bat, but it's better than nothing, she thought as a new attack of rustling stopped her in her tracks. At closer vantage, Allie recognized the noise's odd rhythm and began to suspect the perpetrator might not be human. She darted her attention to the back door at the end of the hallway. The deadbolt was still firmly turned. From there, Allie's gaze slid to the pet flap in the door's bottom half. This special entry would allow a small animal to come and go at will. Normally the pet flap was securely latched. But the latch had somehow come undone.

Allie's mind raced with possibilities, one of which included a skunk. Her lip curled as she imagined being sprayed by her invader. She looked at the hair dryer and knew it was no defense against a skunk. Allie laid the appliance on the hall bench and tiptoed toward the kitchen. Holding her breath, she peered around the doorway to see a raccoon invading her new box of cornflakes.

The phone's shrill ring sent Allie into a jump. The raccoon jerked up from his culinary pursuits, took one look at Allie, and darted toward the doorway. In a blur of gray and white fur, the creature dashed through the pet door with the clap of wood, and the guy was history.

Allie covered her heart with her hand, wilted against the wall, and laughed out loud while the telephone persisted in its demand. Finally she trotted past the spilled cornflakes, grabbed the phone off the counter, and tapped the green button on the phone screen.

"Hello, this is Allie," she chirped through a spontaneous giggle.

"Well, hello!" a familiar male voice responded. "I'm hoping you have caller ID and you're just overjoyed to know I'm calling."

"Uh . . ." Allie tugged her earlobe and tried to place the voice.

"This is Brent," he said. "Brent Everson. Ex-cousin? Just saw you today."

"Oh, yes!" Allie replied through a smile.

"So I take it the joy has nothing to do with me, then," Brent said in a pouty voice.

"This—this raccoon was just in my kitchen," Allie explained and eyed the array of cornflakes on the Italian tile. "At first I thought he was a person, so I got the hair dryer—"

"Oh yeah, now that's a tried-and-true weapon," Brent teased.

Allie chortled. "I know. I know." She leaned against the counter and nudged at the box of cornflakes with the toe of her shoe. "Anyway, I figured it had to be some kind of an animal and was just glad it turned out to be a raccoon and not a skunk."

"Whoa! Now *that* would have made for a fragrant evening," Brent said.

"No joke," Allie replied as a series of questions nibbled at her, like why Brent was calling her and how he'd gotten her phone number.

After a meaningful pause, Brent said, "Listen, Allie, sorry to be calling so late, but I just wanted to let you know how much I enjoyed seeing you today. It's been a long time since I, well . . . er . . . enjoyed a lady's company as much as I did yours."

"Oh!" Allie straightened and touched the headband as if he could see her.

"I actually called your dad to get your number," he admitted.

"You did?"

"Uh-huh. He seemed thrilled to hear from me. You know, I haven't talked to him in a while. I still had his cell number from a few years ago and wasn't sure the number was right or what kind of a reception I might get even if the number was right, if you know what I mean."

Allie strained for his meaning as the implications of his call sank in. She had thought Brent was a grieving widower, much like Jim Bennington. Now she wasn't so sure. Nevertheless,

Allie couldn't fathom that Brent Everson was really interested in *her*, especially not when she considered his former wife's beauty or even that of Evelyn, whom he'd once dated.

"I guess the last time I talked with your dad was when Evelyn and I were dating—if that's what you want to call it—before I married Chrissy."

"Oh, yes!" Allie replied and finally understood the undercurrents of Brent's words. Evelyn had been certain she and Brent would marry until she threw that birthday party for him and invited their fair-haired cousin, Chrissy Elton. That night Brent had ignored Evelyn in preference for her guest. Within weeks they received news that Brent and Chrissy had eloped. Allie doubted Evelyn was over the whole ordeal even now. Like Louise, she'd not been denied a thing and had assumed she would marry her husband of choice. Never did she contemplate that her husband of choice would choose someone else.

Finally the purpose of Brent's call became clear. He was interested in a reconciliation with Evelyn and probably wanted to know Allie's opinion. *He's just being nice to me to find out more about Evelyn,* Allie decided. "Did you get a chance to talk with Evelyn when you called Dad?" she questioned.

"No. Why would I want to do that?" Brent replied and destroyed her assumption.

"Well, I just thought . . ."

"Ooooohhhhh, I see! You always were the modest one, weren't you?" Brent teased. "No, I got the phone number for the sister I wanted to talk to—and she isn't Evelyn," he flirted.

Allie moved toward one of the high-backed bar stools and plopped therein. She covered her face with her hand and swallowed a groan. The *last* thing she needed was for Frederick to think she had a relationship with Brent or any other man for that matter. She brainstormed about a way to tell Brent she wasn't interested without blurting something like "Get lost!"

When the hinges on the pet door creaked, Allie looked toward her back door. A black nose nudged past the door and two ringed eyes soon appeared. The call of cornflakes must have been too much for the coon. He scouted out the kitchen and was halfway through the door when Allie suddenly spoke, "Brent, I've got to go. The coon is back!"

Before he had the chance to reply, Allie disconnected the call. She stood, clapped her hands, and bellowed, "Get outta here!"

The startled raccoon fell to the floor on his face. He then proceeded to scramble back out the pet flap with the grace of a pig on ice skates. The trap door clapped shut behind him, and Allie scurried forward to fasten the latch. With the door secure, she straightened, looked at the phone in her hand, and hoped Brent might be as easy to discourage.

Twenty-One

The next day Frederick placed the last bottled drink in his plane's cooler and closed the door. He picked up a scrap of paper lying beside one of the seats and crumpled it. Jim was using the portable vacuum, which hummed from the back of the plane. The guy had accidentally spilled half a box of carpet deodorizer, and the smell was strong enough to choke a Tyrannosaurus Rex. At least the mini cleanup endeavor had given Jim something to do.

He'd been nothing but a listless piece of humanity last night. Frederick had even stayed awake until he was certain Jim was asleep. After his bout with Robert Frost, Frederick hadn't trusted Jim not to try something desperate. Thankfully he hadn't.

Frederick yawned and stretched and planned another dose of caffeine via Coca-Cola. After waiting on Jim to go to sleep, Frederick had awakened periodically through the night to check on the guy. Then he had to get up by six to catch the shuttle flight to Charlotte to fly the Beechcraft to Atlanta. Frederick's body was now reminding him he needed a nap.

The afternoon sunshine splashed through the open passenger door, which ushered in the inviting spring breeze. Frederick walked toward the doorway, gripped both sides, leaned out, and looked toward the cloudless sky. He gulped the clean air. The day couldn't be more perfect. Neither could Frederick's expectations. Despite the sleep deprivation, his restless anticipation brought new meaning to spring fever. He had it and had it bad. Either that or he was lovesick.

Maybe both, he thought and strained against the sunbeams for any sign of Allie's Mercedes or the Groves' Lincoln. Jim had driven to Atlanta this morning and taken their luggage back to his townhouse. The rest of the group was supposed to meet them here at this small county airport.

The place reminded Frederick of the one back home. It was simple, functional, and not highly trafficked. Exactly the kind of setup Frederick enjoyed. There were six other planes parked near the runway, ten in the hangar, and only minimal employees taking care of business. A lazy lowing reverberated from the pasture of cattle grazing near a pond. And Frederick was tempted to bring his fishing gear the next time he came and ask permission to fish. The pond screamed of trophy bass.

He checked his watch and counted the minutes until Allie would arrive. Per his trusty Timex, she should be here in five. According to Frederick's plan, everyone else should be gone within three hours. After the flight, the group would go to dinner together. Then they'd go home . . . everyone except Allie.

That's when she'd be all his. They'd talk. He'd explain everything; tell her he'd never stopped loving her. She'd say the same. He'd kiss her like there was no tomorrow. Then he'd ask her to marry him. The very thought sent Frederick into a heady tailspin. He never even questioned she'd say yes. And this time, they'd immediately elope—maybe go crazy and fly to Las Vegas tonight. They could buy a change of clothing and some toiletries once they got there. No one in her family would have to know until after they'd said "I do."

Louise was probably going to need therapy though. But even after his guilt trip last night, Frederick was too hyped to let the Louise business get him down. He glanced toward Jim and decided maybe he and Louise could get together after all. But try as he might, Frederick couldn't seem to get Jim to say he'd even noticed Louise. Frederick prayed today would change all that.

The young doctor turned off the vacuum and peered around him. "Looks good," he declared with more spunk than Frederick expected. "I think I got all the carpet cleaner up."

"Whew! Smells like a perfume factory," Frederick joked and straightened from the door.

"Yeah." Jim put his hands on his hips and shook his head. "Sorry 'bout that."

Frederick chuckled. "No prob," he replied and was tempted to slap himself. *I'm starting to sound like Louise,* he thought.

"I guess I should stick to treating patients and forget the housekeeping scene. I'm no good." Jim rubbed his hand along the front of the faded green scrub shirt he wore with a pair of baggy jeans and thick-soled sandals. Frederick had started calling Jim's present clothing his uniform. The doctor had two sets of scrubs leftover from med school, a couple pairs of favorite jeans, and a closet full of clothes Frederick now thought of as his "prefuneral" clothes. After Felicity's death, Jim had simply stopped caring.

At least he did wear something else yesterday and Saturday, Frederick remembered, *and his uniform is clean and ironed today.*

He glanced down at his own blue jeans. The things were worn in all the right places, frayed around the pockets and hem. And Frederick was as committed to them as Jim was his scrubs. The three-year-old cowboy boots and faded cotton shirt were no exception.

The distant hum of a car's engine ended Frederick's musings about his and Jim's lack of fashion savvy.

"I'll put the vacuum up," Jim said. "That's probably them coming now."

Frederick leaned against the door and gazed toward the two-lane road that led to the airport. Sure enough, a Lincoln Town Car slowed at the airport's drive. A pale blue Mercedes followed; behind the Mercedes, a red Corvette. Frederick's attention settled upon the Mercedes. So did his heart. The very fact that Allie had driven her own vehicle alone said a resounding yes to everything he wanted to ask her.

"Yes!" Frederick hollered and thrust his fists upward.

"What's the deal, man?" Jim asked and looked at Frederick like he'd gone bonkers.

High on adrenaline, Frederick lifted both hands and moved toward Jim, who halfheartedly met his friend in a double high-five.

"Yes!" Frederick repeated like a football enthusiast whose team just won. All drowsiness vanished.

Ignoring Jim's question, Frederick hustled back to the plane's doorway. His palms began to ooze perspiration. His heart in his throat, he grabbed the stair's support cable and descended. Frederick waved at the approaching vehicles until they drove toward the parking area that serviced this section of airport.

Soon the whole Grove clan was bustling toward Frederick with Allie following at a distance, her head bent. The shy tilt of her head coupled with her flowing skirt and blouse increased her feminine appeal. Frederick's adrenaline kicked up a notch and stimulated his masculine desire to protect Allie . . . for life.

He wished for the engagement ring he'd bought ten years ago. But the diamond was at his place in Charlotte in the safe.

His desire to keep the ring all these years now made perfect sense. Even if he didn't give the diamond to Allie tonight, he would definitely surprise her with it soon. She was so sweet-spirited he knew she would be thrilled even if she received it *following* their marriage.

After a distracted welcome for the rest of the group and a brief handshake with Charlie Grove, he was in the middle of sidestepping Helena and Louise when Louise grabbed his arm.

"I get to ride up front with you today. Don't forget." She wagged her index finger back and forth and smiled as if they had a secret agreement and their conversation last night had never happened.

"No, not this time," Frederick said with what he hoped was an apologetic grin.

"But I thought you said I could!" she huffed and crossed her arms. For once she was dressed decently in a pair of cotton capris and a shirt that actually covered her stomach.

"Are you sure?" he gently questioned and offered a fatherly smile. "Because I don't remember that."

She pouted. "Well, this was my idea, so I just thought—"

"Yes, but the front seat is kinda reserved already." Frederick shrugged and glanced toward Allie again. He hoped she would accept the invitation and Louise would take the hint.

"If it's up for grabs, I'm all over it!" Helena declared and bounced into the conversation with no warning.

"No, I was just saying it *isn't* up for grabs," Frederick explained.

He eyed Louise's redheaded counterpart. She'd been less focused on Frederick all day yesterday because Craig had been present. But with his absence today, it appeared that Helena was resuming her leech status. She grabbed Frederick's arm and gushed a smile up at him.

"Bummer!" she exclaimed. "You're looking awfully handsome today."

"I'm sure Craig would probably agree," Frederick teased, but hoped Helena read between the lines. He was getting to be a near pro at well-aimed hints these days.

"Craig? Who's he?" she countered.

"You know. Tall guy. The one who's falling all over himself in love with you." Frederick disentangled himself from Helena.

"Oh, him. Don't know if he's the right one, if you know what I mean," she chattered and placed her hand on her miniskirt-clad hip. "When we first met, I thought he was going to play pro basketball. Scouts were even looking at him. But now with his knee injury, it looks like he's going to have to resort to just coaching."

"Really?" Louise questioned and eyed her sister like a feline guarding her territory. "Last I heard, he thought the injury wasn't going to stop him."

"Well, that's the latest," Helena replied. "He just told me last night. Now . . . I don't know about him and me. He *has* mentioned marriage, but being married to a pro basketball star is one thing. Marrying a high school coach is something else." She pulled her petite handbag off her shoulder and began scratching through it.

"If you really love him, does any of that matter?" Frederick queried and couldn't believe he was urging an immature nineteen-year-old to consider marriage. But anything was better than Helena and Louise fighting over him like a couple of hens after the same beetle.

Helena, busy unwrapping a stick of gum, looked up and said, "Did you say something?" She popped the gum into her mouth and chewed, her bronze-tinted lips puckering with every chomp.

Louise snorted.

"Never mind," Frederick said and backed away. "I'll talk to you later, okay?"

"No, wait!" Louise caught up with him and gripped his arm.

Frederick faced her. Given the stubborn set of her mouth, he began to think he was going to have to use a more direct approach in getting some space.

"I'm sitting up front with you, and that's all there is to it!" She darted a hostile glance toward Allie. "Don't think I don't see what's going on," Louise snarled, her voice barely audible. She doubled her fist and leaned closer. "And I'm not going to let my man go without a fight. You either let me ride up front or there's going to be a really nasty scene." She shifted back, crossed her arms, and lifted her chin.

Up until now, Louise's antics had amused him at best and irritated him at worst. But this move sent a flash of heat through his gut. Frederick hadn't ever allowed himself to be manipulated or controlled, and he wasn't about to start now. Apparently Louise really was going to have to have the direct approach. Whatever it took, Frederick was feeling more cornered by the minute and was ready for some freedom.

"And I mean it," she whispered, her blue eyes hard. "You're *mine*, and you'd better get that into your head and keep it in your head!" Her eyes slid toward Allie again.

Frederick clenched his jaw and ground his teeth together. His spine went rigid while heat crept up his face. He checked out the rest of the group to validate they didn't have an audience and decided to make himself so clear Louise would know exactly where she stood.

"Louise, it's time we get something straight," he said and moved his face closer to hers. "I am *not* your man," he jabbed his index finger against his chest, "nor have I ever been. I told you the day you invited me to your place that I was a family friend, and that's all. That's *still* all I am and nothing more. You have no claims on me."

Her face grew pale, but Frederick took no chances on being misunderstood. "You need to find a boyfriend your own age," he stated. "And I'm not him. End of discussion!" He lifted his hands for emphasis.

"You're dumping me for *her*!" she accused. Her ashen face flushing red, Louise stomped her foot and pointed toward Allie.

"I'm not dumping you, Louise," Frederick insisted. "We never were a couple. How can you dump someone you never dated in the first place?"

"What do you mean we never dated?" Louise raged. "You've courted me for weeks—been at my house all the time. We've gone to dinner. We've—"

"Yes," Frederick nodded, "with your family and friends all around us. Think about it, Louise. I've never even kissed you."

"Well, if you haven't been there for me, then why have you been there?" she demanded.

Frederick looked down and wondered how to get around that question. Even though Louise had angered him, he still hated to tell her he'd been after Allie and used her to get to Allie. The longer the seconds stretched, the more he felt like a cad. But then, Louise had said that Frederick was her "catch of the day" and that she changed boyfriends like some changed socks. If he'd known Louise was going to get so serious about him, Frederick would have certainly devised a more honorable plan.

"Louise, you told me when we met that you changed boyfriends like some people change socks. I had no idea you were going to get so serious here. If I had . . ." He shrugged and tried to appear remorseful enough to communicate genuine regret without her thinking he wanted to kiss and make up.

He glanced back toward the group. Thankfully they were mesmerized with the plane, and it appeared that Jim was doing a good job of answering their questions.

"Oh my word . . ." Louise breathed.

Frederick snapped his attention back to her. She was glaring bullets toward Allie.

"You were after her the whole time, weren't you?" she accused.

"Louise, I—"

"Yes, you were!" She pointed her finger at his nose. "That's why you were at that roadside park in the first place and why you told me to tell everyone you and I just bumped into each other. You didn't want anyone to know you were chasing her."

"Now listen! I never—"

"Don't lie to me, Frederick Wently," she challenged.

"Who says I'm lying?" He stepped back and placed his hands on his hips. "I might be a lot of things, but I am *not* a liar!"

"That's right. You are a lot of things!" She stepped forward. "You're a woman user, that's what you are. And you've used me!"

Frederick's face went cold. Never did he imagine Louise would be sophisticated enough to detect his plan or verbalize the accusations he'd hurled at himself.

"No one uses me and gets away with it," she whispered, her lips stiff. "And you'll either let me have my place beside you today—and for the rest of your life—or I'll make you so miserable you'll wish you were *dead.*"

The flames eating at Frederick's gut roared to an inferno. His control snapped, and he uttered the first thing that came to his mind: "I am not going to marry you! You can't force me to. I'm not afraid of you, Louise, not even a little bit. I don't care what you do. You can crawl through the escape hatch, tap dance on top of the plane, scream to the world about me, then fall off and break your neck, and it's not going to make one shred of difference in my final decision. Listen to me and listen closely. We are *not* together. We have *never* been together. And we are not *going* to be together. Got it?"

Her eye twitched. Her lips trembled. She lifted her hand to slap him, and Frederick stopped her mid-swing.

"Uuuuhhh!" Louise growled, then pulled her hand from his grasp and stomped toward the plane.

Twenty-Two

On the heels of her nocturnal boldness, Allie met the morning with an attack of insecurities that would not stop. She'd been so overtaken by doubts she nearly backed out of coming altogether. All morning she had second-guessed everything—even Frederick's direct invitation for her to stay after everyone left. By the time she drove into the airport, Allie decided she'd be Louise's laughingstock for life if she *had* somehow misunderstood Frederick.

Maybe he was just trying to be nice, she thought as her heart began to hammer and she pretended a deep interest in the plane's front propeller. The last she dared check, Frederick had been chatting up Louise and Helena as if nothing happened between them last night. No special invitation. Nothing.

All the way to Atlanta, Allie had rationalized every move he'd made from yesterday evening—right down to his kissing her hand. Frederick always had been a high-quality gentleman, and Allie began to think maybe the kiss was just a gallant way of inviting her on the flight along with everyone else.

Afraid to look at him again, afraid not to, Allie finally sneaked a quick peek, only to discover Frederick was walking straight toward her while Louise stomped up the aircraft's steps. She dismissed Louise and concentrated on Frederick. One look into his dark, adoring eyes was all Allie needed to

189

sweep aside her doubts. She lifted her head as her confidence soared. She might be "just Allie" to her family, but with Frederick she was *Allie!*

Why did I ever let Aunt Landon talk me out of him? she wondered and realized Frederick was dressed much like he had been when she first fell in love with him. Furthermore, the shirt he wore showed off his muscles as nicely now as the ones he'd worn all those years ago. Even Landon had commented that his muscles would knock the socks off a saint. Allie indisputably agreed.

She recalled the email from Aunt Landon she'd received this morning while drinking her first cup of tea. The message was filled with subtle inquiries about the Frederick situation and hints about his breaking her heart. Allie had deleted it without answering, and picked up her phone to type out a quick text to Sarah Hamilton instead. Allie told Sarah she'd been right about Frederick's not being a womanizer. And now, in the face of his adoration, she wondered if her morning insecurities had been rooted in her aunt's message. Somehow her aunt seemed to know every move Allie was making.

"Hiya!" Frederick said.

"Hi," Allie replied with a shy smile.

He shoved his hands into his jeans pockets like a high school senior about to ask the new girl to the prom. "So, what do ya think?" He waved toward the plane.

"It's great!" Allie said through a grin that felt as goofy as Frederick's looked. She admired the plane and noted Jim acting as host for the rest of the group. Thankfully he looked much less forlorn now than he had last night. Mr. and Mrs. Grove were climbing the steps that led into the aircraft with Helena close behind.

"Would you like to ride up front with me?" Frederick queried.

A warm flash swooped through Allie. Her acceptance would make a bold proclamation to the rest of the group about her position in Frederick's life. Hopefully, Louise would accept defeat and find another catch. A heady wave of victory washed over Allie. For once she had won. She won her man. And despite Louise's temper tantrums and proclamations, she couldn't do a thing about it.

"I'd love to," Allie agreed.

"And you're still staying after everyone leaves?"

"For sure." She nodded.

"Good." He grabbed her hand and tugged her toward the plane. "Come on."

Allie beamed up at Frederick and squeezed his hand tight. For the first time in ten years her world felt complete. And this time Allie decided she'd marry him if they had to elope. Nothing would stop them—absolutely nothing.

With confidence, she walked in sync with Frederick and nearly fell over laughing when she noticed Macy's blatant gape. Charlie and Jim were involved in a discussion. Mr. and Mrs. Grove were disappearing into the plane with Helena on their heels. That left Macy alone at the bottom of the steps. And she didn't even attempt to hide her shock. In a fit of bravado, Allie winked at her sister. Macy's mouth fell open.

Fleetingly, Allie wondered how many minutes would lapse before Aunt Landon had the scoop, and she just didn't care. Allie had her man . . . the man of her dreams . . . her very own American hero. And nobody was going to stop them this time. *Nobody!*

"Hey, Frederick!" Louise's high-pitched call exploded into Allie's victory. "What do you think of me now, huh?"

She glanced in the direction of Louise's voice and didn't spot her for several seconds. Finally movement on top of the plane pulled Allie's attention upward. There the willowy blonde stood, her hands on her hips like the queen of the airways. The wind tossed her hair in all directions, and she cocked her head at an arrogant angle.

"Oh my word," Frederick growled.

A horrid sense of impending disaster shook Allie to the core.

"You're a *jerk*, Frederick Wently!" Louise screamed.

"Louise!" Frederick yelled and dropped Allie's hand. "Get down from there now!"

Her face a mask of mockery, she bent forward and bellowed, "Wanna see me tap dance now? Do ya?" And she started a soft-shoe routine.

Stunned, Frederick wondered if he was going to have to go up there and drag her off.

The Groves and Helena scurried down the stairs. "She was crawling through the safety hatch, and we tried to stop her," Charlie Grove declared with a "do something" look at Frederick.

"Crazy woman!" Frederick moaned and raced toward the plane. "Get down now, Louise!" he commanded through clenched teeth.

"No!" she said and flounced into a more intense tap dance session. "Not until you let me sit up front with you!"

"You're going to fall and break your neck!" Frederick hollered and wanted to choke himself for even suggesting there was an escape hatch.

"No, I'm not," she challenged. "Because you're going to catch me."

"I can't catch you, Louise Grove!" Frederick screamed. "Now get down before you get hurt!" He pointed downward and wondered if the woman had had any discipline at all growing up.

"You caught me when I jumped off the picnic table," she challenged. "You can catch me now."

He braced himself in case she did jump and wondered if his back would *ever* recover this time. "It's too high. And remember, I've got a bad back." He lifted his hands and imagined her toppling down the plane and hitting the concrete head first.

Frederick shot a furtive glance toward the rest of the group. They were all imagining the same thing, if their expressions were anything to go by.

"Come on and get down, Louise," Jim coaxed. "You can ride by me, okay?"

She eyed Jim for a few seconds and her hard expression eased, but soon she was back to Frederick and flaming furious once more. "I want to ride up front with Frederick, not you." She crossed her arms, tapped her toe, and looked skyward.

So far Louise had done nearly everything Frederick suggested. She'd crawled up on the plane, screamed about him, and tap danced. Now all that was left was breaking her neck. Horror mingled with ire.

"Okay, okay," Frederick acquiesced and didn't even want to admit she'd won the control game. "I'll let you ride up front for a while if you'll just crawl back through the escape hatch."

"Okay!" she said with a smirk that said, *I won!* She lifted her chin and glared toward Allie.

Frederick could only imagine what Allie was thinking.

"Just be a good girl and crawl back down the way you came." Martha's maternal encouragement was all Louise needed.

She turned around and took several baby steps toward the edge.

Relaxing a bit, Frederick began walking around the plane. Once Louise got on the wing, he could help her down to safety and the whole episode would be over. Frederick rubbed his face and dreaded the thought of being chained to Louise Grove for life. The poor guy who did say "I do" had better be ready to have a tiger by the tail. He gazed toward the tower and shook his head.

When a throaty scream ripped across the airport, Frederick stopped and looked at Louise. Wildly, she waved her arms and teetered toward the asphalt below. Her gaze met Frederick's, and he recognized the raw panic ravaging her soul. The terror was genuine, and it was exactly what engulfed him in cold dread.

The airport swayed. Frederick's face chilled. He scrambled forward just as she tumbled onto the wing. Another ear-piercing scream accompanied her hitting her neck against the nacelle's ridge. Then she toppled to the concrete in a silent heap.

"Nooooo!" Martha's shriek mingled with dismayed yelling as the rest of the group crowded Frederick.

Stunned by the crumpled form, Frederick hustled forward and collapsed at her side while his own words pummeled his brain: *I don't care what you do. You can crawl through the escape hatch, tap dance on top of the plane, scream to the world about me, then fall off and break your neck, and it's not going to make one shred of difference in my final decision.*

The family's yelling and talking and confusion mingled with the war in his mind and became secondary to his need to know if she was alive. He kept telling himself that dead people usually have their eyes open in a blank stare—at least the ones he'd encountered in Afghanistan. Louise's eyes were closed. He picked up her wrist, held his breath, and checked her pulse. Thankfully, her heart's soft tattoo met his fingers, and her chest moved gently with the intake of air.

"Don't touch her! Don't touch her!" Jim's frantic cry penetrated Frederick's horror. He looked up into the young doctor's face and realized he was surrounded by a huddle of panic-stricken family members.

Spreading his arms, Jim wedged himself between the family and Louise. "Somebody call 9-1-1!" he insisted.

"I already did!" Allie's urgent voice floated from outside the circle.

Frederick stood and inched away from Louise, his stomach rolling. *I shouldn't have said what I did. How could I have been so cruel? I should have been faster. How could this have happened? Oh, Lord, please don't let her neck be broken. Please, God, I take it all back!*

"The paramedics will need to stabilize her spine and neck before they move her," Jim explained, his voice strong and sure. "If there's a fracture, we can do more harm if we move her."

Martha Grove's cry erupted from near Jim. "My baby!" she shrieked. "My baby! Oh, dear God, please tell me she won't die!" Martha stumbled and Frederick jolted forward, but Charlie Sr. appeared from behind and stabilized his wife before she collapsed to her knees.

A movement to the left snared Frederick's attention. Macy was dragging herself up from the concrete and examining her knees. Allie, right at her side, was helping her stand. *Macy must have tripped*, he thought.

"I've got a first-aid kit in my car," Allie said.

Frederick looked back at Martha's flushed face as she hovered near Jim and peered at her unconscious daughter. Shaking his head, he backed away even farther. He'd told Louise he wasn't scared of her. But right now Frederick's fear was rising to epic proportions.

"I'm sorry," he mumbled. "I'm so, so sorry."

Twenty-Three

Frederick paced the emergency room waiting area as he'd done years ago when Allie broke her leg. Ironically, this was the exact same hospital. Not much had changed, except this time the patient was Louise. And this time, the body part that was broken was her neck. Jim was right in his diagnosis. So were the paramedics. Their latest report from the ER X-rays validated their professional evaluation. The doctor also said Louise had yet to gain consciousness and was showing no signs of reflexes.

Oh, Lord, help her, Frederick prayed and paused near the Coke machine. No one was saying "paralyzed" right now, but the word hung between them like an unspoken omen. Frederick well understood the hopelessness that diagnosis could bring. He'd been told he'd never walk again. The doctors said his sheer willpower had overcome the odds. Frederick knew there was a power much higher than his who had played a vital part.

He eyed the choices on the drink machine and pulled out two dollars. When the cold bottle of Coca-Cola thumped out, he retrieved it, unscrewed the lid, and guzzled a third of the liquid. The acidic burn brought a sting to his heavy eyes and a satisfying tingle to the back of his throat.

But nothing could wipe away the horrid reality that this

accident was his fault. He'd allowed Louise to believe he was interested in her so he could get closer to Allie. Last night he'd done a lousy job of explaining that they really weren't in a relationship. Today he'd brutally given her the instructions for how to break her neck. And she'd done it. Like a small child, she was desperate for Frederick's attention and willing to resort to anything—even tap dancing on top of a plane—to divert him from Allie. This only fueled Frederick's awareness of her immaturity and his greater need to wisely handle the mess. So far his performance had been anything *but* wise.

Frederick glanced toward the distraught family on the other side of the waiting room. Martha Grove's forlorn sniffles and Helena's less-controlled crying mingled with Allie's gentle encouragement. Her shoulders hunched, Martha mopped at her face and nodded at whatever Allie was saying. Helena, on Allie's other side, was piling up tissue and paid little attention to Allie. Mr. Grove sat apart from the ladies and stared into space.

Charlie Jr. and Macy had left once they received the medical report. Dinnertime had come and gone. They had to relieve their baby-sitter and prepare the twins for school tomorrow.

As for Jim, the guy had been given bedside privileges because his practice was associated with Atlanta Mercy Hospital. He'd known the doctor on duty and half the staff. Frederick hadn't seen him since he trotted down the hallway beside Louise's gurney. Impatient for some news, Frederick pulled his cell phone from his pocket and pressed Jim's speed dial number.

He answered immediately with, "Frederick, I'm just around the corner . . . coming to get you. She's awake and wants to see you."

"Me?" he gasped.

"Yes, you. And her mom. They're moving her to ICU."

Jim appeared at the waiting room's doorway and disconnected the call. His face was stiff; his eyes, grim.

Uh-oh, Frederick thought, and the nausea returned. He looked toward Martha, and then his focus trailed to Allie. She and Martha and Helena all focused on him.

"Louise is awake," he said.

Martha jumped up. "She's awake? May I see her?"

"Yes." Jim's firm reply came from beside Frederick. "She's asking for you and for Frederick. You can both see her for just a few minutes, and then they're moving her to ICU."

"ICU?" Helena wailed. Charlie Grove stood. His fists balled but he said nothing, just stared at Jim in red-faced agony, his handlebar mustache as askew as his hair.

"She's unable to move right now." Jim's gaze faltered. "And in these situations, it's important to monitor her breathing. Sometimes these patients can just, well, stop." He shrugged.

"Is she paralyzed?" Allie questioned.

"For right now, yes. It looks that way . . . from her neck down." Jim held on to the ends of the stethoscope around his neck and gazed at the floor.

"Is it permanent?" Allie asked.

"They don't know. In these situations it's hard to tell." Jim's expression suggested he didn't want to say too much. "Well . . ." he added, "it's best to say you'll need to talk to her regular doctor. I'm just a helper at this point."

Frederick felt as if he were trying to breathe through a wet sponge. The air was too heavy, and the guilt constricted his lungs past the point of function.

This is all my fault, he thought and rammed his fingers against his scalp.

Martha's wail began slow and weak and gradually escalated

to that of a mourner saying her last good-byes. Charlie Grove's bulky form slumped onto the edge of his seat, and then slid to the floor. Frederick didn't realize the guy had passed out until he flopped over in a limp wilt.

"Oh my word, he fainted!" Allie exclaimed and left Martha.

"I'll see to him," Jim commanded and knelt at Charlie's side. He looked up at Frederick. "You go ahead and take Mrs. Grove to see Louise. You only have a few minutes."

"Yes, okay," Frederick said and tossed his Coke into an empty chair. He dubiously observed Helena, who had gone strangely quiet. She had stopped crying and was staring straight ahead as her father had been only minutes before. Frederick hoped this was not an indicator that she would faint next.

He stepped to Mrs. Grove's side, put his arm across her shoulders, and said, "I'm sure everything's going to be okay." But the whole time Frederick had the gut-wrenching feeling that everything was a long way from okay.

"She's got to calm down before she goes in there," Jim advised. "Otherwise they won't let her in."

Allie looked up from her post near Mr. Grove. For the first time since this ordeal sprang upon them, Frederick made eye contact with her. Her soft, brown eyes were full of compassion and understanding . . . and a plea. Frederick knew what she was thinking. He just knew. She was telling him not to blame himself, that the whole thing was Louise's fault, that she was young and rash and irresponsible, and she reaped the consequences. But nothing could alleviate Frederick's self-reproach, not even Allie's silent encouragement.

Mrs. Grove laid her head on Frederick's shoulder, and he stroked her temple. "Mrs. Grove, do you think you can stop crying long enough to smile for Louise?" he coaxed.

Her broken sobs slowed, and Frederick ushered her forward. "She needs you to be brave for her right now. She needs to see your smile," he added and felt like a hypocrite. He was asking Louise's mother to do something he was incapable of. Frederick had just contributed to a very young, very beautiful woman becoming paralyzed. Smiling was the last thing on his to-do list.

"Allie, you brace him," Jim commanded. "I'll go get something that will rouse him. I'll be right back."

She nodded and gazed after Frederick as he ushered Mrs. Grove toward the hallway. Jim passed them on the way out and motioned them to follow. Allie wanted to stroke Frederick's face just as he was stroking Mrs. Grove's. Whether or not anybody else noticed that he was eaten up with remorse, Allie knew.

Once she got him alone, Allie planned to talk him out of it. What Louise did was of her own making. Frederick hadn't forced her on top of that plane. She'd gone of her own free will. Just as Louise had been irrational in her anger last night, so she had been irrational in her actions today.

From all Allie could gather, Louise lived dangerously. She had for years. How she'd managed to avoid detrimental accidents this far was anybody's guess. And while Allie certainly felt sorry for the young beauty—especially if she was paralyzed for life—she simply could not allow Frederick to pin the blame on himself.

Mr. Grove moaned and shifted. Allie turned her attention to him. His eyes slid open. He blankly stared up at Allie.

"It's me, Allie, Mr. Grove," she said.

He straightened and rubbed his forehead. "I passed out, didn't I?" he questioned.

"Yes." Allie looked toward the red-eyed Helena. Allie didn't think Helena would notice if a gang of apes marched through the room.

"Louise." Charlie straightened his legs then prepared to stand.

"Mrs. Grove and Frederick are going in to see her now."

"Good." He struggled to his feet and settled back into the chair. "I know she's crazy about—about Frederick. I've never seen her so in—in love before." He lowered his head. "If anyone can help her, he . . . he can . . . he can."

Twenty-Four

Mrs. Grove clung to Frederick until he reached Louise's room. All the way he held her up and wished for someone to hold *him* up. The stone-faced nurse that led them to the room opened Louise's door and said, "You've got three minutes."

Frederick eyed the swathed figure lying motionless in the elevated bed. Louise's limp hair, sprawled against the pillow, lacked the life of a vivacious young woman in a convertible. Louise was hooked up to an IV along with a variety of other monitors. One screen featured the steady rhythm of her heart. A severe neck brace gave her the appearance of being choked. Her face was pale except for the twin splotches of rouge that once blended with her complexion. The room's antiseptic smell took on the odd undertone of funeral flowers. Frederick would have vowed Louise were dead if he hadn't known better.

A technician near the bed's head looked up from his duties and said, "We're getting ready to move her. You need to hurry."

So I've heard, Frederick thought and nodded as the man swept past them.

"My baby, my baby," Mrs. Grove moaned.

Frederick gripped her arm. "Stay calm," he encouraged as a hard tremor wracked his body. After the land mine shrapnel pierced his spine and he'd been rushed into surgery, Frederick recalled awakening in a hospital bed alone. He'd tried to move his legs but couldn't. He fought with the covers until his arms were free, but his legs refused to budge. He'd barely been able to wiggle his toes.

Frederick relived the agony that blazed through his veins. He'd imagined life in a wheelchair, being totally dependent upon others—on his parents, on his sister. He had no wife to meet him at the airport or help him, like many of the injured did. He didn't need the doctor to tell him he'd have to have a miracle to ever walk again. Frederick knew long before the doctor's prognosis. And he'd already decided that, with God as his helper, he'd walk again. And he had. Even though he'd live with a bad back the rest of his life, he walked and walked with determination.

As he looked at Louise, Frederick identified with her as he never imagined he could. His story was a chance-of-a-lifetime miracle. He had no clue if Louise would ever overcome this tragedy. But he did know that she would feel a level of panic she never imagined existed. At least he'd had the use of his arms. She was immobile from the neck down. He swallowed a groan and recognized that whether she ever walked again or not, she'd need a strong network of people to stand beside her.

He imagined the blonde being strapped in a wheelchair, unable to move or feed herself for the rest of her life. Alone. Totally alone. Except for her parents. One day, they'd be gone. Then what? Her brother and sister-in-law hardly took care of their own children. How would they manage a quadriplegic?

He thought of the flighty Helena. She was barely responsible enough to guard her own safety, let alone a paralyzed dependent's. Frederick imagined her accidentally tipping Louise's wheelchair down a massive flight of stairs. Then he saw himself pulling the wheelchair back to safety and keeping Louise from flopping down the steps.

Wrapping his fingers around the cold bedrail, Frederick paused near Louise while Mrs. Grove touched her cheek. "Honey?" she crooned.

Louise's lids drifted open. She focused on Frederick and offered a weak smile. "Hi," she whispered, her eyes dull.

"Hi." Frederick's eyes stung, and the weight of responsibility would not be denied.

"Oh, Louise," Martha whimpered. "I'm right here. Mama's right here," she added as if Louise were three.

Louise never acknowledged her mother. Her attention remained on Frederick. "Don't leave me," she begged. "I love you. We—we were going to get married. I just *knew* it." Her face crumpled. "Please don't leave me for *her*," she cried.

Martha fell silent. Frederick glimpsed her from the corner of his eyes. She'd traded tears for a gawk.

His face stiffened.

"Please say you'll marry me like you promised."

"Louise, I . . ." Frederick shook his head and garbled out something that made no sense. How Louise could have ever convinced herself that he'd promised to marry her was an enigma.

"I'd *love* to have you as a son-in-law," Martha said, her voice thick. "I know Charlie would, too. And you're as good as gold to stand by Louise like this even though—"

Eyes wide, Frederick looked at Martha, who was once again absorbed with Louise. Like her daughter, she'd already assumed the marriage was a done deal. The weight of the moment overpowered him as the responsibility piled up in stifling conviction. He imagined the horror of being a quadriplegic, especially if you *really believed* a man loved you and dropped you because you were crippled. He understood what it felt like to be alone in such a situation, even if Allie had dumped him before the land mine explosion. He also knew the heartbreak of dreaming of Allie, reaching for her, only to remember he was stranded in bed and she was never coming back.

In the desperation of the moment, he believed the most honorable thing to do was be there for Louise—even if it meant sacrificing his own happiness. After all, she wouldn't be paralyzed if he hadn't used her and then told her how to get on top of the plane.

"Please . . ." Louise begged as tears slipped from the corners of her eyes. "Please don't leave me. I promise if you'll marry me, I'll make you the best wife ever."

Frederick's sleep-deprived mind struggled with a ragged jumble of "shoulds" and "what ifs." He wondered if he could live with himself if he left the twenty-year-old with no options of matrimony and no future. Even if he and Allie became blissfully wed, Frederick wouldn't be able to sleep at night knowing what he'd done to Louise . . . knowing he'd abandoned her.

"Of course," he whispered and gently kissed her hairline.

Martha wept. "Such a wonderful young man. So wonderful," she said between sniffles. "I could never ask for a better son-in-law. Just wonderful."

Louise's face relaxed. She licked her dry lips, swallowed, and closed her eyes. A satisfied smile played around her mouth.

The nurse reentered and moved to the head of Louise's bed. "I'm sorry but your time's up," she stated, her eyes compassionate, her words as unyielding as her face. "She's going to ICU. Please check with them about their visitation schedule."

Frederick urged Martha away from the bed and walked into the hallway. Clinging to Frederick, Martha once again rested her head against his shoulder. She dabbed at her nose with a tattered tissue and mumbled something about Frederick's being a prince.

A surreal numbness seeping into his soul, Frederick steered his future mother-in-law back toward the waiting room. While his remorseful heart convinced him he'd done the honorable thing, his mind insisted he'd fallen into a dreadful trap he had no way of avoiding. When he spotted Allie sitting by Mr. Grove in the waiting room, a swell of confusion nearly took him down. Frederick knew the crazy circumstances had overtaken his life like a rapid river flood that sweeps through and destroys in seconds.

His exhaustion from earlier that day attacked him tenfold. Frederick's gritty eyes grew heavy with fatigue and grief.

Mrs. Grove slumped in the chair next to her husband and said, "Frederick Wently is the most wonderful man who ever lived. He just told Louise he'd still marry her no matter what." She gripped Frederick's hand and looked up at him as if he were Superman.

Charlie Grove turned his flushed face toward Frederick. A trickle of tears collected in the creases under one eye. Not even the flood of admiration crossing his features could bolster Frederick.

"You have no idea what a relief that is," Charlie said. "As long as we're alive, we'll be there for her, but then what?"

"I know," Frederick mumbled, and finally had the nerve to look at Allie.

Her stricken expression added to Frederick's frustration. Minutes before, he'd wondered how he could sleep at night knowing he'd left a woman who was a quadriplegic because of him. Now he wondered how he'd ever sleep knowing what he'd done to Allie.

"I—I'm sorry," he gasped and shook his head. "I—I—"

Frederick gripped the back of his neck with both hands and stared at the floor. "If it hadn't been for me this wouldn't have—"

"No!" Allie exclaimed.

Both the Groves jumped.

Frederick's gaze snapped back to her. He never remembered Allie sounding so forceful.

She leaped to her feet and doubled her fists. "You can't blame yourself!" She stomped her foot and the sound filled the room with a *slap*.

"But you don't know everything, Allie! You just don't know." Frederick lifted his hands. He teetered on the precipice of blurting everything . . . about how he'd used Louise . . . about his brutally telling her he didn't care if she broke her neck . . . about how all this had driven someone so immature and fragile into doing exactly what he'd said.

Frederick clenched his teeth and decided he didn't have the stomach to tell the awful truth. Not now anyway. In Afghanistan, flinging his body between his crew and that land mine had ranked him an American hero. His treatment of Louise was anything *but* heroic.

"I've got to go," he mumbled and strode from the waiting room.

"Frederick, wait!" Allie called.

"No! I can't!" he barked over his shoulder and rushed toward the exit.

"Frederick!" she cried. *"Please!"*

Frederick lunged into the star-studded night, and the automatic door blocked Allie's voice.

Twenty-Five

Allie was certain this ordeal was a nightmare she'd awaken from. But as she stood at the closed hospital doors, she understood that the dream scenario was nothing but wishful thinking. A siren's screaming raked along her nerves and insisted that all was reality, right down to the bizarre fact that Frederick had agreed to marry Louise. Allie felt like she was going to throw up.

A paramedic pushed a gurney through the hospital's automatic doors, on it a screaming infant and a bruised and bedraggled mother. Allie couldn't take any more trauma. She turned her back on the victims and decided the time had come for her to go home. When she stepped back into the waiting room, Jim Bennington was talking with Louise's parents.

His face shadowed, Jim glanced toward Allie and then walked closer. "They said Frederick is marrying Louise," he said, his voice low. "I didn't even know they were that serious."

Allie shrugged and was so disheartened she couldn't even cry. "I guess there was more there than any of us knew," she said.

"Guess so." Jim shook his head and glanced toward Louise's family. "These guys all need a place for the night. I'd offer my townhouse, but Frederick's there and I've only got two bedrooms. Anyway, Frederick was supposed to call his sister and see if they can stay at Elton Mansion."

"Oh, of course they can," Allie replied, before remembering the mansion was no longer hers to offer. She could have really used her third-floor haven tonight. The ache for her old home plus the Frederick–Louise business left Allie nearly unable to talk.

Finally she said, "I meant, uh . . ." she smoothed her icy fingers along the front of her blouse, "that's—that's a great idea. I'm sure Darren and Sophia won't mind in the least. They seem like a nice couple." Her smile felt as sincere as plastic.

"Are you going to be okay?" Jim asked.

Allie peered at the alert man before her. Last night Jim was but a shadow of a soul compared to tonight. When he began exercising his medical authority, the man had fallen into his element and taken charge. The change in his demeanor was nearly miraculous. Ironically, Allie could better relate to last night's Jim . . . the forlorn guy who could find something depressing in every rhyme.

"Allie?" Jim prompted.

"I . . . I'm not feeling very well." She eyed Mr. and Mrs. Grove and Helena, who'd moved to her parents' side. The three of them had finally stopped staring and crying and fainting long enough to talk to each other. "Would you be able to take care of them—make sure they get to Elton Mansion? I need to go home—back to Macon." Allie's face felt wooden; her heart, like stone.

"Sure, but are you going to drive all the way back alone?" Jim checked his watch, and his straight hair fell over one eye.

"You need a haircut," Allie mumbled and didn't realize she'd voiced her thoughts until Jim chuckled.

"How right you are," he said. "I was going to try to make that happen tomorrow."

"Sorry." Allie looked down and thought she might have gotten embarrassed if she hadn't been so distraught. "I didn't even realize I said it."

Jim put his hand on her shoulder. "Believe it or not, Allie, you've helped me more in the last couple of days than you will ever know."

"I have?" she asked, her voice dull.

"Yep. And I'd let you shave me bald if you wanted to."

Allie managed a tired smile. "All I did was listen, I guess." She shrugged.

"You did more than that. Last night you told me it's time to get on with my life. Nobody else has said that."

"Really?"

"No. Not even the counselor. At first I was aggravated at you. Then sometime last night after all that Robert Frost business—I think it was about three or so—I realized you were right. I've decided tonight to go back to work full time." He toyed with the stethoscope. "The head nurse just told me they need an ER doctor here. I might apply. I think it would be a good change for me. Help to get my mind off of Felicity and onto making a difference."

Even though his words sounded solid and his face held more light, Jim's eyes still reflected a trace of the darkness. And Allie knew that he was having a good evening, but his future still held its share of struggles.

"Well, good," she said and couldn't believe the turn in their fortunes. Last night Allie had been thinking that Jim was nearing the edge. Now he seemed to be regaining some balance, and *she* was the one nearing the edge.

The baby's distant screaming accompanied the sounds of a

frenzied staff working to save lives. The waiting room smelled like stale coffee and stagnant cleaning fluid. Mrs. Grove had started weeping again. The fluorescent glare off the over-polished floors threatened to give Allie a headache. And every bit of it pushed her to the brink of hysteria.

"I . . . I really need to go," she repeated and backed toward the exit.

"Sure," Jim replied. "Like I said, I'll take care of everything here." He looked around. "Whatever happened to Frederick, anyway?"

"He left," Allie stated and stiffly walked toward the exit.

"Oh." Jim's hollow reply was loaded with all sorts of questions that Allie didn't even want to think about. "Well, he probably didn't get far," Jim said. "We're in my truck, and I've got the keys."

Within an hour and a half, Allie entered the guesthouse. She slung her canvas bag onto the couch and kicked her backless sandals across the room. They slammed into the coffee table and flopped against the area rug. Allie looked down at the spring outfit she'd donned this morning and was tempted to tear the thing off and rip it to shreds. She'd bought the gauzy blouse after her haircut and hadn't worn it until today. Allie never wanted to look at the top again; it would forever remind her of the day Frederick promised to marry Louise Grove.

This morning when she left for the flight with Frederick, Allie had twirled around in the dress and hoped the feminine appeal wasn't lost on him. His appreciative grin and the invitation for her to ride in the copilot's seat had fueled her hopes. But now Louise would forever be riding next to Frederick.

Allie slammed the door and pulled at the hair she'd so meticulously styled before leaving for Atlanta. Somewhere in the middle of her journey home, she had begun to cry. And she'd wept until her eyes were bleary, her lids puffy. Even now, new tears streamed down her cheeks and marred her vision.

Blindly she stumbled into the kitchen, only to step on something crunchy that cracked beneath her weight. Allie looked down to encounter a floor strewn with food. Crackers, bread, and a box of Cheerios cluttered the path between the kitchen cabinets and the back door. At the pet flap, a hunched-over, ring-tailed visitor stared at her like a disobedient child waiting for his parents' verdict.

"Great!" Allie hollered. "Just great!" She picked up the box of Cheerios and hurled it at the coon. "Go ahead!" she screamed. "Eat it! Eat all of it!" As the cereal box crashed against the door and slammed to the floor, the coon was just slipping out the pet flap. Allie ran to the door, kicked the Cheerios out of the way, and examined the sorry excuse for a latch. To say the thing was defective was a joke.

Her face heating, Allie twisted the deadbolt, whipped open the door, and snatched up the box of cereal. She threw the Cheerios onto the back porch and yelled, "Just eat me out of house and home, why don't you! Now I don't have *any* cereal left!"

She slammed the door, fell against it, and slid to the floor. Allie pulled her knees to her chest, wrapped her arms around her legs, and tilted to her side. Fresh sobs wracked her body. And in the middle of all the misery, Allie knew this must be Frederick's way of paying her back for what she did to him. Aunt Landon was right. He really was a heartbreaker.

Twenty-Six

The next morning at ten, Allie sat in her bed with her laptop and tried to decipher today's emails. After deleting the usual junk mail, she rubbed her swollen eyes and focused on the remaining messages. Allie peered at Aunt Landon's latest email a full ten seconds before deciding not to open it right now. Another one from Sarah Hamilton appeared more inviting and much safer.

Allie clicked on the message and waited to read Sarah's brief communiqué. As the message opened, Allie remembered sending her friend an email yesterday morning stating that Sarah had been right about Frederick's not being a womanizer. Now she absorbed Sarah's response and wished she'd read Aunt Landon's email instead.

Like I said, Allie, I think Frederick's gold. If he's still interested, grab him and don't let him go. You know I know a good man when I see one. I married Larry, didn't I?

Over & Out!
Diana Ross

Under normal circumstances, Allie would have chuckled over Sarah's signature. But today she found no humor in it.

Instead, her eyes filled with fresh tears while her stomach felt full of lead. Her face tightening, Allie hit Reply and typed, "It's all over. He's marrying Louise." She pressed Send without even bothering to sign her name.

Allie swiped away the tears and clicked on Aunt Landon's email. As usual, she was singing the same tune:

Allie,

I haven't heard a peep from you, and that worries me. I know you're probably aggravated at me because I keep warning you against Frederick. But I can't tell you enough how strongly I feel. Call it women's intuition or what you like; I just have a hunch he'll eventually hurt you. Honey, please don't do something we'll all regret later!

Much love,
Aunt L

Allie hiccoughed over a sob. She grabbed the box of tissue from her nightstand, pulled out a wad, and scrubbed at her cheeks. When the tissue was wet, she used the freshly laundered sheet to dry the last round of tears.

After hitting Reply, Allie's trembling fingers rested on the keys. "Not to worry," she wrote. "He's marrying Louise Grove, Macy's sister-in-law." As with Sarah's message, she didn't bother to sign it.

The phone rang. Allie looked at her cell phone and debated whether or not to answer. There was no name to indicate who it was—only a number. After Brent's phone call Sunday night, she cringed every time the phone rang.

But the reason she'd cringed was because she didn't want Brent to interfere with her relationship with Frederick. Presently there *was* no relationship with Frederick, so there was no need to hesitate—except for the fact that Allie wasn't interested in *any* romance right now.

She answered the phone on the sixth ring and wasn't surprised when Brent's voice floated over the line. Allie forced her words to a normal tenor and commended herself for sounding only stuffy-nosed. After the usual "Hellos," "How-are-yous," and "Isn't the weather nice?" Brent cleared his throat and hesitantly said, "I was wondering, um, if you aren't busy tonight, if you'd like to go out for dinner and a movie."

"Tonight?" Allie echoed.

"Yes, tonight," he replied with a smile in his voice.

Allie allowed the laptop to slip to the mattress. She propped up her leg, rested her elbow on her knee, and rubbed at her damp, burning eyes. Her sleep experience last night had been sporadic, filled with weeping and tormented by nightmares about Frederick and Louise's wedding. Allie glanced down at her beige, satin PJs and far preferred the thought of staying in them until tomorrow rather than dressing for a dinner date tonight.

"Allie?" Brent prompted. "Are you still there?"

"Yes," she replied. "Sorry. I just . . . you caught me by surprise, that's all."

"Ah, being your usual modest self, I guess, huh?"

"Well . . ." Allie hedged as an animated duck marched to the center of her laptop screen and quacked at her.

"Did I just hear a duck?" Brent asked over a chuckle.

"It's my email notifier," Allie explained. "I'm at my laptop, checking my email. Every time a new email comes, this duck quacks at me."

He laughed. "I love that. Maybe you could get me signed up for that program. Would you tell me more about it tonight?"

"Uh . . . sure," Allie absently agreed while she noted who the email was from. Landon Russ's name appeared in her inbox.

"Great, then!" Brent exclaimed. "I'll pick you up at five thirty. Is that okay?"

"Excuse me?" Allie bleated and sat straight up.

"I'll pick you up for dinner at five-thirty. You just said you'd go out with me, didn't you?" Brent's voice took on an unsure, insecure note that reminded Allie of a little boy.

She gazed across the room into the dresser mirror. The colonial-style dresser looked as if it belonged to royalty, but the woman in the mirror resembled a street person. Her hair could have been a Brillo pad. Her face was ashen; her eyes bulging. In a fit of despair, Allie wondered how she'd ever stop crying long enough to pull her look together for a date.

"Allie, please?" Brent's pleading voice reminded her of the loss of his wife and his obvious need for some new friends.

"Okay," Allie heard herself say and wondered if she'd lost her mind.

"Great!" Brent exclaimed. "I can't wait. Will you give me your address so I can map it?"

Forcing her voice to remain steady and polite, Allie rattled off her address, then excused herself from the call as swiftly as she could.

Once she set down her phone, she looked toward the ceiling and said, "How did I get myself into this?" Allie pulled both knees toward her chest, rested her elbows on her knees, and cradled her face in her hands.

Then the duck quacked at her again. Allie lifted her face. "I forgot all about Aunt Landon," she mumbled and pulled the laptop back onto her lap. Allie clicked on the message, which immediately sent the animated duck into a quacking fit as he waddled off the screen. In seconds, Allie read the brief missive:

I am so relieved! Why don't you come stay with me awhile? It will get you away from that place. I wasn't really sold on your going there anyway.

Much love,
Aunt L

Allie closed the email program without responding and closed the lid on her laptop. She set the computer on her nightstand and picked up the tumbler of ice water with lemon slices she'd been sipping on since she awoke an hour ago. Allie downed the last of the tart liquid, stood, and walked into the kitchen. After setting the glass on the counter, she was overtaken with a yawn and a new onslaught of exhaustion.

She slumped against the kitchen counter and pondered Aunt Landon's request. Staying with her aunt in Atlanta held way more appeal than remaining here while Frederick and Louise planned their wedding. She imagined a gloating Louise sitting in her wheelchair, her makeup as flawless as ever, her expression saying, "I won!" Allie didn't have a grain of empathy for the paralyzed woman.

"This is awful," she groaned and despised herself for not pitying Louise. But no matter how hard she tried, all Allie could feel was frustration and jealousy—a jealousy that burned into her soul and consumed her with a fire that wouldn't be quenched. And Allie knew she really had no choice in leaving the guesthouse. She could not remain at Grove Acres while Frederick hovered over a triumphant Louise.

In a fit of desperation, Allie wondered how in the world she'd make it through the rest of the day without falling apart, much less through an evening with Brent.

"Oh, God, why?" she prayed, repeating the prayer that had been her bedmate all night long.

~~~~~

Brent stretched out on the hotel bed and tapped Penny's name on his phone. She answered on the first ring.

"Can you talk?" Brent questioned.

"Yes. Just for a few. I'm alone, but not for long," Penny replied, her voice low and intense.

"Okay. I'll keep it short, then. I've got good news."

"You got a date with her?" Penny asked.

"How'd you guess?" he drawled. Picking up the remote from the nightstand, Brent flipped on the TV and muted the volume.

"I could tell by your voice. It sounded like money," she shot back.

"I like the way you think," Brent commented and eyed the tennis match in full swing.

"So do I!" Penny replied with a twist of wicked humor.

Brent grinned. One of the things he'd loved about Penny was her lack of messy emotions. The first time Brent had indulged in a fling that didn't involve her, he'd expected Penny to become irate. But she'd barely flinched. And when Brent explained that he'd been able to steal a huge diamond from the hare-brained heiress, she'd been thrilled with his success. The two had enjoyed the money that diamond brought for several months.

"And how are you doing?" Brent queried. "Any luck in

the last twenty-four hours?" He reached for the flask of rum sitting on the nightstand.

"Nothing. I swear, Evelyn Elton is the most obnoxious person I've ever met. I can't believe you ever dated her. What was wrong with you?"

"Haven't you heard?" Brent asked. "I like money. And if I have to, I'll marry money no matter how obnoxious it is. I just happened to get lucky when I met Chrissy. She was way nicer than Evelyn and just about as rich, so I dumped Evelyn." A tiny tinge of remorse marred his conscience. While Brent had never been madly in love with Chrissy, he hadn't exactly been glad that she died, either. She was easy to look at and not demanding in the least. She never questioned why Brent needed a raise in his allowance or why he was late getting home. Chrissy said she trusted him. Life for Brent had been perfect until those killer bees did their thing.

"Well, Richard Elton is every bit as obnoxious as his daughter," Penny huffed. "He's so conceited, all he can think about is himself and whether or not his tan is even. I can't *stand* him!"

"But he's rolling in green," Brent purred, "and that's the perfect grounds for a successful marriage." He poured the golden liquid into the glass of ice near the lamp. "I think Allie will bore me to tears." He yawned.

"Good. Maybe she'll feel the same about you once you're married, and that will give us more time to play."

Brent's seductive chuckle was answer enough. He downed a generous swallow of rum and relished the burn all the way to his stomach. He looked around the economy motel room. While the place wasn't a "Roach-Way Inn" by any means, it was a far cry from the five-star hotels in which he and Penny had stayed when he and Chrissy were married. His Rolls-Royce, parked at the curb, was as out of place as his Rolex.

"Oh, I have to go." Penny's urgent whisper barely preceded her abruptly ending the call. Brent laid his cell phone aside and enjoyed another nip of rum. Most of their phone conversations ended like this one. Penny sporadically talked to him in a rush. But one way or another, they were keeping each other posted as they progressed in the plan they'd dubbed, "Dupe the Eltons."

Twenty-Seven

Before Brent arrived, Allie managed to dress in jeans and a denim jacket, as well as apply a generous layer of makeup. She put on more Mary Kay than usual in hopes of hiding the ravages of the day-long tears. But now that the date with Brent was ending, Allie wondered if she'd put too much effort in. While Brent hadn't blatantly ogled her, the male appreciation in his eyes made her squirm. Even during the movie, she'd sensed his occasional glances. And he'd not hesitated to tell her how great she looked the second he saw her.

As they pulled up in the guesthouse driveway, Allie felt his stare once more. The Rolls-Royce purred to a luxurious stop behind her Mercedes, and she detected Brent's anticipation. He wanted her to ask him in. But all Allie wanted was to crawl under the covers and cry some more. Everything tonight had reminded Allie of Frederick. Even Brent's telling her she was pretty brought back memories of Frederick's saying, "All hail Mary Kay." Tomorrow she planned to pack and head to Aunt Landon's for a while. The sooner she went to sleep, the sooner tomorrow arrived.

Before Allie could piece together a polite rejection, Brent was opening her door and helping her from the vehicle's supple leather and into the cool, spring night. The stars shone as vibrantly as the night Frederick had kissed Allie's hand. The owl sang his usual beat. The yardman had mowed today, and the night smelled of freshly cut grass. Allie remembered a time when Frederick was their yardman—ten years ago, but it seemed like yesterday.

"You said you'd show me your email program," Brent said with an eager smile. "I'm totally intrigued by that duck." Allie focused on Brent and tried to blot Frederick's dark hair and eyes and commanding height from her mind. By sheer willpower, Allie was able to focus on Brent, and she had to admit that the man *was* attractive. His pale green eyes and sandy hair had snared Evelyn's fancy for a reason. Furthermore, he had been the consummate gentleman all evening. He deserved more than her distracted attention. Nevertheless, Allie hesitated about inviting a man into her home . . . alone.

"You know . . ." Allie hedged, "I normally don't have men in when I'm alone."

"Of course," Brent said with an assuring grin. "Normally I wouldn't invite myself in like this, and I certainly don't entertain women at my place alone." The full moon highlighted the sincerity in his eyes. "But the way I see it, we've known each other for years. You were my cousin-in-law when I was married to Chrissy. So we're as good as family. And I *do* want to see that duck." He leaned forward and smiled like a child eager for a new toy.

"Well . . ." Allie said as her anxiety eased. Brent seemed like the decent sort, and even though he'd certainly appreciated her beauty, he hadn't even offered to hold her hand, let alone threatened to violate her. "I guess it wouldn't hurt just this once," she agreed. He *did* have a good point. They'd known each other for years. He'd been married to her cousin. It wasn't like Brent was a total stranger she couldn't trust.

Like a true gentleman, he walked beside her to the front porch and kept a respectable distance. By the time Allie opened the front door and entered, she'd convinced herself that Brent would maintain the same gentlemanly manner he'd manifested all evening. She'd show him the duck and tell him how to get his own email program just like hers. They'd share a handshake. He would leave.

Allie walked toward the kitchen and tossed her purse on the service bar. "My laptop is in my bedroom," she said over her shoulder. "Make yourself comfortable. I'll be right back."

She hurried through the kitchen and dubiously eyed the pet flap at the bottom of the back door. So far the latch was still in place and there was no sign of her ring-tailed visitor. Nonetheless, Allie had placed all her food in the upper cabinets, just in case the critter made another appearance.

Allie stepped into her bedroom, hurried toward the night-stand, and picked up the laptop. When she rounded the end of the bed and looked up, she noticed someone in her doorway. Allie jumped and squealed before she realized the person was Brent.

"Hey, it's just me." Brent lifted both hands, palms outward.

"Oh!" An uneasy doubt attacked Allie. She gripped her laptop and wondered if she'd grossly misjudged Brent. Dressed in a polo shirt and a pair of perfectly faded designer jeans, he looked like a next-door neighbor you'd trust with your kid sister. Nevertheless, Allie couldn't shake the unease . . . or the daunting awareness that he'd followed her to her bedroom.

"Didn't you tell me to come in here with you?" he asked and raised his brows.

"No." Allie shook her head. "I asked you to make yourself comfortable in the living room."

Brent's eyes widened. "My word, I'm so sorry," he apologized. "What must you think? I thought your laptop was back here and so . . ." He helplessly shrugged.

"It's okay. Really," Allie said, and her tension eased.

"Look, I can tell you aren't comfortable. Why don't I just go home for tonight. You can show me the email program another time. I'd *die* before I'd make you feel—"

"It's quite all right," Allie rushed and walked toward the hallway. The last thing she wanted was to leave him a reason for another visit. He stepped aside and allowed her to pass. "I'm on edge tonight anyway." She glanced behind and saw that he was close. "Let's just go back to the living room."

"Works for me if it works for you," Brent replied.

Her heels tapped across the tile in sequence with his loafers, and the two made their way into the living room. Deciding to keep this as businesslike as possible, Allie settled onto the sofa, pushed aside the potpourri dish, and placed the laptop on the coffee table.

"This is actually an email manager program, and you can choose from all sorts of notifiers," she said, and turned on the computer. "There's a butler, a dog, a bouncy ball, a flower, an actual mailbox, and all sorts of other things. In fact, if you'll give me your email address, I'll send you the link."

Brent told her his address. When Allie looked at him, his focus was intent on her. In this dim lighting, his pale green eyes looked sharper than they had tonight, and the distrust teased her mind anew.

She vaguely smiled and prayed he didn't ask her out again. Allie had never been so ready to see a person leave. Attractive as he might be, Brent's main flaw was that of every other man who'd pursued Allie. He wasn't Frederick Wently. When she looked back into his eyes, the sharpness was gone. Nothing remained but a genteel respect, and Allie decided she must have projected her worries upon the poor man . . . all because he wasn't Frederick. Her eyes burned, and she forced herself to swallow the burst of tears that threatened a fresh eruption.

Allie clicked on the email icon and prepared for the short wait until the program opened. She noted the time in the lower right corner of her laptop—nine-thirty. An unexpected yawn attacked her, and she politely covered it.

"Sorry," she said through a grin. "I didn't sleep well last night."

"I feel your pain," Brent said and yawned himself. "Here I go, too. I guess it's catching."

"I guess," Allie replied and hoped he didn't stay much longer.

Just as the email program opened, a firm knock sounded at her door. Allie jerked her gaze toward it. "Who could that be at this hour?" she mumbled and then wondered if her sister had seen Brent's car and sent Charlie to check on her. It wouldn't be the first time Macy hid her nosiness behind the pretense of caring.

"Want me to get it?" Brent asked and scooted to the edge of the seat.

Allie nearly declined his offer but considered the alternative of leaving Brent with her opened email program. She did not want to return to the computer to find that he'd read her private correspondence.

"Sure," she said and decided to send Brent the promised email that would give him the link to the email manager. She clicked on the line to the left that read, "Tell a Friend," and heard a muffled male voice ask if she was home.

"Of course," Brent responded. "She's right here."

Fully expecting Charlie, Allie glanced up from the laptop as Frederick stepped into the room.

"Frederick!" she gasped.

"Allie." His mouth hard, he nodded and shot a barely civilized greeting toward Brent.

Allie stood and smoothed her hands along the front of her jacket. "Louise! Is she—"

"Everyone wondered where you've been all day," he snapped, his dark eyes hostile.

"I . . . I . . . I . . ." Allie groped for words and found none. She'd been so distressed over her own pain, she hadn't imagined going to see Louise. That, plus trying to deal with Brent, had left Allie distracted to the point of irresponsibility. When the phone rang midafternoon, she had decided the caller must be Macy, asking her to pick up Barry and Bart. Allie hadn't even answered the phone. She'd felt a twinge of guilt over that.

Now the weight of not even checking on Louise hung around her neck like a yoke of accusation. All she could imagine was how insensitive and uncaring she must look to the whole family. But then, no one had left a voice mail about Louise, so she had assumed everything was the same with her.

Frederick eyed Brent again and then gazed back at Allie. "You don't look like you're worried about Louise in the least," he accused, and she noted that his rumpled T-shirt and jeans were yesterday's.

Allie stiffened. "What exactly did you want me to do?"

"Oh, I don't know, Allie." He waved his hand. "Maybe call! Maybe just ask if she lived through the night!"

Her heart pounded and Allie forgot to breathe. "Is she— did she—"

"No!" Frederick replied and shook his head. "She's fine. I guess as fine as someone paralyzed from the neck down can be." He rubbed his face with both hands. When he pulled his hands away Allie noticed just how haggard he appeared. If Frederick got any sleep at all last night, he didn't show it.

"I—we—I drove Mr. and Mrs. Grove home to get some sleep. We're going to take some of her things to her in the morning. If she continues to improve, they'll move her out of ICU tomorrow."

"So she's improving?" Allie asked.

"Yes. I said she was still paralyzed from her neck down, but technically that's wrong now. She's actually regaining some movement in her arms and fingers."

"Really? That's great!" Allie said and genuinely meant it. As much as losing Frederick hurt, Allie still couldn't wish ill upon one so young and so alive.

"Yeah." Frederick gazed past Allie. "The doctors are saying the legs are another matter. That might never happen."

"Oh." Allie crossed her arms, hugged herself, and stared at the laptop.

"Well, I'm sorry to interrupt you," Frederick stated, his words stilted. "I—we were all concerned about you, but I can see we shouldn't have been." A new thrust of accusation hurled his words straight into her heart.

Her legs shaking, Allie tightened her self-hug and didn't even look at Frederick. When the door banged shut, she looked up. He was gone. Despite Brent's presence, Allie could hold her emotions no longer. A sob tore from her throat. She covered her face and collapsed onto the couch.

Muttering an oath, Brent plopped beside Allie and gently patted her shoulder. Somehow that gentle pat grew into a full-blown hug, and she was crying in his arms.

"That jerk!" Brent muttered. "If you want me to, I'll chase him down and—"

"Nooooooo!" Allie wailed. "It's okay! Reeeeaaaallllly!"

"Yeah, it looks okay to me," Brent growled. "He had no right!"

"But I should have at least—at least called today, and I-I-I didn't!" Allie hiccoughed and inched away from Brent.

"Here, darling," he said and Allie accepted the wad of tissue he offered. After a few blinks, she recognized the Kleenex box from the end table.

"This has been the worst day ever!" she wailed.

"And all because of that creep, right?"

When Allie didn't answer, he continued, "What has he done to you, Allie? He didn't . . . *hurt* you in any way, did he?"

Allie looked up to see a protective light in Brent's eyes she never expected. "No." She shook her head. "Not unless you count my heart," she blurted and realized she'd said too much. Allie jumped up and balled her fists. "Brent, I don't mean to be rude," she stammered, "but I really need some—some time alone."

"Of course you do, sweetheart," he crooned and stood. "I totally understand. I'll just talk to you about the email later." Brent wrapped his arms around her again for a brief hug before placing a gentle kiss on her forehead and then on her cheek.

In her weakened state, Allie didn't have the strength to resist when he finished with a lingering brush of his lips against hers. "I'll be here for you, honey," he breathed against her ear. "Just call me anytime, you hear?"

Despite her overwrought emotions, Allie's feminine alarm system swung to full operation. Keeping her head lowered, she stiffened and backed away.

"I'll just let myself out, okay?" Brent purred and squeezed her hand.

Allie nodded.

"But if you need someone to talk to in the night," he lifted her chin and bathed her in an adoring gaze, "you call me."

She nodded again, barely comprehending his words.

"It's a deal, then," he said before stepping through the front door.

The second the door clicked shut, Allie hurried forward, turned the deadbolt, and stumbled back to the sofa. She flung herself against the pile of pillows and allowed her emotions to flow. This time she was as genuinely ashamed of herself as she was hurt by Frederick.

To some degree, Frederick's exasperation was warranted. Allie hadn't done anything all day long but lounge around, cry, sleep, and lick her wounds. This morning, she couldn't even talk herself into pitying Louise. She pictured the young woman strapped to a wheelchair for life and tried to imagine how she would feel if she were paralyzed. The panic. The anger. The desperation.

"Oh, God," Allie groaned and buried her face into a pillow, "please forgive me for being so selfish. I've thought of no one but myself. I'm not the only one who's been hurt here. Please, Lord, please help Louise . . . and help Frederick help her." Allie dug her fingers into the pillow and wondered if she'd survive losing him a second time.

Frederick ran toward the bridge that spanned the creek between the guesthouse and the Groveses' mansion. When his boots slammed into the wooden floor, the narrow bridge shivered. Gulping for air, he slowed to a stop. He grabbed the handrail, doubled over it, and stared into the stream merrily jogging among the rocks. The full moon cast gold dust upon the wavelets, and the water looked warm and inviting. But when Louise had talked Frederick into wading a few days ago, he'd learned the inches-deep water was anything but warm and inviting.

A chill started in Frederick's soul and shook his body. He looked toward the guesthouse, whose lights were visible through the maples and oaks lining the creek. When he'd seen the Rolls-Royce in Allie's driveway, he'd suspected the vehicle belonged to Landon Russ. Frederick recalled that she'd driven a Rolls years ago. He'd never forget the times she stepped out of the luxury car and barely acknowledged him in the mansion's yard.

Even though Frederick believed he'd have to face Landon, he wanted to see Allie badly enough to put up with her snobby aunt. He'd been overcome with the need to explain everything and prayed Allie would understand. As he knocked on the door, Frederick had convinced himself that maybe Landon was spending the night, had already gone to bed, and Allie would be up alone. Then Brent Everson answered the door, and Frederick had never been so disgusted to see that church wolf. From there, the whole thing went sour.

Frederick straightened and rubbed his face. He writhed in the memory of his accusations and wouldn't blame Allie if she never spoke to him again. There wasn't a kinder soul on the planet, and he understood her need for some space from Louise.

"I'd feel the same way," he admitted and wondered what had possessed him. One word surfaced in his mind: *jealousy*. Even though he'd chosen to marry Louise, he still didn't want anyone else to have Allie—especially not Brent.

He looked toward the Grove mansion, in full view from the bridge. Inside, a grief-stricken set of parents had already declared him a saint and vowed their undying loyalty. He was dubbed a hero by the national press after he returned from the war. But the one person who mattered most probably thought he was a cad right now. He rested his elbows on the railing and stared into the gold-lined water.

Fleetingly, Frederick thought of throwing himself off the bridge and drowning. Then he reminded himself that the water was only inches deep, and he'd have to find a spot between the rocks to immerse his nose and mouth. Somehow drowning lost its theatrical appeal when the victim had to work to die.

His chuckle was involuntary . . . so was his eyes' stinging. Frederick clenched his teeth and rammed his fist against the handrail. He bolted toward the guesthouse, but stopped as abruptly as he began. Whirling back around, Frederick faced the mansion. The lighted yard and balcony implied that all was well; the owl's soul-chilling hoots belied the light and echoed through the night like an omen of doom. Frederick pressed the heels of his hands against his temples and swallowed the agonized cry swelling from his spirit.

"Oh, God!" he cried and fell to his hands and knees. "Oh, dear God!" The grass's cold dampness seeped between his fingers. *What have I done? What am I doing? Is it the right thing?* "Jesus . . . help me!" he groaned. Frederick rolled to his side and then to his back. He pulled his knees up and rested his feet against the earth at an angle that ended the twinge of pain in his lower back. He stared at the black sky full of stars and the moon's satin glow. Warm tears silently flowed down his temples and trickled to his ears until Frederick no longer saw the stars or the moon. All he could see was the darkness.

Twenty-Eight

"What are you doing?" Macy's question exploded upon Allie and shattered the focus she'd maintained all morning. One mission and one mission alone had driven her since she awoke at seven: Get packed and get away from Grove Acres.

Allie observed her sister. Arms folded, Macy stood on the edge of her yard. Her silent accusation reminded Allie of a five-year-old who's mad because her elder sister is going away to college and leaving her stranded.

"I'm going to stay with Aunt Landon for a while," Allie replied and dropped the last duffle bag into the opened trunk.

"You mean you're leaving for good?" Macy's canvas shoes crunched along the graveled drive until she stopped within feet of Allie.

"Yes. For now." Allie refused to show even a little doubt. Macy could fall into a pity party and pouting session that had a way of changing the stoniest of hearts.

"Weren't you even going to say good-bye?" Macy's voice broke, and she raised her hands.

"Of course," Allie said, keeping her tone as practical as possible. "I was just getting my car loaded first." She pointed to the trunk full of her belongings. "Just so you know, I left a few things in the freezer. I tried to get everything, but I'm out of room in the cooler." She pointed to the ice chest.

"Why are you leaving?" Macy pressed, her words now steady.

"I just need a change of scenery," Allie replied, and glanced toward the guesthouse. When she'd arrived here weeks ago, Allie had welcomed nature's haven. Now she couldn't get away fast enough.

"But who's going to be here to pick up the boys if I've got a headache or I'm sick?"

Allie's gaze flicked over Macy in her white shorts and red-striped sweater. The red sandals finished off an outfit that heightened Macy's color, brought out the highlights in her hair, and made her look like the picture of health.

"I don't know," Allie said. "Who picked them up before I came? Martha?"

"Sometimes," Macy said. "But she isn't here right now because of Louise. I had to go pick them up yesterday. Where were you, anyway? I tried to call you. Your car was here, but . . ."

"I was here," Allie admitted and shut the Mercedes' trunk. "I just wasn't taking any calls."

"Oh. Well," Macy snapped. "Isn't that convenient!"

Not as convenient as a perpetual headache, Allie thought but didn't vocalize her remark. She pulled a tissue from the pocket of her linen shorts and dabbed at the perspiration along her forehead. The sun burned high and promised today would offer a preview of the coming summer. All cool spring breezes were off.

Allie marched toward the porch to retrieve her final bag. Macy followed.

"Just so you know, I sent some flowers to Louise this morning," Allie said. "I called and they said she'd been moved from ICU and could receive flowers now."

"I know—I mean about her being moved from ICU," Macy said. "She's doing better, but we're all still really worried about her. Charlie's there now. He spent last night up there. I stayed home and got the kids off to school. We're going to take turns spending the day with her. Tomorrow will be my day."

"Great!" Allie picked up the makeup case and didn't express how glad she was that Macy was thinking of someone else and actually taking her sons to school. Usually Charlie dropped them off, and Macy foisted pick-up duties onto whoever was available.

"I'm sure Louise is thankful to have such strong support," Allie said, her words stilted.

"Yes. We all want to be there for her." Macy eyed Allie, who looked away. "Frederick's been a lifesaver. He's been up there most of the time, too. But he drove the Groves back home last night, and they went back to Atlanta this morning. The doctor says they might be able to move her to a hospital here in Macon in a few days."

"Great!" Allie repeated and walked toward her vehicle. The way the conversation was going, Allie wouldn't be surprised if Macy announced that Frederick and Louise had set the date for their wedding.

Macy matched Allie's swift pace. "You're leaving because of Frederick, aren't you?" she asked.

Keeping her head bent, Allie hid her shock and refused to acknowledge the question.

"I don't know what was going on with you two, but it looked to me like you were getting awfully cozy. Then Louise breaks her neck and Frederick is suddenly devoted to *her*."

Halting, Allie looked Macy in the eyes and stated the facts before she even realized what was spilling from her mouth.

"If you want the truth, Macy, Frederick and I nearly got married ten years ago."

Macy's mouth dropped open.

"And, yes, we were on the verge of getting back together, and yes, his engagement to Louise is the reason I want to get away from here. Happy now?" she challenged.

Macy stared at her sister. Allie held her gaze and didn't blink.

"You're not yourself," Macy blurted. "I've never seen you like this! What's gotten into you?"

Striding the few feet to her vehicle, Allie doubted the wisdom of telling Macy everything. But she'd released the unadulterated truth, and it was too late. No telling who all Macy would tell or how long it would take for Louise to find out.

Allie swung around and nearly bumped into her sister. "I shouldn't have said all that," she admitted. "Promise me you won't repeat it."

"I promise." Macy looked like she was in court, pledging to solemnly tell the truth, the whole truth, and nothing but.

Oddly, Allie believed she really meant her promise. The fact that Macy had told no one—not even Charlie—about the Eltons' financial crisis added to Allie's optimism.

"Good," she affirmed and walked to her Mercedes. "Because I'm really not doing well." Allie opened the back door and set the case on the seat near the piles of luggage.

Her eyes threatened to go teary, but Allie refused. She'd cried herself to sleep two nights in a row. Her forehead and teeth hurt because of the pressure on her sinuses. Allie had taken a non-drowsy antihistamine and a couple of aspirin that were just now taking effect. Unfortunately, there was no pill for her heartache, and Allie hoped she could maintain her wits enough to concentrate on driving.

She closed the back car door and opened the front one. After retrieving her purse from the driver's seat, she dug out the keys and pitched her bag into the passenger seat.

"You aren't even going to say good-bye to the boys?" Macy asked, her voice wobbly again.

Allie rested her forehead on the top of the open door and gripped the side. "Yes. I had planned to come see you now and tell you I was leaving. Then I was going to see if it was okay if I took Barry and Bart to lunch—if the school would let them go. If they couldn't leave campus, I was going to go pick up a pizza and surprise them at school."

"Oh," Macy replied. "Of course the school will let them go for something special like this—especially if I call ahead or go with you." Macy checked her watch. "It's eleven," she said. "They don't have lunch for another hour, but if I went I'm sure I could get permission for them to go now and take a long lunch." The pregnant request hung between them.

"Want to go with me, then?" Somehow Allie managed a genuine smile.

Macy brightened and nodded. "Sure!"

"Well, go ahead and get in." She pointed toward the passenger side.

"Okay, but can you drive me back home quick to get my purse?" Macy asked as she rounded the car.

"Of course."

Even though Macy could be trying, she was still Allie's little sister, and Allie was beginning to think she might miss her. She settled behind the wheel and gazed at the pine guesthouse. The place looked like it came out of a brochure for a Swiss resort, and she realized she'd miss the house, too.

The invader coon waddled through her mind and Allie chuckled.

"What's so funny?" Macy asked as she moved Allie's purse from the passenger seat to the console and plopped into the car.

"You need to get someone to fix the pet flap on the guesthouse's back door," she explained. "There's a coon that keeps getting into the house."

"Oh my word!" Macy slammed the passenger door. "Did he come in on you?"

"Yes. Ate my Cheerios and my cornflakes." Allie nodded.

Macy squealed and covered her mouth, her eyes bulging. "That is *too funny!*"

Allie laughed. "Yeah, I guess it is now. But at the time it was highly exasperating. The thing is like a big rat with lots of fur."

"Stop it!" Macy wheezed. She rapidly stomped her feet and cackled.

Cranking the ignition, Allie looked at her sister and caught a glimpse of the carefree little girl Macy once had been. But she hadn't been the same since their mother's death, and Allie wondered if she'd ever gotten over that shock. In some ways Macy seemed frozen at age twelve.

Looking back, Allie suspected that Macy's getting married so young might have been linked to the death of their mom. From the time Charlie Grove took an interest in Macy, his mother had lavishly pampered her. She still did. Allie couldn't remember a time when Martha had ever voiced a negative remark about Macy except in regard to the way she and Charlie handled the twins. And that was usually so subtle Macy had no clue that her mother-in-law disapproved of her. Martha had become the mother Macy so desperately needed, and Charlie Grove was a ticket to having that need met.

As this reality settled upon Allie, she focused on the guesthouse porch and wondered about her own life . . . her own choices . . . and how her mother's early death had affected her. In seconds, Allie felt as if God had placed a mirror in front of her soul and bade her to look closely. What Allie saw took her breath.

I'm thirty-five, she thought, *and I've never been my own woman because . . . because . . .* She groped for the underlying reason and finally stumbled upon a theory. *Because I'm scared to death to go against my family because I'm afraid I'll lose them just like I lost Mom.*

But do I even have them? she wondered. Her dad and Evelyn had only emailed once the whole time she'd been in Macon. Aunt Landon was the one family member Allie could always depend upon, and she'd even hinted about disinheriting Allie if she got too involved with Frederick.

Allie curled her toes, concentrated hard, and begged the Lord for more insight. *So I've let them make my decisions,* she thought. *I didn't marry Frederick ten years ago because of Aunt Landon. Even though I've wanted a career for years, I haven't gotten a job because Dad doesn't believe an Elton should work.*

I came here because Dad and Evelyn would rather go to the beach than deal with Macy in her sick mode. Of course, they didn't seem to care what I wanted to do. They never do. Fleetingly, Allie wondered if Macy felt the same. If so, perhaps that was the root of her perpetual illnesses. In order to get some love and support, she concocted all sorts of physical problems just as Allie played the part of the family mouse in order to please everyone.

Closing her puffy eyes, Allie groaned. *Sarah Hamilton is more of a sister to me than either Evelyn or Macy,* she thought and relived the supportive phone call Sarah had placed this morning. She hadn't read Allie's email about Frederick's marrying Louise until she went to the office, and Sarah had stopped her whole schedule to place an emergency call to her friend. She'd been loving, supportive, and had insisted that Allie plan a long visit at her place in Atlanta. Allie had agreed.

"Allie?" Macy touched her shoulder. "Are you all right?"

Allie opened her eyes, propped her head against the head-rest, and gazed at her sister. "No, I'm not," she said. "And I don't think I've been okay since Mom died, really."

Macy looked down, picked at her thumbnail. "Why'd you have to bring that up? We were laughing and having a good time."

"Maybe because it's *time* we bring that up," Allie responded, "and bring it up regularly." She flipped on the air conditioner and enjoyed the blast of cooler air. The car was getting stuffy.

Averting her gaze out the window, Macy said, "I'd rather not."

"I know. But I don't think any of us is going to come to terms with it until we start talking it through."

Macy's only response was clenching her hands into a tight ball.

Allie covered Macy's fists with her fingers and squeezed. "I love you, Macy," she whispered. "And I don't think I say it enough."

Her eyes watery, Macy turned toward her sister. "I love you, too," she responded. "And I'm going to miss you s-so bad."

"I know . . . I know," Allie soothed and pulled Macy into her arms. She rested her head against Macy's and tried to sound cheerful when she said, "Hey! Why don't you bring the twins up and spend a weekend or two with me and Aunt Landon? Who knows, I might get really wild and get a job and a townhouse. Then you could come up every weekend if you wanted."

Macy laughed out loud and pulled away. "That's the most

hilarious thing I've ever heard," she said and rubbed at her damp cheeks. "Dad would never let you do that! You're an Elton, remember? Eltons don't work," she added, mimicking their father's tone syllable for syllable.

"Maybe it's time one does," Allie responded and gazed past Macy toward the rose garden, now in full bloom.

"You're serious?" Macy prompted.

"Maybe." Allie ran her fingertips along the top of the floor gearshift covered in leather. "What happens if this whole plan to save the estate fails and we have to file for bankruptcy?" Allie asked. "I'd feel much better if I was already supporting myself."

"Why don't you do what I did and marry somebody with money?" Macy snapped her fingers as if she were a magician calling a rich bachelor into existence.

"You're starting to sound like Aunt Landon," Allie replied.

"What about Brent Everson?" Macy asked. "He couldn't stop looking at you Sunday. He's driving a Rolls, and you know Chrissy was loaded when she died. He's probably making salads out of hundred-dollar-bills these days."

"No." Allie shook her head.

"Really? I thought I saw his car over here last night." Macy toyed with her seat belt.

"You did. But he's not the one." Although her tone was soft, Allie laced it with strong resolve.

And Macy didn't push the subject. Instead she said, "But you've got your trust fund still, don't you? You could live off that interest."

Allie examined the car's radio. Sarah's trip through medical school had put a huge dent in her trust fund. The interest on her investments would help pad her earnings and nothing more. Presently, Allie was allowing the interest to stay within her investment account while she lived off the Elton allowance.

"You *do* still have your trust fund, don't you?" Macy asked, her eyes dubious.

"Since we're getting so honest here, I might as well tell you. . . ." Allie sighed. "I helped pay Sarah Hamilton's way through med school and, well, a couple of other students, too."

"What?!"

"Yes." Allie nodded. "Nobody knows. Not even Sarah. So *please.*" Allie gripped Macy's arm. "*Please* don't tell anyone this, either, okay?"

"So is it, like, all gone?" Macy pulled on a strand of her hair.

"No." Allie shook her head. "I've still got some of it. Just not what you or Evelyn have—unless Evelyn's already blown hers."

"I haven't even *touched* mine!" Macy asserted and released the lock of hair.

Allie laughed at the irony. She'd have figured Macy's trust fund was history by now.

"What's so funny?" Macy raised her brows.

"Oh, nothing." Allie put the engine in reverse. "Enough about all my problems. Let's go get your purse and see my nephews, okay?" she said and hoped the visit with them went as well as her chat with Macy.

Twenty-Nine

A week later, Allie stooped over Aunt Landon's flowerbed, trying to decide if she should add a row of geraniums or ferns next in the huge circular bed. A flat of each of the plants rested near her feet. Even though her aunt had a yardman, Allie had been eager to dig her hands into some project that would help get her mind off of Frederick and Louise. Carving out a new flowerbed started with a garden tiller three days ago and had kept her busy.

Unfortunately nothing seemed able to stop her thinking about Frederick. At least she *had* stopped crying, but the emptiness remained. Allie felt as if she'd been given a glimpse of heaven, only to have it snatched away.

She hiked up her baggy work jeans, dropped to her knees, and decided the ferns were next. They'd be a perfect balance between the geraniums and azaleas that served as the focal point around the birdbath in the center. The earth smelled great and felt just as good against her fingers. She'd added peat moss, and the rich black mixture mingled with brown earth for a combination high in nutrients. Noticing a cracked nail and marred manicure, Allie came close to regretting her decision not to use gloves. But then she wouldn't feel the dirt, and she so enjoyed that connection with nature.

Deciding manicures were made to be repaired, Allie picked

up her miniature spade and began tackling the soil. On her third overturn, a bumblebee zoomed by her ear. Allie jumped back. When the winged bomb targeted her for another swoop, she swung her spade at him and jumped to her feet. Her left leg protested the swift movement, and Allie shifted her weight to the right.

Aunt Landon had given her some body lotion, and Allie lavished her skin with it this morning. Even though she looked like a bum, Allie wanted to at least smell good. When the bee arrived for another round, she wondered if he thought she was a potential pollen factory.

"Yoo-hoo! Allie dear!" Aunt Landon's high-pitched call stopped Allie on the verge of all-out war.

She pivoted to face her aunt, who was exiting the home's sunroom. The moderate-sized house featured all the latest in modern architecture and bespoke taste, class, and money. The large sunroom, replete with floor-to-ceiling windows, offered a perfect view of anyone inside. Allie spotted an "anyone" whom she never expected.

Brent Everson followed Landon from the sunroom into the yard. *Oh no!* Allie thought, and she was so distraught she ignored the bee as it hummed closer.

"There's a *wonderful* young man who's come to see you!" Beaming, Landon stopped on the edge of the circle and lifted her hand toward Brent as if he were royalty. "I had just let Tiffany in when I saw the most gorgeous Rolls-Royce driving up, and wouldn't you know, Prince Charming got out!"

His ever-deepening tan made his hair's blond streaks appear even blonder. The sand-colored shorts and white polo shirt heightened the effect. And Allie didn't have to wonder why Aunt Landon smiled like a cat who'd captured the most succulent mouse on the planet.

"We've already been chatting for absolutely ages!" Landon said. "At first I didn't remember him, and then he reminded me he once dated Evelyn. I can't believe how long it's been since we've seen each other!" Landon laid her diamond-crusted hand upon her chest and fluttered her eyelashes at Brent. Allie wondered if her aunt might like him for herself, even though he was about ten years younger.

"And I must say," Brent purred, "you've never looked younger or more beautiful."

Oh brother! Allie thought and narrowed her eyes. While Aunt Landon was an absolute fashion plate in her linen capris and gold sandals, Allie recognized thick flattery. And Brent was laying it on.

His satisfied smile was miles removed from the "mourning widower" image he'd portrayed in Macon. Today Brent reminded Allie more of a pampered sheik. She thought of Jim Bennington. Allie hadn't heard from him since the night Louise broke her neck. She fully believed that Jim was indeed grieving the loss of his beloved, but a new series of doubts popped up regarding Brent.

When Brent turned his attention back to Allie, his smile morphed into gaping horror.

A shock of alarm flashed through Allie. She looked around, fully expecting a monstrous viper or some other evil beast that would invoke Brent's reaction.

"Be still, Allie!" Brent bellowed and lunged forward.

Allie stiffened. Her eyes wide, she braced herself against Brent's attack. Waving wildly, the man went for her head, and Allie stumbled back.

"Bee!" Brent screamed.

Her canvas shoe caught on a flat of plants, and Allie tripped backward. Arms flailing, she plopped onto the dirt, bottom first. Her teeth jarred against each other. When she looked up, Brent hovered over her.

"There was this huge bumblebee sitting on your head," he panted.

A nearing buzz announced the flower seeker was zooming in for another look.

"Here he comes again!" Brent shrieked. He snatched up Allie's garden spade and charged the bee.

"Why don't we just go in?" Landon suggested.

"I think he likes my body lotion." Allie hoisted herself up. Brent swatted at the bee while Allie hustled toward the sunroom, brushing the soil from her seat with every step. "I'm going to have to remember not to use that stuff when I'm working outside. It's lethal!"

Laughing, Landon followed Allie inside.

Like a combat soldier with a machete, Brent backed toward the door, the spade held in both hands.

Allie nearly laughed out loud at his stance until the guy whipped around and ducked inside. His ashen face suggested he'd been fighting a livid cobra.

"Oh my word," he said and grabbed Allie by the shoulders. "Are you okay? Did that thing sting you?"

"No, not at all," Allie said and waved aside his bizarre concern.

"Thank God," Brent breathed, his eyes rolling shut. "I promise, I thought I was having a flashback to Chrissy." His lips shook, and Allie realized the man was genuinely disturbed. The mourning widower was back, and Allie was driven to a supportive response.

"I'm so sorry," she whispered and covered his hand with hers. "Look, sit here." She tugged him to the wicker settee and glanced toward her aunt. "Maybe a glass of iced tea?" she prompted.

"Of course!" Landon agreed, her face full of questions and curiosity. She got up and headed toward the kitchen.

Brent dropped into a chair, propped his elbows on his knees, and covered his face with his hands. "All I could see was you being *swarmed* by those things. I flashed back to Chrissy." He shivered. "She was so covered in stings her eyes swelled shut."

"I'm okay," Allie soothed and knelt next to him. While she already knew the history of Chrissy's death, she figured it did Brent good to vent some, especially after such a scare. Allie also repented of her judgmental thoughts from moments ago. Even if he had acted like a satisfied sheik, Aunt Landon was treating him like he *should* act that way.

"Really, bumblebees have never scared me that much," Allie said and tried a cheerful smile. "They're more annoying than anything else."

"A bee is a bee in my book," Brent said.

Landon breezed into the sunroom. "Here's some tea for everyone," she chirped and set the bamboo service tray on the wicker coffee table. "The cook left us with a full pitcher of mango madness last night. That ought to liven us up." She wiggled her brows, and Allie smiled a bit.

Brent chuckled. "I've had about all the liveliness I can stand for a while."

"I'm just going to step into the bathroom and wash my hands now," Allie said and lifted her dirt-smudged fingers.

"Please do, dear," Landon admonished. "Why you refuse to wear gardening gloves is anybody's guess."

Allie didn't bother to tell her aunt how much she enjoyed the feel of dirt. She'd already told her dozens of times to no avail.

As Allie walked away, Landon was using silver tongs to

grab ice cubes from the bucket and plunk them into the tall, crystal tumblers. After a quick hand-scrub and change into clean clothes, Allie settled into the corner chair near Brent and sipped her mango madness, glad for the break. Even though the morning was cool, she'd nearly worked herself into a fit of perspiration before the bee attack.

"I'm sorry I went ballistic out there," Brent said, his gaze taking in first Allie and then Landon. "Did you know my first wife was killed by a swarm of killer bees?"

"You're kidding!" Landon exclaimed.

"No." Brent's expression was as serious as the day of the funeral. "Any time I see a bee, I see death, more or less."

"I am *so sorry*," Landon crooned. "You know, now that I'm thinking about it, I believe I do remember Allie going to that funeral a couple of years ago, but I didn't connect it to you."

"Yes," Brent replied. "Chrissy was my wife."

"My cousin," Allie supplied and followed with a long swallow of the honey-laden liquid. "Dad's brother's daughter."

"Right." Landon nodded. "I remember everything now. I even thought about going to that funeral, but I'd already bought my plane ticket for my trip to Canada." She crossed her legs, rested her elbow on her chair's armrest, and leaned toward Brent. "I have a good friend who lives there."

Brent nodded and sipped his sweet tea. As the chitchat continued, he tried to get control of himself. He couldn't keep his tea glass from trembling as fiercely as his legs. He'd nearly had a stroke when he saw that huge bee sitting on Allie's head like it was staking territory. All he could see was a Chrissy repeat and Allie's millions being snatched from his grasp. Of course, if she were attacked by bees after their wedding, then Brent would be less worried. At least he'd get some of what she was worth at her death, just as he had with Chrissy.

He attempted a smile at Landon, who wasn't bad to look at herself. She had that spoiled-rich-lady appeal that Brent could spot ten miles away. Her pale hair was perfectly highlighted, her makeup immaculate. Her fingernails bore a flawless French manicure with toenails to match. And Brent decided if he totally failed with Allie, he might place Landon as the next attempt on his list. She had to be at least a decade older than he. But Brent wouldn't have cared if she were *two* decades older, as long as she had plenty of green. That color had such a way of softening a woman's age.

A black Persian cat strolled into the sunroom and rubbed her body against a ficus tree's brass pot. After a pitiful meow, the creature twined her way toward Landon, who set her tea on the Italian tile and scooped up the feline.

"There you are, you sweet darlin'," Landon crooned and scratched the cat's neck. "How's Mama's baby?"

That's when Brent spotted the thin cat collar studded in diamonds. He sputtered through a swallow of tea and nearly choked.

"Are you okay?" Allie asked.

Hacking, Brent nodded and wheezed "Yes," while adding Landon Russ to his list of definite matrimonial candidates. But first he needed to concentrate on snaring Allie. Today she wore no makeup but still had a sun-kissed appeal that wasn't half bad. Of course, she could have warts on her nose and purple skin and Brent would have thought she was beautiful. Any woman as rich as an Elton was a supermodel to him.

After draining his tea glass, Brent set it on the coffee table and smiled toward Allie. "Actually, the reason I came was to ask you to lunch."

"Oh!" Allie said and gazed toward her aunt.

"What are you looking at me for?" Landon encouraged while stroking the cat. "Go get ready. The man wants to take you to lunch!" She aimed a sassy wink at Brent.

He winked back.

"But I was going to change clothes and finish the flower-bed," Allie protested and avoided eye contact with Brent.

"Oh nonsense!" Landon waved aside the whole protest. "That's what yardmen are for. Let John battle the bees. Go on and enjoy yourself. It'll do you good!"

"Well . . ." Allie hedged and looked down.

Even though she'd kept him at arm's length during their last date, Brent had expected a little more enthusiasm over his offer. He'd already prepared himself to move at a snail's pace with Allie, but her hesitancy would exasperate Job himself.

"Why don't you go with us, Aunt Landon?" she finally said.

"I can't think of a better idea!" Brent seconded and lifted his tea glass. "A toast to the most beautiful ladies in town. And *I'm* the lucky guy who gets to take them out."

"Oh you!" Landon said as her color rose. "How can we refuse?"

Allie looked at herself in the dresser mirror and decided she'd done enough to prepare for the lunch date with Brent. Her hair was less than perfect, she'd barely slapped on her makeup, but she reapplied that body lotion. Fleetingly she hoped there were no bees between here and the restaurant. She stepped away from the mirror, considered changing into something dressier, but decided to remain in the casual lounging pants and cotton top. No sense in making Brent think she was dressing up for him. Allie had already given that impression once and reaped a kiss as the result.

Memories of her last encounter with Brent evoked Allie's dumbfounded stare. She slumped onto the nearby settee, gazed at the ceiling fan, and hoped Brent didn't mention what happened with Frederick in front of Aunt Landon. She hadn't brought up Frederick since she arrived at her aunt's home. As far as Allie suspected, Aunt Landon didn't know how close her niece had come to a full-blown reunion with her old flame. Allie didn't want to live through an interrogation over it. The less her aunt knew, the better.

Allie hurried from the plush suite and scurried toward the living room. Halfway down the hall, she realized she'd left her purse on the end of the bed. She turned to get it but decided to wait. More than anything else, she needed to chat with Brent before Landon entered the living room. Her aunt had gone into her suite to freshen up just as Allie had, and Allie was banking on Landon's taking her usual sweet time to get ready.

When Allie stepped into the living room, Brent was sitting on the sofa with Landon's cat in his lap. This room, like the others, looked like a photo out of *Better Homes and Gardens.* Already Allie was missing the more rustic appeal of the guesthouse.

Brent smiled at Allie and said, "She's taken to me. What's her name again?"

"Tiffany," Allie replied.

"Ah, like the jewelers," Brent observed. "And it looks like she's got her own piece here." He lifted the collar with his index finger.

"I guess," Allie said. "Actually, I think those are just cubic zirconiums," she added.

Brent dropped the collar. "Oh," he said.

Allie hurried forward and sat near Brent. In her haste to

speak with him, she landed on the couch with too much momentum and nearly toppled into his lap.

"Hey, now this is a great change of pace," he crooned and reached for her hand.

The cat moved to Allie's lap, and she avoided Brent by picking up Tiffany. "Sorry to crowd you," Allie scooted away, "but I just wanted to ask you to not say anything about Frederick Wently in front of my aunt."

Brent offered nothing but a blank stare.

"I'm talking about what happened last week after you and I went to dinner."

"Oh, that!" Brent said. "Actually, I've been so determined to forget that jerk I didn't even register who he was at first. I was hoping you'd feel the same," he added and snatched her hand from Tiffany's fur. Before Allie could stop him, Brent kissed the backs of her fingers.

"No way would I bring *him* up. I want your thoughts to be all for me." His breath fanned her skin.

"Good," Allie breathed and pulled her fingers away to stroke Tiffany again.

"Glad you feel that way, too," Brent said and inched so close she smelled his minty breath.

"Oh!" Allie stood and took the cat with her. "I didn't mean it that way. I mean I'm just glad you're not going to bring Frederick up. That's all."

Brent bathed her in pouty appraisal that suggested the mourning widower was gone. He was back to his I-want-to-be-a-pampered-sheik mode. "And here I thought you were getting all warm and fuzzy after I saved you from that awful bee." He stood next to her and wrapped his arm around her waist. "Don't I at least get one little kiss for going to battle for you?" He moved in, and Allie placed her hand on his chest.

"Not right now," she said while Tiffany squirmed for release.

"Oops!" Landon's exclamation from the doorway hinted at all kinds of assumptions. "Should I go back to my room for a while?" she teased.

"No," Allie said and hurried to the other side of the room. She placed Tiffany in her favorite spot, right in the middle of the leather love seat, and observed her aunt. As she suspected, Landon's blue eyes offered the approval she'd never extended to Frederick. But then, Frederick didn't have the money Brent so obviously possessed.

"I need to go get my purse," Allie announced as she hurried up the hallway.

By the time she picked up her bag from the end of the brass bed, Allie relived last week's revelation. During the conversation with Macy, she had realized she'd never been her own woman. *And as long as I stay here, I don't stand a chance*, she thought. Allie already suspected the next few weeks would be marked by Brent on her trail with Landon cheering him on. Allie had never wanted her own place more than now.

Thirty

By the time April merged to May, Frederick could almost fly the route from Charlotte to Macon if he were in a coma. Since Frederick's list of clients hadn't repented of the need to fly here, there, and everywhere, he'd been required to develop a routine. So Frederick had blocked out two days a week for Louise. Traveling schedules varied from week to week, so each week was different. However, he remained faithful to his promise to be there for Louise, despite feeling like he was trapped in a room that grew smaller every day.

This week's routine was no different; neither were the feelings of entrapment.

He strode to the front door of the Grove mansion, the usual roses in one hand, the mystery novel in the other. Louise said his reading voice reminded her of low-rumbling thunder on a lazy summer evening. Frederick wondered where Louise came up with some of her flattery. Her drama queen tendencies, although dampened, had yet to be conquered. Frederick suspected only death or senility would put an end to those inclinations.

And I've got a lifetime of it to look forward to, he thought and wondered how his strength had been such a contributor to his weakness. While far from perfect, Frederick had spent his life trying to do the most honorable thing. With the Louise scenario, the most honorable thing had seemed right at the time, but now it felt so wrong. However, Frederick could see no way out of the situation without breaking Louise's heart and devastating the Groves. They'd all come to depend upon him, his loyalty, and his honor.

Frederick rang the doorbell and wiped at the sweat dotting his cheekbones. The temperature reached 90 degrees today, and the Georgia humidity did little to minimize the heat. While he waited, he idly glanced around the landscaped yard. His gaze eventually roamed to the Dodge truck parked near the six-car garage. Because he didn't want to block the driveway, Frederick had pulled his rental car along the drive that led to Macy and Charlie's house. He'd parked in the grass beside the lane, so he hadn't noticed the truck until now.

The vehicle looked exactly like Jim Bennington's. The man was a fool for pickups and, until Felicity died, he usually bought a new truck every couple of years in order to get all the latest in gadgets and accessories. This Dodge Ram was a deep burgundy that nearly looked black. Frederick wondered if perhaps Mr. Grove had bought Jim's truck or one like it.

Maybe it belongs to Craig Hayden, Frederick mused. He and Helena certainly were getting cozier the last few weeks. The one good thing that had come out of Frederick's engagement with Louise was Helena's reaction. She'd stopped vying for his attention and was apparently realizing what a good catch Craig was, whether he was a pro basketball star or a high school coach. Martha was forever saying they were out together and what a fine Christian man Craig was. While Frederick didn't think marriage at the age of nineteen was appropriate for most young ladies, he was beginning to think Helena might be the exception. Hopefully Craig's level-headed tendencies and his ring on her finger would protect Helena from herself.

Frederick lifted his hand to press the doorbell again when the door opened. The new maid, a short German lady who guarded the premises like a Doberman pinscher, eyed Frederick without greeting or smile.

Having learned her routine early, Frederick stepped inside and simply said, "I'm here for Louise."

"Vou are not supposed to be here dis day," the maid said.

"Yes. This is my day." Frederick nodded and didn't give any sign of retreat. He'd learned to stand his ground with this woman, and do it with resolve. "I left a voicemail for Louise saying I'd be here a day early this veek," he said and threw in a wry smile.

The maid narrowed her eyes and crossed her arms. She didn't appreciate Frederick's humor today or any day of the week. With her iron-gray hair pulled into a bun at the nape of her neck, the woman reminded him of a prison warden. The faint, dark mustache rounded off the effect, and Frederick expected her to pull out a club any day. If he hadn't been nine inches taller than she, he might have been tempted to fear her. What she lacked in physical size, she made up for in strength of will. In order to keep her from thinking she could boss him around, Frederick had learned to occasionally give her a little grief—just to keep their understanding clear.

The maid had detested Frederick from the day she arrived because he'd made the fatal mistake of laughing out loud at her name—Buffy. Even now Frederick was hard pressed not to cackle at the very thought. Naming this woman Buffy was like calling a mad grizzly bear Tootsie.

"Dis is not vour day," Buffy insisted, her voice rising. She placed her hands on her hips and hunched forward like a linebacker preparing to make a clean sweep.

Mrs. Grove appeared in the hallway, balancing a silver tea

tray laden with all sorts of goodies. "Oh, Buffy, there you are! I was wondering what was taking you so long." Mrs. Grove waddled forward, her muumuu swaying. Then she spotted Frederick.

"Frederick!" she exclaimed. "Is this your day to be here?"

"Yes." Frederick nodded. "I left a voicemail for Louise. I had some scheduling problems I couldn't get around." He dropped the novel and wrapped roses on the foyer table and hurried forward to relieve Mrs. Grove of her burden.

"Thank you, thank you," she said with smiling lips as red as her dress. "You're such a wonderful gentleman."

Buffy shut the front door and picked up the flowers and novel. "I tell him dis is not his day, but he von't listen." She glared at Frederick, and he blasted her with his most charming grin.

"Oh, it doesn't matter!" Mrs. Grove waved her pudgy fingers. "It's just that this is Louise's physical therapy day. They are just finishing up," she explained, "and I promised them some snacks. Buffy's just worried we'll tire Louise." Mrs. Grove hustled toward the game room that had been adapted into a suite for Louise since her bedroom was upstairs.

Knowing the path well, Frederick followed and eyed the sugar cookies and halved strawberries. The fast food burrito he'd downed at lunch was wearing thin. His stomach growled. When he stepped into the sunroom, he fully expected Louise to be swathed in covers, holding a TV remote in one hand, a Sprite in the other, and ruling the roost as always. Instead she was standing beside her bed, reaching toward Jim Bennington with no walker for support.

"Come on, Louise!" Jim encouraged.

"Oh my goodness!" Mrs. Grove shrieked. "What are you doing? She can't! She mustn't! Not without a—"

Louise lunged at Jim. She screamed as he caught her, and the two slammed into the wall. Jim, supporting Louise's fall, hit the floor with a plop and held her tight all the way down. Frederick dropped the tea tray on the bed's end and rushed toward the two, only to discover she and Jim both were laughing.

"I did it!" Louise bellowed. "I did it! I took a step!"

"I told her she could!" Jim crowed. Still cradling Louise, he beamed up at Frederick and Mrs. Grove.

"Are you *crazy*?" Frederick demanded. "You're a doctor, man! Don't you understand she could be *hurt*!"

Like a small child, Louise reached for Frederick. He bent and slipped one arm under her knees and the other supported her shoulders.

"So what hurts her worse?" Jim asked as he stood. "Taking a risk on her first step, or safely staying in bed the rest of her life?"

"I did it!" Louise rested her arms around Frederick's neck.

Frederick noted her exultant face and the smell of baby powder. Louise gazed up at Frederick with all the adoration of a girl in her first crush. Her green satin house robe accented her peaches-and-cream complexion and made her golden hair look like honey. Try as he might, Frederick couldn't generate any feelings for her other than that of a fond elder brother exasperated with a daredevil kid sister.

"You did it, all right," he scolded and hoped she couldn't read his mind. "You nearly gave me a heart attack."

"That makes two of us!" Mrs. Grove fussed and pulled back the hospital bed's covers.

Frederick laid Louise on the elevated bed and glanced toward the end where he'd dumped the tea tray. Buffy-the-mustache-maiden was picking up the damp mess.

"I vill redo dis," she declared and glared at Frederick.

He winked.

Her spine stiff, Buffy marched out of the room holding the tray like she was the martyr of teatime.

"Now," Frederick said as Martha covered Louise, "you'll probably need a nap after all that."

"I was thinking of maybe some tango lessons," Jim quipped and settled on the end of the bed.

"Where did you come from, anyway?" Frederick demanded and directed a mock glare toward his friend.

"I've been around awhile," he claimed and smiled at Louise. "Are you going to defend me here or let your fiancé kick me out?"

"He's been coming with the physical therapist," Louise explained through a yawn.

"Yes," Mrs. Grove confirmed. "He dropped by to visit one day when the therapist was here and has been back once a week since."

"See!" Jim waved toward the Grove matron. "My honor has been defended."

Louise giggled.

"So where is this physical therapist?" Frederick looked around the spacious room.

"Oh, she left a while ago," Jim explained and stood. "I was just hanging out seeing if—"

"If you could get Louise to kill herself?" Frederick asked and delivered a playful shove at his friend.

"Something like that." Jim smiled and returned the favor with a punch of his own. "Don't you remember *I* was the one who was there for your first step?"

"Yep, I remember!" Frederick barked. "You pushed me out in the middle of the room and I had to walk or flop."

"Now, now, let's don't exaggerate." Jim wrinkled his nose at Louise. "You need to watch this guy when you get married. He likes to lie."

"Will you two stop it?" Mrs. Grove admonished and bustled around the room like a mama hummingbird.

Louise languidly smiled and snared Frederick's hand in hers. He rubbed his finger along her fingers, void of an engagement ring. Amazingly Louise had yet to press for a jeweled sign of their verbal agreement, and Frederick couldn't bring himself to purchase a ring. He attributed her not mentioning a ring to her distraction with the paralysis and wondered how long she would go before pressuring him into buying a diamond.

"I *am* sleepy," Louise mumbled, her eyes heavy. "I missed my nap today."

"Well, okay then." Jim held up his hands. "I know when I'm not wanted."

"No . . ." Louise begged and reached for him. "You stay and have dinner with Frederick and me. Maybe I can take another step even."

Jim took her hand and kissed it. "It will be my honor, fair maiden," he said.

Louise giggled again.

"Such a flirt!" Martha rolled her eyes at Frederick.

And all Frederick could think was, *Since when did Jim-the-depressed-one turn into a flirt?*

"Now shoo! Shoo!" Martha said and waved the men toward the door. "Out with the both of you now. She needs sleep! We'll have our tea in the front room."

"I'd prefer a Coke, actually," Frederick asserted.

"Me too," Jim added. "I haven't had my overdose of artificial color and sugar today."

Frederick narrowed his eyes at his health-nut friend. "Are you mocking me?" he challenged.

"Only if you want me to," Jim replied and never blinked.

"We're out of Coke," Martha whispered from behind. "All we have is Sprite right now."

"I have a couple in my car," Frederick said and was thankful he'd bought a stash along with a tiny Styrofoam cooler when he gassed up the rental car. "I'd rather drink muddy water than Sprite," he absently complained and watched Jim walk toward the hallway. The guy was dressed in some of his prefuneral clothes—a pair of wrinkle-free Dockers and a starched shirt, to be exact. Frederick looked down at his own clothing, the standard jeans, boots, and T-shirt. At least this time the T-shirt was new.

Then Frederick cast another glance at Louise, who was already dozing. He scratched his head, looked back at Jim, and wondered when the guy had gone and gotten so cheerful. Frederick had been so busy he hadn't seen Jim in more than six weeks. And those weeks had certainly brought a change.

He meandered down the hallway as Martha closed the game room door. When he passed the living room, he eyed Jim again. The doctor was standing at the window swaying to some unheard melody.

"Martha says they're out of Cokes. I've got a couple in my car," he said. "Do you really want one?"

"Yeah, I heard her," Jim answered. "And no thanks on the offer." He shook his head. "You know I don't drink that stuff. I was just giving you grief."

"Okay," Frederick said and studied Jim some more.

"Are you okay?" Jim asked.

"Yeah, why?"

"You keep looking at me weird."

"Maybe because you're acting weird."

"Am I?" Jim gazed back out the window and laughed.

Suddenly Frederick no longer felt like hanging out, nibbling cookies and strawberries, and watching Buffy protect
her territory until Louise woke up. He needed some space. He
needed to think about what he hadn't allowed himself to think
about in weeks—like how in the world he'd been talked into
an engagement with a woman he didn't love who was nearly
young enough to be his daughter, how he was going to get
out of it, and what his chances were of ever getting Allie back.

"Hey, Jim, will you please tell Mrs. G. I'm going for a
walk?" Frederick asked. "I'll be back in time for dinner."

"What? Did you say something?" Jim queried, turning his
nonplussed gaze toward Frederick.

"A walk," Frederick replied. "I'm going for a walk. Be back
in an hour. Tell Mrs. Grove. Okay?"

"Gotcha covered." Jim gave Frederick a thumbs-up along
with a grin that was way too goofy.

Frederick narrowed his eyes, looked toward the game room,
and strode outside. He retrieved his icy Coke from the mini
cooler in the backseat and marched down the lane that led to
the guesthouse where Allie had stayed. When the lane crossed
the stream, he hung a left and followed the stream until the
bridge came into view.

After unscrewing the Coke lid, Frederick slowed, took a
long swallow, closed his eyes, and relished the burn. He moved
closer to the bridge, squatted beside it, and picked up a pebble.
Pitching the stone into the gurgling water, he watched it sink
to the bottom. Standing, he walked onto the bridge, placed
his elbows on the handrail, and stared into the water. The
Coke chilled his hand as his new decision chilled his heart.

"I can't marry her," he whispered and shook his head. "I

just can't." *It doesn't matter that I was partly responsible for what happened. But I can't accept full blame. I didn't force Louise to get on top of that plane. And even if it is the most honorable thing to marry her . . . I don't love her, and I never will.*

"I can't do this to myself," Frederick whispered. He straightened and turned toward the guesthouse, allowing memories of Allie to flow unchecked. His hands shaking, he downed a fourth of the Coke and wondered what the possibilities were of Allie Elton giving him another chance and God granting him a graceful way out of this engagement.

Thoughts of Jim's goofy grin teased Frederick's mind. He closed his eyes and considered the implications. From the first, Frederick thought Jim and Louise would be good for each other. Louise would liven Jim up and help him heal, while he would hopefully bring some maturity and balance to her life. Frederick still held to that conviction.

Fleetingly he recalled the day Louise broke her neck. He'd prayed that very day that Jim might become attracted to Louise. Given Jim's cheerful flirting now, Frederick wondered what the chances were that God was answering his prayer.

Maybe I'm being two-timed, he thought and never imagined he'd be so thrilled at such a prospect. If he wasn't being two-timed, Frederick wondered how much the chances would improve if he got out of the way and let nature take its course.

He smiled and decided an immediate change in schedule was in order. Darren had originally wanted to fly to Dallas this evening for a meeting with their adoption agency tomorrow afternoon. After years of trying to have a baby, he and Sophia had finally decided to go ahead and adopt some children—as in three of them from South Korea. They'd wanted to fly to Dallas tonight, spend the night, and get rested up for the meeting tomorrow, but Darren had agreed to wait and fly out in the morning so Frederick could pay a quick visit to Louise.

If Darren still wanted to go to Dallas tonight, Frederick was going to make himself available for the flight. That would put Jim and Louise together all evening. Then, if Frederick was conveniently busy the next couple of weeks, he could call Jim and ask him to please visit Louise more often—as a favor for a friend, of course.

With a sly smile, Frederick pulled his cell phone from his pocket. He'd recently read that sometimes God answers our prayers through us, if we'll just take the time to listen. Frederick believed he had listened. And he now had a plan. Never had he felt so God-inspired as he tapped the screen for Darren's number.

Thirty-One

Two weeks later Allie twirled around the empty townhouse's living room until her long skirt fanned away from her legs. She couldn't believe she'd finally done it. Allie had leased her own place. No one knew. No one. Not Aunt Landon or even Sarah Hamilton. At least, Sarah didn't know *yet*. Allie was awaiting her return call. She'd spent last weekend at Sarah's place and received the support and encouragement she needed to finally fulfill her dream. Sarah even told her about the new apartments several streets over.

Now all Allie needed was the courage to tell her family she was moving out on her own. Once she established her freedom, Allie planned to apply for a job. If her family found out, fine. If they didn't, fine. Allie would be her own woman by then, and she could do what she liked with her life.

After collapsing to the floor, she flopped back onto the cottony carpet and moved her arms and legs in broad arcs as if she were a child in the snow making an angel. The smells of new carpet and wood and paint blended together for a heady rush of delight. Allie laughed out loud and hopped up. Construction had just been completed on this block of upscale townhouses, and Allie was one of the first tenants to lease a place. She'd chosen the one on the corner because it was closest to the flower garden.

Allie skipped to the window, opened the wooden blinds,

and peered onto the garden, bright with the blooms of early June. Petunias and periwinkles, geraniums and roses offered their beauty to the world in a showcase of color that heightened her spirits.

A trio of bumblebees, zipping from one bloom to the next, reminded Allie of Brent's episode with her bee and his subsequent intrusion into her life. As she'd predicted, the guy just would not go away, and Aunt Landon was fully on his side. Once she forwarded him the information on the duck email program, he then possessed her email address. Seldom a day went by that she didn't get a message from him. Most of the time Allie deleted his notes without answering.

Meanwhile, Aunt Landon had all but proposed to him for Allie, and Allie was convinced that if Brent had been ten years older, Landon would have proposed for herself. Allie frowned and wondered what it would take to once and for all remove Brent from her life. She certainly didn't want him coming to her new place—especially not when Macy and the twins were visiting.

Since she'd left the guesthouse, Allie and Macy had kept in closer touch than ever. Macy and the twins had even come for a visit to Aunt Landon's several weeks ago. During the visit, Allie had discreetly probed for news of Frederick and learned what she feared most. He was a regular visitor at Grove Acres and was fully devoted to Louise. Macy had delivered the news with her heart in her eyes and hadn't elaborated. Allie had been thankful that her sister had pretended not to notice Allie's red-rimmed eyes the next morning. In the last few days, Allie had resigned herself to the fact that Frederick was just not coming back. Despite all her hoping and praying, Allie understood that she'd lost him forever.

She swallowed against the lump in her throat and decided

not to allow the Frederick issues to cloud her moment. Sometime during the last few weeks, Allie had decided she should take her own advice to Jim. It was time for her to move on with her life. She'd pined for Frederick enough. And even though she would never stop loving him and would probably never get married because of that love, Allie knew the time had come for some closure on the ten-year yearning. And part of being her own woman involved knowing she could carve out a life without Frederick. She'd have much preferred to live in matrimonial bliss from now on, but since that was denied her, she would embrace her independence and make the best of it.

She gazed around the room again and envisioned Macy visiting with the twins. Macy hadn't been convinced Allie would actually go through with her plan.

"Boy, will she be surprised," Allie said through a broad grin.

Everything was perfect. Everything. Now all Allie needed was furniture.

Her cell burst into a round of short dings, and Allie ran to her purse near the front door to retrieve the phone. A quick glance at the screen proved the caller to be Sarah.

Allie answered the call with a high-pitched squeak before she burst out, "I did it! I leased one of the townhouses!"

"You did!" Sarah exclaimed.

"Yes, I did it! I'm here in Atlanta now, and I am *so excited*! Now all I need is furniture! Want to go shopping with me?"

"You're not going to believe this," Sarah interjected, "but I just got off the phone with Mom. You know she stayed on at Elton Mansion as cook after you guys left."

"Yes, I remember," Allie said. "You were exasperated because she wouldn't take early retirement and let you lease her an apartment near your place."

"Right, right, right," Sarah hurried, then paused and said, "I can't get her to take a dime! She's as hardheaded as—"

"As you are?" Allie teased. Sarah's mom was every bit as spunky as Sarah and then some. Once she set her mind, there was no turning back.

Sarah cleared her throat. "I owe you one," she growled and continued her spiel. "Anyway, I just got off the phone with Mom. She said Sophia Cosby wants to totally redo the third floor because she and her husband are adopting three siblings from South Korea, and they want the top floor to be all for them—a game room and the whole nine yards."

"You're kidding!" Allie breathed. "What are they going to do with all my furniture, then?"

"Mom says Sophia's going to call your dad to find out what he wants to do—put it in storage or what."

Allie began to run in place. "They can just bring it over here!" she exclaimed and imagined the whole place decorated in rich, classic pieces.

"That's exactly what I was thinking. I didn't know if you'd already leased the place, but I thought you might want to know before she actually calls your father."

"By all means yes!" Allie shouted. "Most everything on the third floor belongs to me. What I didn't buy, Aunt Landon gave me. I can't believe this!"

"I think it's a God thing," Sarah said. "He knows you've been wanting to move out on your own. Now that you're finally taking the steps, He's right there with you to make it all work out. Go claim your stuff!"

"Okay, I will. I'll go right away. If she calls Dad and then I say I have a place for the stuff, he'll want to know all the details. And, well . . ." Allie huffed and worriedly rubbed her forehead. "I'm not ready to tell him yet. I don't have my speech planned or anything!"

Sarah chuckled. "Okay, look, I'll call my mom back right now. She's at the mansion. I'll tell her to tell Sophia you're on your way, okay?"

"Yes! By all means yes!" Allie hollered again and disconnected the call without bidding adieu. "Oh!" she said and looked at the screen to read the words "Call Ended." *Sarah will understand,* she decided.

Allie snatched up her purse, grabbed her keys, and darted for the front door. And with every step she prayed Sophia Cosby hadn't already called her dad.

Thirty-Two

Frederick paced the hospital office suite like an expectant father. Jim had texted yesterday, asking if Frederick would meet him at his new office at the hospital. As things turned out, Jim had just been invited to work as an understudy to the head of ER. The older gentleman planned to retire in a couple years. He'd taken an immediate liking to Jim, and the administrator and hospital board loved the idea of the physician grooming Jim for his position. When Jim agreed, he'd been given an in-hospital office and a secretary.

The secretary was long gone today, and Jim's office was locked. Frederick wondered if he'd misunderstood the time. He sat on the edge of a leather chair and checked his watch. He'd been gone for two weeks; the least Jim could do was meet him on time for this impromptu meeting. Frederick leaned back, crossed his legs, and began shaking his foot. The laces on his running shoe flopped with the movement, and Frederick picked a piece of lint off his athletic shorts. The early June temperature was promising that July was going to be blazing hot, and Frederick hadn't felt like dressing in anything but shorts and a light shirt this morning.

His back immediately notified him that it didn't appreciate the shaking or the way he'd slouched into the chair. Frederick carefully stood and tried to straighten. When his back caught, he winced and gradually stood erect. He'd allowed his prescription-strength ibuprofen to wear off and had just swallowed a couple over-the-counters at the water fountain in the hallway. The medication couldn't begin to work fast enough.

He decided it was time to call Jim. When Jim had texted Frederick to request the meeting, his words had seemed somewhat formal and a little uncertain. Frederick had instantly responded and assured Jim he didn't mind flying down for the meeting. He was scheduled to shuttle Darren and Sophia back to Dallas tomorrow anyway.

Two weeks ago, Frederick had gone through with his plan, right down to asking Jim to check on Louise in his absence. Playing the part of the clueless fiancé, Frederick called Louise regularly, all the while praying that sparks were flying between her and Jim. So it was with great anticipation that Frederick agreed to this meeting with Jim. He hoped Jim's unnatural tone in the text could be attributed to a true friend who was as nervous as a long-tailed cat at a rocking chair convention. If Jim and Louise were falling in love and Jim believed Frederick loved Louise, then his nervousness would be a given.

Frederick prepared to press Jim's number on his cell when the door flew open and Jim breezed into the room.

"Oh man, I'm so sorry to have kept you waiting," Jim said. He shifted a manila folder to his left hand and extended his right hand to Frederick as if he were a new acquaintance.

Frederick shook his hand.

"Great to see you," Jim continued and fidgeted with the manila folder.

"You too," Frederick said and tried to smile into Jim's eyes, but Jim averted his gaze to the corner snack shelf.

"Want some coffee?" He dropped the folder on the secretary's desk and hurried toward the pot.

"No, that's fine. You know me—I never touch that stuff. I've heard it's not good for you."

Jim's laugh held an anxious edge. He removed the stethoscope from beneath his lab coat's collar and dropped it on top of the folder. "Yeah, neither is Coke," Jim shot back and moved to the edge of the desk. He sat on the edge with one foot still on the floor for support. Jim crossed his arms and swung his other leg. Still he refused to look Frederick in the eyes.

Frederick's hopes soared to such a level of certainty that he had to stop himself from bursting into cheers. He rubbed his hands together. While he was able to suppress the cheering, he couldn't stop the broad grin.

"So what's up? Why the meeting?" he asked, his words thick with the smile.

Jim jumped up, walked around the secretary's desk, and then back again. He placed one hand on his hip, started to say something, then whipped around and landed in the rolling chair behind the desk. "We need to talk," he finally said, and for the first time leveled a direct gaze at Frederick. Whatever had happened, the poor guy was eaten up with guilt.

"Okay," Frederick said and nearly laughed.

Slumping back in the chair, Jim gripped the arms and stared at the ceiling. "Man, oh man, oh man," he groaned.

"What's the deal?" Frederick prompted and hoped he sounded encouraging. If Jim would just come out with it, and if "it" was what Frederick hoped, the poor guy could be put out of his misery. But on the one percent chance that Jim wasn't trying to say "it," then Frederick didn't want to assume something that would insult his friend.

Carefully Frederick settled back onto the edge of the chair, squared his feet, supported his spine, and hoped he looked as nonthreatening as a lamb. "Look, Jim," he encouraged, "we've been friends since we were kids. . . ."

"Do you have to remind me of that?" Jim challenged and stood. His face reddening, he clenched and unclenched his fists. "I . . . I . . ." Jim garbled out and sounded like he was drowning in his own remorse. His face blanched as swiftly as it had reddened, and horror came over his features.

"I've got to go," he said and hustled around the desk.

Frederick jumped up, stood in front of his friend, and placed his hands on Jim's shoulders. This was *not* a good back day, and his spine wasn't happy about much of anything. It certainly hadn't agreed with his jumping up so fast. Frederick gritted his teeth to keep from hollering against the pain.

"Does this have anything to do with Louise?" he asked in an attempt to relieve Jim's fears. Unfortunately he sounded more angry than anything else.

Jim's eyes grew wider by the second. "How did you know?" he wheezed and didn't give Frederick time to answer. "You're furious, and I don't—I don't blame you! I'm nothing but a cad! A low-life worm! You're one of my best friends and I—I—"

Frederick's spine kicked him, and he couldn't hold the verbal release. "Aaaahhhh!" he groaned and leaned against the desk.

"Oh man, *please* don't start crying!" Jim begged, and Frederick was sure the guy was about to wet his pants. "This is worse than I ever thought it could be."

Even in the middle of the pain, Frederick couldn't ignore the hilarity. "I'm not crying," he said through a pain-ridden chuckle. "It's my back. It's giving me all sorts of grief today."

"Well, why didn't you say so?" Jim gripped Frederick's arm.

"Just help me to the chair, okay?" Frederick pleaded.

Once he was settled, Frederick scooted all the way back and squared his feet on the floor. His spine liked that move. He released his breath and said, "There. I think I can talk now." He looked up at Jim, who hovered over him. The guy had dark circles under his eyes, and he didn't look like he'd slept in a week.

"You're like a brother to me, you know that," Jim said. "And I never dreamed I'd—" He gazed downward.

Finally Frederick decided to just put him out of his misery. "You and Louise like each other, don't you?" he said.

Jim looked up. His agonized soul answered for him.

Frederick barked out a joyous laugh. Jim jumped, and a veil of confusion covered his face. Frederick placed a flattened hand on each side of Jim's face, pulled him close, kissed his forehead, and laughed again.

"What's the *matter* with you?" Jim croaked and jerked away. "Are you *crazy*?" He grabbed a napkin from near the coffeepot and scrubbed at his forehead.

"No, I'm *thrilled*!" Frederick exclaimed and tried to thrust both fists into the air. His back caught, and Frederick minimized the thrust. "I was hoping this would happen."

"You were?" Jim squeaked.

"Yes! Yes! Yes!" Frederick vigorously nodded. "Listen to me! I am *not* in love with Louise, and I *don't* want to marry her."

"You don't? But I thought . . ." Jim shook his head. "I mean even before the accident, she and you were flirting. . . ."

"No!" Frederick said. "She was. I wasn't."

Jim leaned against the wall and reminded Frederick of a tire slowing deflating.

"I think Louise just had a really hard crush on me, and that's about it," Frederick said.

"I think it's more than that with me," Jim said. "I really do. At least it is on my part."

"I'm sure it is on hers, too," Frederick assured him and prayed Louise didn't break his friend's heart.

"She says it is," he nodded, "and I believe her. I guess I should, anyway, because I'm going to ask her to marry me."

"You are! Congratulations, man!" Frederick eased forward, slowly stood, and extended his hand.

Jim pumped it, and his smile couldn't have been more exultant. "I'm hoping we can set a date next year—once she really gets back on her feet. She's doing so well, you know. She's taking several steps at a time now." He finally quit shaking Frederick's hand.

As the relief rolled through Frederick, he'd never felt so free. He covered his face with his hands and heaved through a fit of hilarity.

After a few nervous laughs, Jim finally said, "Is there, like, something I'm missing here?"

Frederick nodded his head. "Yes, all sorts of stuff," he said and lowered his hands. "You never knew this," he explained. "It all happened when you were up to your neck in pre-med at school. . . ." And he told Jim the whole story of his love for Allie.

Thirty-Three

From the time Allie told her aunt she was going to visit her father and sister in Atlantic Beach, Landon insisted on going with her. That didn't surprise Allie. Her aunt had subtly pried for any hint of what Allie was up to. Despite Landon's nonchalance, her suspicious eyes had clued Allie to her awareness that something was underway. But Allie had remained steadfast in keeping her townhouse a secret until she could develop the best approach to the subject.

When all her furniture arrived and she was ready to move in, Allie had nearly spilled the truth to her aunt. But she had held off because she wanted to tell her father, sister, and Landon at the same time. She knew if she leaked the information to her aunt, Landon would tell Allie's sister and father before Allie had the chance. This way, Allie would make her announcement once, and they would all find out together. However, having arrived at Atlantic Beach, Allie was finding it difficult to pull together the courage to drop the news.

Brent Everson's showing up the second day of her visit surprised Allie as little as her own reticence to broach the townhouse subject. Allie certainly hadn't invited him, so she assumed Aunt Landon had. He'd dined with the family last night and dazzled her father as thoroughly as he had Landon.

Evelyn was another story. As Sarah's mom would have put it, Evelyn was fit to be tied and eaten up with jealousy. Allie understood the source of her father's bedazzlement and Evelyn's envy: Brent's obvious money.

Before dinner was over, Allie sensed that Landon thought the big secret involved Allie's announcing her engagement to Brent. This nearly catapulted Allie into blurting the truth about her townhouse right there over the chocolate mousse. But she didn't. She held her tongue and continued to work on her emancipation proclamation and the courage to deliver it.

The next morning, a phone call from Macy proved to be the catalyst that sparked Allie's courage. Her cell phone began its series of beeps at seven-thirty that fine Friday, and Allie covered her head. She'd lain awake half the night in the luxury condominium's bedroom, working on her freedom statement. The whole mental scenario always exploded into a family upheaval that ranked a nine on the Richter scale, which led Allie to scrap the latest version of the speech and start over.

Despite Allie's need for sleep, the cell phone refused to cease ringing. Finally, she extended her hand from beneath the covers and felt for the phone on her nightstand. Once she found it, she uncovered her head and opened one eye only enough to see who it was and swipe to answer.

Allie placed the cell to her ear, mumbled a groggy hello, and grimaced. Her mouth tasted like glue gone bad.

"Rise and shine, sleepyhead!" Macy chirped. "Do I have news for you!"

Pulling the phone away from her ear, Allie frowned. Macy's voice could slice concrete when she was excited.

"Hi," Allie mumbled.

"You are *not* going to believe this!" Macy continued.

"Oh really?" Allie said through a yawn.

"Yes. I found out last night late, and I didn't want to call so late so I waited."

"Mm-hmm. . . ." Allie replied.

"Okay, you!" Macy declared. "If this doesn't wake you up, nothing will. Louise has dumped Frederick. She and Jim Bennington are engaged!"

Allie's eyes popped open. The shadowed room came into focus. She held her breath and decided she must be dreaming. But after flexing her fingers against the phone, wiggling her toes, and sitting straight up, Allie determined this was no dream. The dreadful taste in her mouth confirmed she was awake. She wondered if she'd misunderstood Macy.

"What did you just say?" she asked and held her breath.

"Awake now?" Macy's laughter gurgled over the line.

"Yes," Allie confirmed. "Did I hear you right? Louise and Jim Bennington?"

"Correct!" Macy sang. "Helena called late last night to tell me. They're not setting a date until next year, but—"

"Frederick!" Allie shouted and covered her eyes. "What about him?"

"Jim's saying Frederick gave his blessing and is gracefully bowing out."

Allie flopped back on the pillow. She wanted to laugh and cry and drop to her knees in thanksgiving all at once. Instead she stared at the ceiling in dumbfounded silence.

"And guess what else?" Macy continued.

"What?"

"Helena and Craig Hayden are engaged, too."

"Really?" Allie replied as this bit of news barely registered.

"Helena says they might have a double wedding."

"Frederick!" Allie said again. "Where is he?"

"How should I know?" Macy responded. "Probably at home in Charlotte. He hasn't been here in ages."

"He hasn't?"

"I mean, like, weeks."

"Weeks?" Allie echoed and tried to piece together the situation.

Macy began a deluge of ceaseless chatter that Allie tuned out. With all her faults and constant need of headache-induced naps, Macy usually woke up with the birds and acted about as cheerful as one until about eleven, when she could become "deathly" ill. However, Macy hadn't even offered to cry "headache" during her recent visit with Allie and Landon. She'd even played croquet with the twins in the backyard. While Macy continued her chirping, Allie's mind raced with the implications of the latest and most pressing news.

Frederick was free! She recalled those sweet minutes before Louise broke her neck. He'd asked Allie to ride in the copilot's seat. He'd taken her hand. His eyes held promise, excitement, expectation. And Allie had been ready to elope with him that second and let her family just deal with it. Then he'd pledged allegiance to Louise and left *Allie* to deal with it. His only condolences involved yelling at her about not being more attentive to Louise.

By the time the phone call with Macy ended, Allie was trapped in the winds of anticipation. Yet the anticipation was not without clouds. *Sure, Frederick is free*, she thought, *but would he have still married Louise if she hadn't dumped him for Jim? But then, why hasn't Frederick visited Louise for weeks if he's so devoted to her?*

A still, soft voice suggested that the news Allie received was only bits of a bigger story. And on the heels of that revelation came the desire to discover the whole truth. Only one person could supply that information to the fullest accuracy: Frederick.

A fresh surge of confidence and hope flowed through Allie. She swung her legs out of bed, stood, and dropped her cell phone back into her purse. Today she would do what she should have done ten years ago. Allie would go after her man.

But first, her emancipation proclamation. If she and Frederick *did* get back together, Allie figured her family would take the news better if she'd already staked out her freedom. Breakfast would provide the perfect opportunity to do exactly that.

After slipping into shorts and a tank top, Brent stepped out of the bathroom to the tune of a high-pitched jazz song flowing from his cell phone. Still toweling his hair dry, he picked up the phone and checked the caller's identity. He smiled when he noted Penny's cell number. She had said she'd call this morning. She was punctual as usual.

After the warm reception from Allie's father last night, Brent had been encouraged to go ahead and ask Allie to marry him. Even though Allie was still keeping him at arm's length, Brent suspected that her family would pressure her to accept. Allie was such a pliable creature, he was certain she would bend to their wishes. Landon had already given Brent her approval, and Richard had all but assumed Brent and Allie were already engaged. Evelyn was another story. She'd spent the whole evening sullenly glaring at Brent and snapping at Allie.

Penny was calling to report on the aftermath of last night.

If her report was as positive as Brent hoped, he would pop the question very soon . . . possibly even tonight.

He swiped to answer, placed the receiver to his ear, and said, "Hello, beautiful," in his most seductive tone.

Penny's sensuous laugh assured Brent his effort was not wasted. "Hello, yourself," she replied in a throaty voice.

"What do you know this morning?" he purred.

"You're going to love this," she replied.

"Oh, really? As much as I love you?" Brent lied.

"Don't know," she crooned. "Depends on how much you love me these days."

"The way things are going, I'm lovin' you more all the time," he teased and knew Penny probably didn't believe a word he said. But the good part was she didn't care. Like Brent, as long as her pockets were lined with green, Penny Clayton could live without love.

"You're lying," Penny said through a knowing laugh.

"And *you* love that," he shot back.

Brent settled onto the end of the bed and looked at himself in the mirror. As usual, he was satisfied with what he saw. Very satisfied. And he couldn't imagine that Allie was immune to his classic good looks.

"So what gives?" he prompted and detested the smell of the cheap shampoo he'd been sentenced to.

"Last night after you left, I overheard Landon and Richard talking. You're right in your assumptions. They're *dying* for you to ask Allie to marry you."

"Oh, really? Dying?"

"*Dying!*" Penny drawled. "All I heard was the first of their conversation though. Evelyn came down the hall, and I had to duck into the bathroom."

"How's she taking all this?"

"She's furious!" Penny said.

Brent snickered. "Good. I'll look forward to spending the rest of my life making her eat her snotty attitude."

Penny joined his laughter. "Good. Can I help you force feed her?"

"Anytime, doll, anytime," Brent replied. "I think I'll go ahead and pop the question tonight," he mused and dug his toes into the short-napped carpet.

"It can't be soon enough for me," Penny pined. "I'm ready to get out of here and be a kept woman again."

"Hold that thought!" Brent replied before suavely bidding adieu.

He cut the call off and thoughtfully tapped the phone against the palm of his hand. Gazing around the cheap hotel room, he was tempted to leave this place and switch to a luxury suite tonight. His days of being on a budget were almost over. He smiled at his own reflection in the mirror.

Thirty-Four

Allie sat on the condominium's terrace and awaited her family's arrival for breakfast. Once she made her decision, she had immediately showered and dressed. She finished her makeup just in time to allow room service access to their condo. Room service was part of the sweet package deal on the condo. Allie sat at one of the glass-topped tables sipping her cinnamon tea while the Atlantic licked the beach in time with the heartbeat of the ocean. She'd alerted the family to breakfast and expected them to appear any minute with their yawns and house robes intact. The only Elton who ever claimed to be an early and graceful riser was, ironically, Macy.

Gazing onto the ocean kissed by the sun's eastern ascent, Allie prayed for the Lord to give her the words for the hour. No matter how Allie tried to arrange her spiel, it sounded awkward and invited argument. She didn't know what else to do but commit the speech to the Lord and depend on Him to give her the right words.

She absorbed the salt-laden air, the sound of sea gulls' high-pitched squawks, and exulted in the sun's royal rising. Even at eight-thirty the streaks of indigo and scarlet and mauve were vibrant with life and the promise of new things to come. Allie found the strength and courage she needed to say what she had to say. Freedom lay on the other side of breakfast. Hopefully Frederick Wently waited in the midst of the freedom.

As predicted, the robed family gradually wandered in and helped themselves to breakfast from the heated service dishes. Allie silently sipped her tea until everyone, including Penny Clayton and Aunt Landon, had settled at the table and began eating. Allie couldn't have eaten if someone put a gun to her head; her stomach was in a knot so tight no food could penetrate. There was barely room for even the smells of bacon, eggs, sausage, and hash browns.

"Aren't you going to eat, Allie?" Aunt Landon queried before daintily nibbling a slice of crisp bacon. With no makeup, Landon's translucent complexion and blonde lashes made her appear ghost-like. The pale satin robe accented the effect.

"No, I'm not very hungry this morning," Allie admitted and glanced toward the sun. She picked up her spoon, stirred her tea, laid the spoon down, and repeated the whole process.

"Maybe Allie's lovesick," Richard drawled.

Landon chuckled and squeezed Allie's hand. "Now, Richard," she teased. "You remember what it was like to be young and in love. Don't pressure her."

Allie picked up a package of sweetener and tormented the corner. She gazed into her father's sharp blue eyes. He was the only one who'd fully dressed. All he needed was a ship captain's hat to round off his outfit. His crisp white shirt and pleated cotton slacks made him look like the king of the sea. As always, Allie felt like a dowdy coal girl in his presence. She swallowed hard, cleared her throat, and found her voice. "Actually, this doesn't have anything to do with being in love," she said, and sensed Evelyn's undivided attention.

Allie glanced toward her and at Penny Clayton, who, as usual, seemed about as interested in Allie as she might have been the phone book. Both women wore their housecoats and mussed-by-sleep hairdos.

"What does it have to do with, then?" Aunt Landon prompted.

Allie looked into her aunt's eyes and encountered suspicion laced with fear. Until recently, Allie had held no secrets from her aunt. Landon probably didn't know what to think now.

"It has to do with . . ." Allie dropped the sugar packet, eyed the seagulls, as free as they pleased, and joined them in spirit. "I've leased a townhouse," she announced and looked her father squarely in the eyes.

"What!" he bellowed and plunked down his coffee, which sloshed onto the table's glass top.

"I leased a townhouse in Atlanta," Allie repeated and squared her shoulders.

"I thought we were supposed to be on a budget!" Evelyn squealed. "And you're the one who thought it was such a good idea!"

"Yes, and I still do," Allie said and laced her hands into a tight ball in her lap. Her eye quivered, and she was amazed at her next statement. "And to help you stay on budget, I'm going to stop receiving my allowance."

"She's gone nuts!" Richard spewed.

Allie fixed her gaze on the salt shaker and decided her last admission must have been an answer to her prayer for the right thing to say at the right time. She'd not even considered denouncing her allowance until now. *But who needs it?* Allie thought. *I've still got a chunk in my trust fund. If I have to use some of those funds, it will tide me over until I get a job.*

"Landon, is this your doing?" Richard raged.

"Are *you* nuts?" Landon challenged. "This is the first I've heard of it!"

"How do you possibly think you're going to exist without your allowance?" Evelyn mocked.

Allie never relinquished her gaze from the salt shaker. "I'm going to get a job," she stated simply as a slow tremor attacked her legs. "And until I do, I'll use some of my trust fund—"

"No! No! No! No!" Richard screamed and pounded the table until everyone's eggs were scrambled whether they started out that way or not.

Jumping, Allie stared at her father. He was as red-faced as he'd been when Macy announced she was going to marry into a septic family. It was an odd shade of red beneath his deep tan, and Allie became fixated on why she'd been so terrified of her father in this state. He couldn't do anything to her. She was an adult. What could he do to stop her? She was already relinquishing her allowance, so he couldn't use that as a manipulative tool. The trust fund was legally hers to do with as she chose. And she had made her choice to do exactly that. What was left?

Allie sat up straighter and calmly held her father's gaze, never wavering from his irate stare. Aside from a few leftover tremors, her nerves were miraculously recovering. "Just so you know," she said, "Sophia Cosby is redecorating the third floor of the mansion. I've arranged to have everything that belonged to me moved into my townhouse. She'll be contacting you about the few pieces left—wanting to know what you want to do with them."

"You thief!" Evelyn snarled.

Turning her attention to Evelyn, Allie barely raised her brows. "I'm a thief? For taking the things I bought and what Aunt Landon gave me?"

"Yes, you are!" Evelyn jumped to her feet and slung her

linen napkin onto her plate. "You've taken the man I love, and now you're taking half our furniture!"

"Evelyn, Evelyn, Evelyn," Aunt Landon crooned. "Allie's right. That furniture *does* belong to her. And as for the man thing . . . there are many more out there where he came from. Just be glad one of you is going to get him. Now, calm down."

Landon smiled at Allie and squeezed her hand. "I'm sure Allie knows exactly what she's doing, and we've got to trust her. After all, when Macy got married, she moved out, didn't she?" Landon directed a pointed stare toward Richard. "And what greater *job* is there than being a wife?"

Allie nearly denied the very possibility, but Evelyn cut her off.

"I won't calm down!" she yelled and turned to her father. "Tell her she can't do this. Tell her she can't!" Evelyn pointed toward Allie as if she were Judas Iscariot.

Richard's color had returned to normal. His thoughtful gaze shifted from Landon to Evelyn. "Allie has always had a very level head," he admitted. "Landon's right. I'm sure it will all make perfect sense in a few weeks. Allie probably just isn't free to tell us all the details right now. Am I right, Allie?"

"Well—" Allie said.

"Aaaaaaahhhhhhhh!" Evelyn screamed and raced from the table, leaving Penny behind.

For the first time Allie could remember, Penny's attention was riveted to her in anything but bored disinterest. Allie glanced toward the seagulls and then back to Penny, who was shifting her chair away from the table as if the scrutiny never took place. "If you'll excuse me." She stood and smiled at Richard like he was the most scrumptious thing on the breakfast menu.

"Of course, Penny," Richard replied and watched her sway

toward the terrace doors. "And please see if you can calm her down, will you? You're always so good with her. I don't know what we'd ever do without you."

Allie decided now was a good chance for her escape, as well. Before standing, she considered countering Landon and her father's assumptions about her impending marriage to Brent but decided to take the path of least resistance for the present. One upheaval for the morning was enough. A seagull swooped within inches of the terrace railing, his high-pitched calls prompting her to make her next move.

She picked up her tea mug and prepared for the next step in her well-laid plan. "I need to go make a phone call."

"I'm sure you do, honey." Landon picked up her coffee, took a sip, and smiled across the rim at Richard. "Don't let us stop you."

Scooting back her chair, Allie stood.

"I'm sorry for not understanding at first," Richard purred. A calculating gleam in his eyes, he smiled up at his daughter. "You never have been one to make waves. I should have understood."

"It's okay," Allie mumbled and wondered what her father would do when he found out her potential marriage was to the wrong man.

Keeping her focus downward, Allie swiftly exited the terrace. Before she closed the French doors, her aunt's melodious voice floated in with the breeze. "Well now, Richard, it looks like everything's going to work out just like I said. Maybe one day you'll learn to listen to me."

Allie snapped the door shut and hurried upstairs to her bedroom. Once there, she locked that door and retrieved her cell phone from her purse. Sinking into the broad-backed rattan chair, Allie tapped the number for Elton Mansion.

When the answer came, she declared her identity and asked for Sophia Cosby.

The second Sophia's cheerful greeting sounded over the line, Allie's heart began to thud in her throat. "Hi, Sophia," she said, her voice unsteady. "I'm calling to see if you would give me Frederick's cell phone number."

Thirty-Five

By mid-afternoon Allie strolled at the ocean's edge, allowing the cool water to lap at her ankles. This private strip of beach was occupied by the condominium owners only and featured imported sand as white as crushed pearls. The gray-blue water foamed white on the swelling waves while seagulls screeched and scurried along the waterline in quest of food.

Inserting her hand into the pocket of her linen shorts, Allie felt her cell phone and willed it to ring. With a knowing smile in her voice, Sophia had given Allie Frederick's number. Then she'd informed Allie that Frederick was flying to Atlanta today, so if he was in the air, his cell was off. Allie had fully expected to get his voice mail, and that's what she got. She left a brief message telling him that she was staying at the Atlantic Beach Condo and Resort Center. She also announced that she wanted to talk to him as soon as possible. That had been hours ago, and Allie hadn't parted with her cell phone since.

Turning to face the ocean, Allie paused, allowing the wind to whip at her hair and spray her face with a salt-laden mist. She licked her lips, and the taste of the ocean tinged her tongue. Closing her eyes, she prayed Frederick would call. There was so much she wanted to ask him and so much she wanted to say. Allie looked at her watch. *Three o'clock,* she thought and wondered what she would do if Frederick *never* called. *Maybe he just isn't interested anymore,* she worried as a shroud of the old insecurity covered her spirit. But Allie recalled the love in his eyes when he took her hand and asked her to ride in the copilot's seat. She dismissed the worries and decided if Frederick didn't call her back by tomorrow, she would call him again.

I refuse to let him get away this time! she determined and swiveled back toward the condo. Allie pulled her canvas tote from her shoulder and withdrew her sandals. After rinsing off her feet, she slipped them back into her sandals and gazed toward the boardwalk. A long line of shops and restaurants called her name, and Allie decided a new outfit was in line. If Frederick *did* call and perhaps came to see her, she wanted to be ready. She'd dropped her wallet into her tote just in case she decided to shop.

Within five minutes Allie was strolling along the boardwalk, checking out the various stores and their wares. She paused at an upscale clothing shop and gazed through the window. The chic pantsuits and casual beachwear beckoned her in. After two hours of trying on clothes, Allie settled upon four new outfits—two casual beach outfits and two designer dresses. In the spirit of the moment, Allie decided to leave on the aqua-colored tank top and cotton shorts with the wide-brimmed hat. Once she left the shop, her anticipation for Frederick's call increased with every step.

The smell of fresh coffee wafted in the air, and Allie looked toward the next-door cafe, which serviced customers both indoors and out. She strolled through the sea of tables covered in umbrellas and entered the cafe through the glass doors. After placing her order for a large cappuccino, she sat at a corner table and gazed out the window toward the ocean.

If only life were always this peaceful, she thought and considered how angry Evelyn was and how much Landon and her father were pressuring her to marry Brent. Allie couldn't get moved into her new townhouse soon enough. All that was left was shaking Brent and connecting with Frederick—and then life would be perfect. She rested her elbow on the table, placed her chin in her hand, and sighed.

Idly Allie watched people strolling along the boardwalk and imagined Frederick being one of them. She smiled. Her lips stiffened when she realized she *did* recognize one of the pedestrians—and he wasn't Frederick.

Brent briskly walked from the direction of the condo and looked to be targeting the cafe where Allie sat. Groaning, Allie slumped in her seat and pulled the hat low over her eyes. She hunkered down, held her breath, and waited for the door to open. When it didn't, Allie peeked from beneath her hat and glimpsed Brent entering the narrow alley between the cafe and the shop she'd just been in. Before disappearing, he checked his wristwatch and hurried forward.

That's odd, Allie thought and then dismissed it. She couldn't have cared less what Brent did or where he was.

Then she spotted Penny walking along the boardwalk from the other direction. The wind tossed her hair and her knee-length skirt as she alternated trotting with a swift walk. Fully expecting Evelyn, as well, Allie strained for signs of her sister, but determined Penny was alone. As she neared the cafe, Allie wondered if Penny would be entering. If she did, Allie decided she would take her coffee and leave. But Penny, like Brent, scurried down the narrow alley.

Staring straight ahead, Allie contemplated the implications. *Are Penny and Brent meeting each other?* she wondered. *Or is this just a coincidence?* To her knowledge, Penny and Brent had met for the first time last night. At least they acted like they hadn't known each other.

I guess I could follow them, she contemplated as she looked down at her big bag of clothing and cumbersome beach tote.

A sixth sense urged Allie to act on her impulse. Standing, she pulled her cell phone from her pocket and placed the ringer on vibrate. She approached the counter. After canceling her cappuccino order, Allie dashed back into the dress shop and left her bag of clothing on hold with the clerk. That left only the beach tote to weigh her down.

By the time she slipped down the alley, her curiosity drove her forward, but common sense insisted she use prudence. Halfway down the wooden passage, Allie spotted an open entrance to the left behind the cafe. She hugged the left wall and glanced behind her. None of the pedestrians even noticed her. Allie scurried forward and didn't even want to think about how she'd explain her presence should Brent or Penny appear.

Once at the entryway, Allie discreetly peeked around the corner. What she saw left her blushing. Ten feet away, Brent and Penny sat alone in the lover's alcove that featured only one table surrounded by potted ferns and ivy. With Penny in Brent's lap, the two were in a passionate clutch that would make Hollywood proud. Each was too immersed in the other to even notice a third party or the sea wind that rocked the plants.

Allie gasped and plastered herself against the cafe's outside wall. Her pulse thumped in her temples. She narrowed her eyes. *Either Brent's a very fast mover or those two have a history.* Allie chose the latter option, which opened up all sorts of issues.

Her cell phone vibrated against her leg. *Oh, great!* Allie reached for the phone in her pocket, wondering if the caller might be Frederick. As much as she wanted to talk with him, this was not a convenient time. When Sarah's name appeared on the screen, Allie's fingers relaxed. As she answered the call, she suddenly remembered her phone's digital camera.

Shoulders hunched, Allie tiptoed away from the alcove and stopped halfway up the passage. She placed the phone next to her ear and urgently whispered, "Sarah! Let me call you back."

"You okay, girlfriend?" Sarah asked.

"Yes, I'm fine." Allie glanced over her shoulder. "Just give me thirty minutes. Okay?"

"Will do."

Allie hit the End button and gripped the phone. Before she had time to second-guess herself, she darted back to the alcove, peeked around the corner, and confirmed that the two were still at it. Her hand unsteady, Allie snapped six successive shots. After another glance to make sure they never suspected her presence, she dashed from the walkway, turned the corner, and burst into the clothing store. Breathlessly she retrieved her purchases from the shop and ran toward the condo.

By the time Allie hit the beach, her legs were quivering to the point that she slowed to a trot. With another glance over her shoulder, she hurried across the beach, into the condo, up the stairs, and into her bedroom. Thankfully no one was present to insist upon empty chatter or ask questions about her agitation.

Within fifteen minutes, Allie had uploaded the digital photos onto her laptop and viewed them on her monitor. Only one of the photos was too dark. The rest were bright enough to vividly recognize that Brent and Penny were much more than passing acquaintances. The heady rush of accomplishment had never been sweeter.

Wishing for her portable printer, Allie decided to go with

the second best alternative. She popped up from her computer and hurried through the condo, headed toward the resort center's business office. After signing in with the clerk, Allie sat down at one of the computers and logged into her cloud account. Soon she held printouts of the five photos and breathlessly observed each one.

I can't believe I did this, she thought and was astounded at her own bravado.

Shuffling through the enlarged pictures, Allie wondered when to show the images to Aunt Landon and her father. That would require another serious dose of courage. But Allie knew she had no choice. If this didn't prove that Brent wasn't a fine gentleman solely devoted to her, then nothing would. The photos would also end the potential romance between her father and Penny, which grew more noticeable every time Allie saw them together.

Her phone vibrated against her leg, and Allie's fingers flexed upon the photos. *I forgot Sarah!* She grabbed the cell and saw that sure enough, Sarah's name claimed the screen. Allie answered the vibrating call and placed the phone against her ear.

"Sarah," she said and rolled back the chair with the faint squeak of wheels, "hang on just a minute."

"Are you sure everything's okay, Allie?" Sarah asked.

"Couldn't be better!" Allie logged out of her cloud account. "Just wait a few seconds. I'm in the business center. . . . Got to pay for something." Allie juggled the cell phone, her bag, and the photos while paying the clerk for the photos she'd printed.

With the pictures secure in her tote, Allie walked out of the office and into the sunlight. Like a spy, she looked up one end of the beach and down the other. Spotting no one she knew, Allie placed the phone to her ear and said, "You're *not* going to believe this!" Then she told Sarah everything.

When she finished, Sarah said, "Are you *crazy*, Allie? I can't believe you did that!"

"Neither can I," Allie said through a nervous chuckle. Even the memory of snapping the shots made her nerves quake. "I guess I was temporarily insane."

"You just did what you had to do," Sarah said. "And I'm proud of you."

Allie gazed up the beach and breathed easier. Penny and Brent apparently had no idea they'd been caught in the act.

"You know, I'm remembering something here," Sarah mused. "If I'm not mistaken, my mom is good friends with Chrissy Everson's ex-maid. What if I called Mom to see if she'll call her friend. Maybe she has some information on Brent we're missing."

"You'd do that?" Allie asked.

"I'd do anything for you, Allie Elton," she said. "You paid my way through med school." Sarah disconnected the call.

Allie's mouth fell open. "How did she know that?" she gasped. The ocean's roar was her only answer.

Thirty-Six

Dinner on the terrace was every bit as miserable as Allie imagined it would be. With Brent sitting on one side and Aunt Landon on the other, Allie felt like she was in a cage. Penny remained absorbed with Richard and Evelyn while ignoring Brent and Allie.

As Allie pushed the green beans and roast beef around on her plate, she became increasingly uncomfortable with the implications of Penny's having ignored her every time they'd been together. She obviously tuned out Brent because she didn't want anyone to know they were intimately acquainted. Did that mean Penny's disregarding her was also an act? If so, why?

While the meaningless conversation droned on, Allie gazed toward the ocean and sensed there was something she had yet to discover regarding the Penny–Brent association . . . something to do with her.

Come on, Sarah, she urged, *call!* The cell phone, resting in the pocket of her linen skirt, remained still.

Allie managed to nibble a green bean, and by some miracle forced the thing down her tight throat. Her stomach rebelled against the intrusion, and she gulped her iced tea. She'd not eaten breakfast, barely snacked at lunch, and now couldn't swallow dinner.

Tonight the weather was picturesque—a stark contrast to the storm within Allie. The breeze had died, and the ocean was a lazy mass of lavender-gray that lovingly stroked the sand. A bank of clouds in the west partially hid the sun, and vivid shafts of light burst through the inky blue puffs. The whole placid effect was lost on Allie. All she could think about were the photos she'd slipped into the outside pocket of her purse and when she would display them for family viewing. The answer remained a jumble amid the rumbling worries that troubled Allie's soul.

And why hasn't Sarah called back? Allie wondered. She prayed her friend discovered more evidence of Brent's true nature.

Someone snapped her fingers in front of Allie's face. The sparkle of diamonds suggested that someone was Aunt Landon. Allie blinked, and the family came into focus.

"Hello in there," Landon teased. "We're waiting for your answer."

"Oh, hi," Allie rasped and looked around the table. Everyone's attention rested on her. "Sorry. Did someone ask me something?" She glanced toward Aunt Landon and avoided eye contact with Brent.

"Actually," Brent said and wrapped his hand around hers, "*I* asked if you had a good day at the beach."

Allie's hand trembled. Her attention riveted to him. She scrutinized his eyes and didn't allow the guileless mask to fool her. A spinning blaze of apprehension tore at her mind, and Allie wondered how he'd known she was on the beach. *Did he see me? If so, where? When?*

She blurted the first thing that came to her. "How did you know I was on the beach?"

"Landon just mentioned it, silly," he replied. With an endearing grin he slipped his arm around her.

"Are you okay, Allie?" her dad asked.

She jerked her head toward him and rapidly blinked. "Of course," she squeaked and dropped her fork. It clanged against her plate, and Allie reached for her tea glass but wound up knocking it into her plate instead.

"Oh no!" she wheezed as a splash of icy liquid baptized her lap.

"What is *wrong* with you?" Evelyn challenged.

Allie jumped up and began shaking her skirt. She gazed toward Evelyn, who was perfectly made up and as stunning as ever. But the disdain she wore so overpowered her beauty that even her silk coral dress couldn't compete.

"I . . ." Allie croaked and glanced toward her father.

"She's just nervous, I'm sure," Landon crooned toward Richard. "Most young women are at this point in their lives."

Fully expecting her dad's critical scowl, Allie was mesmerized to the point of no longer fussing with the mess. Her father bathed her in respect and untainted approval. The light in his eyes was everything Allie had longed to see. The irony was that his approval hinged on her marrying Brent, and if she went through with that, she would link herself to a womanizing jerk. That's when Allie also recognized her father's greed. In a fit of panic, she wondered if he would even care that Brent was immoral—just as long as she had access to his money.

Is that all I am to you? she fumed. *Nothing more than bait for a rich man?* Her face went cold.

Richard looked down.

"You're going pale, Allie," Landon fussed and stood. "Are you going to be sick?"

"I think so," Allie whispered and stooped to grab her purse. "If you'll excuse me."

Brent's chair scraped the terrace. "I'll make sure she's okay," he announced.

"No, no, I'll be okay. I . . . really . . ." She turned toward Brent, who now reminded her of a hungry wolf. "There's no need." Allie scurried toward the French doors and fumbled with the doorknob. Somehow she managed to stumble into the elegant living room.

"Allie, wait!" Brent called.

She didn't even look back. With the sound of his footsteps close behind, Allie hurled herself into the downstairs bathroom, slammed the door, and locked it. Heaving for air, she hovered near the door and listened. Brent didn't knock.

Allie's eyes stung. She covered her lips with unsteady fingers and forced herself not to cry. Her stomach growled in a sickening roll. The bathroom tilted in a blur of chrome and tile, and Allie wondered if she was going to vomit.

She dropped her purse, grabbed a disposable cup from the cabinet, filled it with water, and dashed the liquid down her throat. Allie looked in the mirror. Her rosy lipstick looked like it was on a corpse. And she hoped the nausea would subside.

When her cell phone vibrated against her leg, she forgot the nausea. *Sarah!* she thought. After a fumbling battle with her skirt, she retrieved the phone from her pocket to confirm that her prayer had been answered.

Sarah's satisfied drawl soon supplied every missing detail Allie had been groping for. "Girlfriend, you are *never* gonna believe all this."

"Try me," Allie whispered and glanced toward the door. She slipped out of the backless heels and stepped into the shower. The smell of soap engulfed her while the damp tile cooled her toes. Silently she closed the clear glass door and hoped it provided a better sound barrier against eavesdropping.

"I was right about my mom's knowing Chrissy's ex-maid," Sarah said. "I just got off the phone with her. Didn't think she'd *ever* call me back." Allie could just see Sarah rolling her eyes. "Anyway, according to the maid, Brent is a gambling playboy who preys on rich women. She even caught him—" Sarah cleared her throat—"uh . . . *entertaining* a woman once when Chrissy was out of town."

Allie groaned. "Oh my word," she whispered. "Did she tell Chrissy?"

"Are you kidding?" Sarah replied. "He threatened to fire her. He told her he'd make sure she never got another job in Atlanta, so she kept her mouth shut."

Allie closed her eyes and rested her forehead against the tile.

"Mom's friend made a few calls. That's why it took her so long to get back with me. Anyway, the skinny is he's broke."

"Broke?" Allie's eyes popped open. She lifted her head.

"Yes, broke. He blew all the money he got at Chrissy's death, and now he's looking for a new Chrissy."

Allie didn't expect the burst of sarcastic laughter that ricocheted off the bathroom ceiling. She covered her mouth and looked toward the door. "So he's after me because he thinks I'm rich," she said through a mirthless grin. "And Aunt Landon and Dad want me to marry him because they think he's rich."

Sarah chuckled. "Isn't it all just too hilarious?"

"Yes," Allie agreed. "In a sick sort of way, I guess."

"Really." Sarah continued. "Now, here's another tidbit. Didn't you tell me that woman who hangs with your sister—the one you caught him with today—is named Penny?"

"Yes, Penny Clayton," Allie supplied. "Why?"

"Okay, that's the same woman my mom's friend caught him with right before Chrissy died," Sarah said.

"Do you think . . ." Allie rubbed her forehead as the picture gradually came into view.

"They're working together?" Sarah finished Allie's thought.

"Yes."

"Of course. I figure they saw your family as an easy target."

"Penny is after Dad."

"And Brent is after you. They're partners. If and when one catches gold, they both enjoy."

"Oh my word," Allie whispered, her mind a whir of clues and deductions.

A tentative knock sounded at the door.

Allie jumped.

"Are you okay, darling?" Brent's soft voice penetrated the bathroom.

"Yes, fine," Allie called, and his voice had never rankled so severely. "It's Brent," she hissed into the phone. "He's at the door."

"You go, girl," Sarah said. "I'm cheering for you."

"You'd better *pray* for me," Allie whispered.

"That too."

Suddenly a fragment of their last phone call marched through Allie's mind. "And get ready to tell me how you found out about the med school thing," Allie hurriedly added while preparing to open the shower door.

"I'll tell you now," Sarah said.

Allie peered at the door and even the pressure of the moment couldn't abate her desire to know. "Okay, shoot," she said.

"Same way I delivered the story today," Sarah smugly answered. "I turned stones. I found out years ago, actually."

"How?"

Sarah laughed. "I was dating Larry then, remember?"

"Yes."

"He's a computer whiz, right?"

"Uh-huh."

"He hacked into the college files and found out."

"He didn't!" Allie forgot to whisper. She covered her mouth and bit her tongue.

"You can't hide a thang from me, girlfriend," Sarah teased. "You might as well not even try."

"Allie?" Aunt Landon's voice blended with a new round of knocks.

"Coming!" she said and disconnected the call without telling Sarah good-bye. "Oh man!" Allie whispered and touched her temple. But she could almost hear her friend saying, *Don't worry about it. I understand.*

Allie stepped out of the shower and flushed the toilet for effect. *I'm getting really good at being sneaky*, she thought with a sassy grin. She looked into the mirror. The short-haired woman who peered back no longer looked like a corpse. Instead her eyes held the triumphant light of a woman with a plan. Allie knew exactly what she needed to do.

Thirty-Seven

Allie stepped out of the restroom and encountered Landon and Brent whispering in the hallway. They abruptly stopped the second she appeared.

"Wow!" Brent said and walked to her side. "You're looking all better."

"Thanks," Allie replied and smiled into his eyes.

"Are you sure you're okay?" Landon asked and took Allie's hand. "Do you need to lie down?"

"No, I'm fine," Allie replied.

"I'm so glad," Brent affirmed as he slipped his arm around her waist.

This time, she didn't move away. Instead she looked at her aunt and said, "I was wondering if Brent and I could have a little privacy."

Brent's sudden intake of air preceded Landon's raised eyebrows and her swift exit. Trying to decide the best place to talk, Allie dismissed all the bedrooms. The living room was visible from the terrace. Besides, Aunt Landon was probably in there planning to eavesdrop. That left the bathrooms or the kitchen. She chose the kitchen.

"We could go into your bedroom." A hungry gleam in his eyes, Brent tightened his arm around her waist.

Allie nearly choked on the smell of his expensive cologne

and stopped short of ramming her elbow in his ribs. "I don't think so," she answered and stepped away. Without further explanation, she strode from the hallway toward the kitchen, never questioning that he would follow. Once there, she paused near the breakfast nook and set her purse on the table.

Brent didn't stop until he was close enough to kiss her. "My, my, my," he purred, his cologne engulfing her again, "this is a nice change of pace." When he tried to put his arms around her, Allie gritted her teeth and shoved his chest with both hands.

Stumbling back, Brent struggled for balance while saying, "Baby, what'd you do that for?"

Allie pulled the photos from her purse's side pocket and held them up with both hands. "Take a look at this slide show," she challenged and was thankful her voice was steady. Her knees certainly weren't. After giving him time to view each photo, she placed them face up on the table until only one was left.

His face ashen, Brent plucked at the sleeve of his blazer until Allie was certain he'd tear a hole in it. "Where did you get these?" he demanded.

"I took them this afternoon." Allie rested a hand on her hip and placed the final photo on the table. She stacked them together and tapped the bottoms against the table. "And unless you want me to march in there this minute and tell my whole family, you'll take Penny Clayton and leave now—and never show your face again."

"There's—there's been some mistake," Brent babbled. "Please!" His eyes took on a pathetic appeal. "Please, babe. You've got to understand. Penny means nothing to me."

"Oh?" Allie asked. "How long have you known her?"

"We only just met. It was a chance encounter. A one-time

thing. I promise." He moved toward Allie. "If you'll just give me another chance . . ." He reached for her again and offered a beguiling smile.

Allie stepped back. "So you only just met her?" she prompted.

"Yes." His nod was as convincing as the sincere glimmer in his eyes, and Allie couldn't believe she'd ever been naïve enough to let this man into her home.

"Well, isn't that interesting." She crossed her arms. "Because Chrissy's former maid says she caught the two of you together right before Chrissy died."

"That liar!" he snapped, a nasty twist to his lips. "She always hated me. Now she's trying to ruin me!" He shoved his fist into the air.

Gripping the back of the wrought-iron chair, Allie swallowed hard. The magnitude of what she was doing settled upon her and caused more than just her knees to quake.

"She's lying!" he repeated. "Who are you going to believe? Me . . ." he placed both hands on his chest, "or some stupid maid?"

"That stupid maid, as you put it, is a friend to my best friend's mother," Allie replied, her lips twitching. "She also says you're broke, and that you prey on rich women. Sarah and I figure you and Penny are working together. You're after me; she's after Dad. And all for our family's money. Is that true?"

"You witch!" he snarled. "I hate you!" Lifting his fist, he lunged forward.

A scream ripping her throat, Allie stumbled backward and tilted one of the chairs between them. With a bellow, Brent crashed into the chair and tumbled to the floor.

"Allie!" Aunt Landon's cry barely preceded her appearance and validated that she hadn't been far. "Are you okay? What's going on?" She stood in front of the refrigerator, her gaze trailing from Allie to Brent.

"He needs to go," Allie declared and struggled to breathe. She picked up the photos and shoved them into her aunt's hands. "I took these today on the boardwalk."

Before Landon got through the stack, Brent scrambled to his feet and bolted from the kitchen.

"He and Penny were working together," Allie explained. She slumped in a chair, placed her elbows on the table, and rested her face in her chilled hands.

Evelyn's shrill voice rose over a jumble of confused conversation. "What is going on?" she demanded. "Penny! Penny? Why are you going with him?"

The condominium's door slammed. Allie lifted her face and held Aunt Landon's confused gaze for a few seconds before Evelyn stormed the kitchen.

"What's going on here?" she repeated.

Allie's father followed close behind. "Allie?" he barked. "What have you done?"

"I think she's just gotten rid of a scoundrel—maybe two," Aunt Landon said in a deflated voice. She extended the photos to Richard while plopping into a chair herself. Allie haltingly explained everything.

By the time the story was over, Richard was sitting, too. Evelyn softly wept. "He nev-never loved me in the first place," she said. A curtain of blond hair hid her face as she dabbed at the tears.

Allie couldn't stop the pity that pulsed through her.

"Penny wasn't even my friend!" Evelyn wailed. She hunched her shoulders and turned toward her father.

Richard reached for his eldest daughter's hand and silently squeezed it.

"I'm sorry, Allie." Landon's grief-stricken eyes filled with tears. "I thought I was doing what was best for you."

"I know," Allie said. "But—" She pressed her lips together as a decade of heartache rolled between them. Allie looked down. "I know," she repeated and sighed.

Her phone vibrated in her pocket and she wondered if Sarah was calling back with more information. Her hands shook so violently she could barely manage the simple task of retrieving the cell. When she finally looked at the screen, Sarah's number was not displayed. Instead the number identified the caller as Frederick Wently.

"I need to take this alone." Allie jumped up. As she ran from the kitchen, she sensed the appraisal of her family, but she didn't feel obligated to explain a thing. Only when she secured the terrace door behind her did she answer the call and place the phone to her ear.

"Hello, Frederick?" she wobbled out.

"Hi," he said.

The sound of his voice triggered a deluge of nervous tears. She sniffled, swallowed, and tried to squelch the emotions.

"Allie?" he questioned. "Are you all right?"

She sniffed again, pressed her knuckles against her lips, and prayed for self-control—but to no avail.

"Has someone hurt you?" Frederick growled.

"No . . . no . . . oh, Frederick," she cried. "I neeeeeed you."

"I'm here!" he exclaimed. "I'm here, but I can't find you."

"You're here?" she blurted and gripped the top of her head. "At Atlantic Beach?"

"At the resort center you're staying at. The main office gave me instructions to your condo, but I've somehow gotten turned around and must have gotten your number mixed in my head. I've knocked on three doors and they've all been the wrong ones."

"Oh my word!" Allie exclaimed and dashed at the tears. She ran to the terrace railing and strained for any sign of him. "You're here? Now?"

"Yes," he said and chuckled. "Why are you so surprised? I thought you invited me!"

"You did? I did?" she babbled.

"But of course," he replied. "When a lady leaves you a voice mail and tells you exactly where she is, you get the impression she wants to see you."

"I do! I do!" she said. "Do you want to see me?"

"Do I want to see you?" he chided, his voice low and caressing. "No, I don't want to see you at all, Allie," Frederick gently mocked. "That's why I flew to Florida like a madman."

"You're here!" she repeated, stood on her tiptoes, and leaned over the railing. A hard perusal of the beach both ways revealed no sign of him.

He laughed. "Yes, I'm here."

"Where? Where are you?"

"I have no idea. That's the whole point of this call. I'm as turned around as—Whoa!" he exclaimed, and Allie heard the rev and roar of an engine. "Some guy in a Rolls just nearly ran over me. Wait a minute . . . was that—"

"Brent Everson?" Allie supplied.

"Yes. It was, wasn't it?"

"Yes." Allie rubbed away the final tears. "He just left," she explained. "For good. You can't be far," she added without a pause. "Don't hang up. Stay where you are and I'll come find you."

"Those are the most beautiful words I've ever heard," Frederick crooned.

Thirty-Eight

Within three minutes Frederick spotted Allie striding down the sand-swept lane toward him. After he'd described exactly where he was standing—at the end of a row of condos with the beach on one side and a narrow road on the other—Allie promised she'd be to him in minutes. She kept her word.

Frederick waved wildly and said, "I see you!" into the cell phone.

"I see you, too!" she replied and returned the wave.

Frederick disconnected the call, shoved the phone into his jeans pocket, and ran toward her. He didn't even give her a chance to say hello before he pulled her into his arms and laid a kiss on her that had been waiting a decade. The way she clung to him made Frederick more hungry for their wedding than when he'd gotten her phone call.

As the ocean's roar echoed the rush in his veins, Frederick broke the kiss and nearly sank to his knees. "Oh, Allie . . . Allie . . ." he whispered in her ear. "This has been such a mixed-up mess. I love you. I love you! I never stopped loving you. And if there's any way we could ever get married—"

"Yes!" Allie exulted and pressed her lips against his face. Amid a trail of eager kisses, Frederick detected the proclamation of her love before her lips pressed his again.

Frederick's eyes closed as he hugged her tightly and drowned in another kiss. Finally he cupped her face in his hands, pulled away, and groaned. "We've got to stop." Glancing toward the beach, he encountered a trio of teenage males who were far too interested in their embrace. "There's an audience," he explained.

"I don't care!" Allie wrapped her arms around him, placed her head on his chest, and continued, "I've waited ten years for this. I don't care if the whole world is watching."

Frederick glanced back toward the guys and caught sight of an older couple near the condos who were just as interested. He chuckled, rested his head on hers, and decided he didn't care, either. Her hair smelled of the sea. Her lips tasted like nectar from heaven. And Frederick was high on love.

"I never stopped loving you," he repeated. "There's never been anyone else."

"Not for me, either," Allie admitted. "Never. I've even got a scrapbook—all of you and your war hero stuff."

Frederick lifted his head and inched back. "A scrapbook?"

"Yes." Allie nodded. "I went to my room and cried over it when you came to the mansion with Sophia and Darren."

"And I went just to see you," he admitted. "Then I followed you to Grove Acres."

"You followed me?"

"Yes. Louise stopped when she saw me sitting at that roadside park by the turn for their place."

"I thought she said you guys just bumped into each other." Allie tucked a strand of wind-tossed hair behind her ear.

"We did . . . literally," Frederick added. "She nearly ran over me in her Corvette."

Allie laughed. "That doesn't surprise me at all."

Frederick shifted his weight and was thankful for only a mild trace of pain. Today had been a good back day. "I was about to chicken out from just showing up at Grove Acres when she drove up. She gave me an excuse for being there."

"You never were romantically interested in her?"

Frederick threw back his head and laughed. "Not even a little bit! I've barely even looked at a woman since you." He wrapped his fingers around hers. "I should have never left the hospital that day you broke your leg."

"And I should have never listened to Aunt Landon." Allie squeezed his hand and pulled away. "Oh, Frederick, can you ever forgive me?"

"Yes." Frederick nodded. He gripped both her hands. "Absolutely. Irrevocably. I think my forgiveness was complete after I saw you again at Grove Acres. I struggled with love, bitterness, and regret all those years. Then when I saw you again, it was like the negativity just went away, and the only thing I cared about was you and the chance we might get back together."

"I was so young then, and so . . . so . . ." Allie shook her head from side to side, and her eyes revealed her sorrow.

"I know. I know." He lifted her fingers to his lips and eagerly kissed them. "I totally understand. And even though I'd forgiven you, I don't think I would have completely understood how you felt if everything hadn't happened the way it did with Louise."

"What do you mean?" A thin line formed between Allie's brows.

"I felt so responsible for what happened and so *obligated*. And that's when I started understanding how obligated you must have felt to your family."

"But you weren't responsible for what she did," Allie insisted. "You *weren't*, Frederick." She touched his face.

"Ultimately no, but I *did* contribute," he admitted. "Do you know what I told her before she crawled up on the plane?"

"What?" Allie tilted her head.

Frederick gazed toward the ocean. "She'd been pressuring me to let her ride in the copilot's seat with me and insisting we were engaged or something." He glanced at Allie before studying the shell-strewn sand. "*Why* is anybody's guess, but you know how she is."

"Yes."

"Anyway, she'd already made me mad. I was feeling really cornered and came out with something like 'I don't care if you crawl through the escape hatch, get on top of the plane, tap dance, scream about me, and fall off and break your neck—it won't change my decision.'" He shifted his gaze to Allie.

"Oh no," she gasped.

Frederick helplessly looked into her eyes and touched her hair. "Now do you understand?"

"Completely."

"And I was so disgusted with myself I couldn't even bring myself to tell you. Then I decided to try to explain that night. I went to your place and saw you with Brent. I royally blew that encounter." He rubbed the side of his jaw.

"It's okay. Really, it is." The adoration in her eyes would make Frederick believe anything she told him. Anything. "And for whatever it's worth, Brent pressured me into going out with him and then invited himself in. He was like a mosquito I couldn't get rid of." She rolled her eyes. "And I nearly died when you showed up and he was there."

"I was so jealous I went nuts," he admitted.

"You had no reason to be." Allie shook her head, and Frederick didn't question her honesty.

"What is the deal with that guy, anyway?" he asked. "I promise, I think he tried to run over me."

"He probably did," Allie said. "He was livid when he left."

As Allie explained the Brent–Penny situation, Frederick's respect for her grew. "None of that surprises me about *him*," he said when she finished. "But what you did? That took a lot of guts."

Allie chuckled. "Yep. And all I know is that they were guts I never had before and may not ever have again. God guided me through that one."

"Kind of like what happened with Louise," Frederick said. He explained how he'd stepped out of the way and prayed sparks would fly between her and Jim.

"So you set them up to two-time you?" Allie questioned.

"You better believe it." Frederick nodded. "And I'd already decided that if they didn't get married, I still *wasn't*." He jabbed his index finger against his chest. "I didn't care if I had to pay for Louise to go to therapy!"

"So you'd have been after me even if Louise hadn't dumped you?" Allie asked, her voice full of hope and wonder.

"Honey, by the time I got over the shock of what happened to Louise, I decided I was going after *my* woman. Nothing was going to keep us apart."

"I felt the same way when I heard about Jim and Louise getting engaged," Allie said. "That's when I called you."

"I was going to call Macy and get your cell phone number after I landed in Atlanta today." Frederick stroked her cheek with the backs of his fingers.

Allie closed her eyes. "Really?" she breathed.

"I wish we were already married," Frederick whispered, his words thick with longing.

"Me too." She opened her eyes, and Frederick fought for control.

With a reckless smile, he asked, "Want to fly to Las Vegas and make it happen?"

Allie batted her eyelashes. "You mean get married?"

"Why not? What's stopping us?"

"As in *now*?"

"Exactamundo," he drawled. "All I have to do is get a flight landing approval and we're good to go."

"But . . . but . . . but . . ." She pointed toward the condos. "My stuff and my Mercedes."

He shrugged. "Go pack. I took a taxi here. We'll use your car to drive to the airport. We'll fly back tomorrow or the next day or next week and get your car. No problem."

"You mean right this minute?" She checked her watch and looked toward the setting sun. "It's almost eight."

"We can get there in a few hours," he said. "From what I understand, they have all-night chapels there. What's the problem? You do *want* to get married, don't you?"

"Yes!" Allie exclaimed. "By all means. Yes! It's just such a shock!" She pressed her hands on either side of her head. "Let me go get packed," she blurted and whirled around. After running several feet, Allie stopped, twirled back around, and hurried toward Frederick. She grabbed his hand and said, "Come on! You're going with me. My family will have to know why I'm leaving. We'll tell them together."

"Okay," Frederick said, walking in sequence with her. "But they might throw me out on my ear."

"No they won't. I won't let them," she said and stopped at the stairwell she'd come down. "I already told them I was going to meet you when I came out here. They didn't say a word. How could they?" She lifted her chin. "I'm my own woman now!" Allie proclaimed with the glow of pride. "I rented my own townhouse, and I'm going to get a job teaching at a community college somewhere."

"You did? You are?" Frederick asked.

"Absolutely." She nodded with a firmness that dared the world to argue. "I've already got all my furniture moved from the mansion to my townhouse, so we can move in immediately." A worried frown marred her features. "That is, if you're okay with everything."

"I'm happy if you're happy," he said. "I *had* hoped you could come on some of my flights with me."

Allie dimpled. "Of course," she acquiesced. "Maybe I'll hold off on the job for a while."

"No." Frederick held up his hand. "I wouldn't stop that for anything. You wanted to teach college when we first met. That was ten years ago."

"Maybe I could start part-time, then," Allie responded, her grin growing broader by the second. "Just teach a class one or two nights a week."

Frederick nodded. "Works for me if it works for you!"

"And what about the townhouse? Are you okay living in Atlanta?"

"Honey, I don't care *where* I live as long as I can be with you!" He was ready to move in for another kiss when he recalled the small velvet box in his pocket. Frederick looked toward the stairwell and the line of cars nearby. After diagnosing the place as the most unromantic one on the planet, Frederick decided to pull out the box anyway.

"Frederick?" Allie prompted. "What's the matter?"

"Nothing." He shook his head and focused back on her. "It's just that I have something to give you, and I want to do it now but this isn't exactly the best place . . . but . . . oh weeeelllllll!" Frederick put his hand into his pocket and wondered if his smile was as goofy as it felt.

He retrieved the velvet box and rubbed his thumb across the top. "If this isn't living proof that I was coming after you today, nothing is," he said. "I picked this up in Charlotte before I got your call."

"Oh, Frederick." Allie sniffled and blotted at the corners of her reddening eyes.

"Recognize the box?" he asked and opened the lid. "And the ring?"

She nodded and whispered, "It's the same one."

"Yes." Frederick removed the ring from its satin bed and tugged her left hand into his. "I never could bring myself to take it back to the jeweler's," he explained as he slipped the diamond onto her finger. "Now I know why." Frederick wrapped his fingers around hers. "I was holding it for you . . . for now."

She gazed up at him with a love that transcended time, a love that promised to grow more fierce as the years unfolded.

Frederick pulled her into his arms and reveled in a kiss that promised their honeymoon would be the sweetest of all.

About the Author

Debra White Smith continues to impact and entertain readers with her life-changing fiction and nonfiction books, including the JANE AUSTEN SERIES and the LONE STAR INTRIGUE series, *Romancing Your Husband*, and *The Divine Romance: Experiencing Intimacy with God*. She has been an award-winning author for years with such honors as Top-10 Reader Favorite, Gold Medallion Finalist (*Romancing Your Husband*), and Retailer's Choice Award Finalist (*First Impressions* and *Reason and Romance*). Debra has 60 titles to her credit and over a million books in print.

Debra and her husband of 35 years co-pastor a small church in East Texas, and she speaks at ministry events across the nation. She has been featured on a variety of media spots, including *The 700 Club*, *At Home Live*, *Getting Together*, *Moody Broadcasting Network*, *Fox News*, *Viewpoint*, and *America's Family Coaches*. She holds two graduate degrees—an MA in English and an EdS in Education—and is a PhD candidate at Northwest Nazarene University.

To write Debra or contact her for speaking engagements, check out her website at www.debrawhitesmith.com.

More Heartwarming Romance for Fans of Jane Austen!

You May Also Like...

The Duke of Riverton has chosen his future wife using logic rather than love. However, his selected bride eludes his suit, while Isabella Breckenridge seems to be everywhere. Will Griffith and Isabella be able to set aside their pride to embrace their very own happily-ever-after?

An Inconvenient Beauty by Kristi Ann Hunter
HAWTHORNE HOUSE
kristiannhunter.com

Julia Bernay has come to London to become a doctor—a glorious new opportunity for women during the reign of Victoria. When she witnesses a serious accident, her quick actions save the life of barrister Michael Stephenson. He rose above his family's stigma, but can he rise to the challenge of the fiercely independent woman who has swept into his life?

The Heart's Appeal by Jennifer Delamere
LONDON BEGINNINGS #2
jenniferdelamere.com

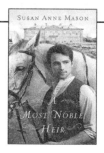

Stable hand Nolan Price's life is upended when he learns that he is the heir of the Earl of Stainsby. Caught between two worlds, Nolan is soon torn between his love for kitchen maid Hannah Burnham and the expectations and chances that come with his rise in station. He longs to marry Hannah, but will his intentions survive the upstairs-downstairs divide?

A Most Noble Heir by Susan Anne Mason
susanannemason.com

BETHANYHOUSE